"You *have* the raw materials—brains, talent, drive. But that's not enough to make it through this place. A thousand kids walked through Thayer Gate four weeks ago, with the same stuff that you have. But guess what? Not all of them are here today! And you know why? Because this place is hard, Davis. It takes more than a high SAT score and a varsity letter. It takes self-discipline. Not the rules that West Point puts on you, but the rules you put on *yourself*. That's what character is all about. Slamming doors when you're mad isn't self-discipline. Making excuses for poor performance, even when they're true, isn't self-discipline. Feeling sorry for yourself isn't self-discipline."

"Yes, sir." I started to feel a little better. This place, I realized, wasn't anything like home. Here, all the name calling and yelling had a purpose, a purpose aimed to give us character, not to hurt us.

"I can't imagine you being a quitter, Davis. But if that's what you want, I can't make you stay. But I can make you think about it."

OTHER BOOKS YOU MAY ENJOY

battle DRESS

amy efaw

Speak
An Imprint of Penguin Group (USA) Inc.

SPEAK
Published by the Penguin Group
Penguin Group (USA) Inc., 345 Hudson Street, New York, New York 10014, U.S.A.
Penguin Group (Canada), 90 Eglinton Avenue East, Suite 700,
Toronto, Ontario, Canada M4P 2Y3 (a division of Pearson Penguin Canada Inc.)
Penguin Books Ltd, 80 Strand, London WC2R 0RL, England
Penguin Ireland, 25 St Stephen's Green, Dublin 2, Ireland (a division of Penguin Books Ltd)
Penguin Group (Australia), 250 Camberwell Road, Camberwell, Victoria 3124, Australia
(a division of Pearson Australia Group Pty Ltd)
Penguin Books India Pvt Ltd, 11 Community Centre,
Panchsheel Park, New Delhi - 110 017, India
Penguin Group (NZ), 67 Apollo Drive, Rosedale, North Shore 0632, New Zealand
(a division of Pearson New Zealand Ltd.)
Penguin Books (South Africa) (Pty) Ltd, 24 Sturdee Avenue, Rosebank,
Johannesburg 2196, South Africa

Registered Offices: Penguin Books Ltd, 80 Strand, London WC2R 0RL, England

First published in the United States of America by HarperCollins Publishers, 2000
Published by Speak, an imprint of Penguin Group (USA) Inc., 2010

1 3 5 7 9 10 8 6 4 2

LIBRARY OF CONGRESS CATALOGING-IN-PUBLICATION DATA
Efaw, Amy
Battle dress / Amy Efaw
p. cm.
Summary: As a newly arrived freshman at West Point, seventeen-year-old Andi
finds herself gaining both confidence and self-esteem as she struggles to get through
the grueling six weeks of training for new cadets known as the Beast.
ISBN: 0-06-027943-5 (hc)
[1. United States Military Academy—Fiction.
2. Military education—New York (State)—West Point—Fiction.
3. Self-confidence—Fiction. 4. Interpersonal relations—Fiction.] 1. Title.
PZ7.E273Bat 2000 99-34516
[Fic]—dc21 CIP AC
Speak ISBN 978-0-14-241397-5

Printed in the United States of America

To all my A's:

THE FIRST FOR BELIEVING,

THE MIDDLE THREE FOR ENDURING,

AND THE LAST FOR WAITING

AUTHOR'S NOTE

Battle Dress is fiction. This is not to say, however, that the story does not contain elements of truth. As my good friend the writer Doris Orgel has said, fiction often draws from an author's memories, imaginings, and aspects of actual people and events. Indeed, one cannot experience a place like West Point and later write about it without reflecting upon that experience in some way. But no character I've portrayed in my story was based exclusively upon any one person I have ever known.

In writing this book, I have simplified West Point's organizational structure. Most notably, nowhere are officers or noncommissioned officers mentioned. Though West Point is largely run by cadets, an entire hierarchy of active-duty officers and noncommissioned officers oversees everything. I have also attempted to minimize confusion about the cadet chain of command by ignoring the many staff positions. Additionally, I've combined the two leadership positions of Platoon Leader and Platoon Sergeant into one; I felt the subtle differences between the two would be lost on readers unfamiliar with the Army structure. Finally, though the cadet leadership normally changes halfway through Cadet Basic Training, I've stuck with Cadet Daily and the rest of H Company's upperclassmen so as not to disrupt the story's trajectory or cause the reader unnecessary confusion.

The writing of this book was not a solitary endeavor but a combined one. I'd like to offer thank-yous to the following people for their contributions, which made my book the best that it could be. To my parents, Elizabeth Moudry and David L. Blanchard, for instilling in me the drive to excel, which led me to West Point in the first place. To my editor, Alix Reid, who, with skilled strokes of her pen, made me dig deeper. To Kristin Gilson, my paperback editor at Penguin/Speak, for so graciously allowing me to make subtle changes to the text, and to Eileen Kreit and all the great designers for giving *Battle Dress* an awesome new look—thank you, thank you, thank you! To my faithful New Jersey critique group: Christine Hill, Dorothy Stanaitis, Barbara Stavetski, and Martha Fenoglio, for all those long-distance critiques. To Jan Cheripko for planting the seed that became this story. To Doris Orgel for her enthusiastic response to my work and for pushing me in the right direction. To Ed Ruggero for his advice and encouragement. To Lieutenant Colonel Julian Olejniczak at the Association of Graduates and to Cadets Kristen Bowles, Scott Akerley, Barbara Antis, Will Canda, Bryan Duncan, B. J. Moore, John Hohng, and Brien

Tsien for their help. To God through Whom all inspiration is given. And, of course, to Andy—'nuff said.

Because "Beast" at its core has changed very little over the years, I have slightly modified the text of the 2010 paperback edition of the book to reflect a more mid-2000s time period rather than the mid-1990s of the 2000 and 2003 versions. But the characters and the story have remained exactly the same. Readers probably won't even notice the changes!

—Amy Efaw

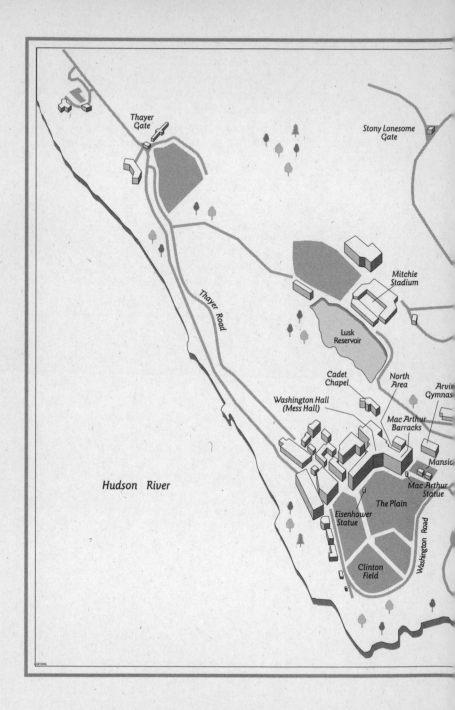

Thayer
Gate

Stony Lonesome
Gate

Thayer Road

Mitchie
Stadium

Lusk
Reservoir

Cadet
Chapel

North
Area

Arvin
Gymnas

Washington Hall
(Mess Hall)

Mac Arthur
Barracks

Mansio

Hudson   River

Mac Arthur
Statue

Eisenhower
Statue

The Plain

Washington Road

Clinton
Field

THE UNITED STATES MILITARY ACADEMY
WEST POINT, N.Y.

to Camp Buckner
and Lake Frederick

Washington Gate

Washington Road

Keller Army Hospital

Washington Road

Eisenhower Hall

Field House

Track

N

Hudson River

BEAST CHAIN OF COMMAND

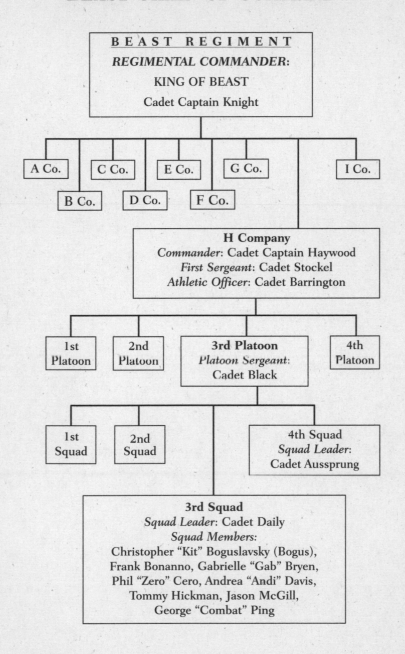

BEAST REGIMENT
REGIMENTAL COMMANDER:
KING OF BEAST
Cadet Captain Knight

A Co.

B Co.

C Co.

D Co.

E Co.

F Co.

G Co.

I Co.

H Company
Commander: Cadet Captain Haywood
First Sergeant: Cadet Stockel
Athletic Officer: Cadet Barrington

1st Platoon

2nd Platoon

3rd Platoon
Platoon Sergeant:
Cadet Black

4th Platoon

1st Squad

2nd Squad

4th Squad
Squad Leader:
Cadet Aussprung

3rd Squad
Squad Leader: Cadet Daily
Squad Members:
Christopher "Kit" Boguslavsky (Bogus),
Frank Bonanno, Gabrielle "Gab" Bryen,
Phil "Zero" Cero, Andrea "Andi" Davis,
Tommy Hickman, Jason McGill,
George "Combat" Ping

You cannot choose your battlefield,
The gods do that for you,
But you can plant a standard
Where a standard never flew.
—NATHALIA CRANE, "THE COLORS"

Your momma was home and you left.
You're right!
Your daddy was home and you left.
You're right!
That's the reason you left.
You're right!
—U.S. Army marching cadence

CHAPTER 1

Friday, June 25
7:15 A.M.

THE MORNING I LEFT for West Point, nobody showed up at my house to say good-bye. I thought that at least someone from the track team—maybe even my coach—might drop by to wish me luck. But nobody did.

So I went to sit on the curb at the bottom of our driveway and waited to leave. I watched my sister and brother get into our blue Volvo station wagon as my dad tossed the last bag into the back and slammed the trunk. He went over to the driver's side and popped the hood. He checked the oil for the second time. Finally, he scowled at the front door and blasted the horn three long times.

My mother stuck her frizzy, uncombed head outside and shrieked, "Do you want to eat today, Ted? I'm throwing some food together. Just sit there and wait."

"I've *been* waiting," he yelled back. "Now it's time to

leave. Didn't we agree we'd leave at seven? Well, now it's almost eight!"

"I'll leave when I'm good and ready. So just shut up! You—" Then her eyes locked on me. "Andi's not even in the car! So what's the big deal? Isn't *she* why we're going in the first place?" Her head disappeared as the door slammed.

My dad glared at me and barked, "You heard your mother. Get in the car!"

I sighed, then got up off the curb and headed for the backseat. *One thousand miles. Can't wait for this trip to be over.*

"Move over!" my sister yelled at my brother as I climbed in. "What's your problem, Randy? You always sit in the middle."

My brother sulked and slid over. Ten years ago, strapped into his car seat, he'd spat into my hair and smeared partially eaten graham crackers on anything within his reach. Now, at least, his annoying car behavior was limited to blowing out his eardrums with heavy metal on his iPod. "Just keep your pile of books on your side—" He smirked. "Mandie."

She shoved him away. "Fine. If you keep your reeking breath on your side. Do you ever brush your teeth? And don't call me Mandie. I told you, from now on it's Amanda. That's what's on my birth certificate. Don't you think it's tacky that all our names rhyme?"

"No, I think it's cool, *Mandie*."

My mother yanked open the door to the passenger's side. "You left the window open in our bedroom," she said to my dad as they both got into the car. "The one over your precious computer. Ever hear of rain?" She crammed a grocery bag on the seat between them and dropped her purse to the floor. Then she turned around and frowned at my brother. "You have that thing on already?"

He shrugged. "Blocks out your voice." He turned up the volume and closed his eyes.

My mother snorted, my dad started the car, and my sister opened her book.

West Point, here we come!

Before we even made it out of the driveway, my mother started complaining to my dad that the radio was too loud, and why did he always have to listen to the sports station? My dad said that she could pick the station when she started doing the driving.

As we whizzed down I-90 past the Sears Tower, my mother turned off the air-conditioning, opened her window, and commanded, "Open your windows, kids. Let's get a nice breeze going." Immediately, hot, sticky air wafted in.

My dad punched the air back on and said in his I'm-trying-to-remain-in-control voice, "Roll up your windows, kids. We need to cool this car off."

My mother shut it off. My dad turned it on. My mother shut it off. He master-locked the windows.

Meanwhile, Mandie, Randy, and I were sweating, our legs sticking to the leather seats.

Finally, Mandie slammed down her paperback and yelled, "Would you stop acting like a couple of babies? Just leave the air on. Stop being so cheap, Mom."

"I'm not being cheap." She stuck her hand out the window. "It's nice outside, and I just want to enjoy it a little. Is that so bad?"

"You call ninety-three degrees with ninety-five percent humidity 'nice'?" Randy asked.

I guess he can't block out her voice after all.

"Just leave it on," Mandie said. "Andi will be gone in a few days. Can't you attempt to limit the amount of misery she is forced to endure?"

I smiled. For as long as I could remember, Mandie had always stuck up for me, like a big sister should. Except she wasn't my big sister. She was two years younger than I. Maybe she felt guilty because I caught so much grief and she rarely did.

"Well," my mother snapped, "you can at least turn it down, Ted. It doesn't have to be on so *hard*." For some reason, my mother always listened to Mandie.

I could tell right away that this bad day was only going to get worse when we stopped to fill up at a Texaco station outside of Hammond, Indiana.

"I think it's crazy that we have to stop so soon," my mother whined. "Why didn't you fill up before we left? You know gas costs more on the expressway."

"Because," my dad said, watching the numbers roll on the pump, "if we would've stopped in town, we never would've gotten out of there! You would've said, 'I need to run into Jewel real quick to get something.' Then it would've been Walmart, then . . .'"

"Oh, just shut up, you dumb—"

"Watch your mouth!" my dad spat.

She finished her sentence anyway.

Shortly after we crossed the Indiana-Ohio border, my mother pointed to a rest stop. "Pull over here, Ted. I have to pee."

"You just went," my dad said as he sped past the stop. "And do you have to be so crass? Say 'urinate.'"

"I told you to pull over! I really have to go!"

"No! We're making terrible time. In a couple of hours we'll need to fill up with gas. We'll stop then."

"A couple of hours?" she howled. "Who do you think you are, *God*? You can't dictate when I can and cannot pee." She emphasized the word "pee."

"Oh, yes I can! I'm driving. *I* decide when we stop."

"Then *I'll* drive!" she screamed, grabbing the steering wheel. The car swerved into the left lane, nearly hitting a red pickup truck. Car horns blared all around us. I grabbed the door handle to brace myself.

My brother's eyes snapped open and he yanked his headphones off his ears. "Hey, what's going on?"

"What do you think you're doing?" my dad yelled. He tried to pry my mother's fingers off the steering wheel. "Do you want to get us all killed?"

"No! I want to drive. I'm sick of you making all the decisions."

"Let go!" He swerved back into the right lane.

Great. Now we'll end up in a ditch.

"Stop at the next exit!"

Why does this stuff always happen in our family? I glanced at my sister. She was just sitting there, reading her book. "Come on, Dad," I said, leaning forward. "Just stop at the next exit. Okay?"

He scowled at me over his shoulder. "Over my dead body!" Then he shoved my mother with his right hand, and she lost her grip on the steering wheel.

My mother screamed in his face. "You animal! You hit me! Did you see that, kids? He hit me!"

"I did not hit you," my dad said, emphasizing every word. "I—"

"Let me out!" she screeched. "Let me out right now!

I'm not going to sit in this car with you a second longer!"
She flung her door open, and it waved to the Ohio pastures
flying by at sixty-five miles per hour.

"For crying out loud!" my dad yelled. As he leaned
across her to pull the door shut, my mother snatched off
his glasses and threw them out the door.

"Ha!" she snorted triumphantly. "What are you going to
do now, Mr. Big Shot?"

Without his glasses, my dad can't see past the tip of his
nose. So he really had no choice but to pull off the road. I
heard gravel ricocheting off the car as we slowly bumped
to a stop. My dad stared at my mother, stunned. She
refused to look back. Instead, she wiped her tears and snot
from her face with the back of her hand and began rummaging through the food bag to find a napkin.

"You should be put away," he finally said. "You know, in
the nineteen years we've been married, I've seen you do a
lot of crazy things. But this . . ." He shook his head and
stared out the window.

He *had* seen a lot of crazy things. We all had. Like her
running around the house at one in the morning in her
nightgown, wielding a kitchen knife and screaming pro-
fanities. Our neighbors called the police that time. Like
trying to burn him out of their bedroom when he locked
himself inside so he could get away from her. The firemen
came that time. Or like hitting him on the head with a fire
poker because he'd rather watch Monday Night Football
than the miniseries of the week with her. I drove him to the
emergency room that time. But she'd never tried to kill us
all before.

My dad took his keys from the ignition and fumbled
around until he found my mother's purse. He dug out her

keys and shook them in her face. "I'm not going to take any chances with you," he said. Then he got out and started walking back along the highway to look for his glasses.

"Hey, wait, Dad! I'll help you!" my sister yelled after him. Then she smirked at my mother. "Great move, Mom. I want to be just like you when *I* grow up."

The car quickly filled with heavy, sun-steamed air. I flung open my door, hoping to get some relief, but the breeze barely stirred the grass in the field beside us. Eight or nine cows ambled in the sun, snacking now and then on the grass and swatting flies with their tails. I got out of the car and stretched each leg, wishing I could go on a long run—pounding the pavement far away from our blue Volvo station wagon.

I heard my mother sniff. "Do you see how your daddy treats me? Taking my keys away like I'm a child or something."

"Well . . ." I picked at my thumbnail. *You act like one.*

"You see how violent he is?" She rubbed her shoulder. "He thinks he can hit me whenever he wants."

"He didn't really hit you, Mom. He *pushed* you."

"What's the difference? It hurt." She stared at me, looking for sympathy. When she didn't find any, she started to cry again. "That man disgusts me. He's nothing but a . . ." She started stringing curse words together. "He thinks he's so perfect. Well, he's not. He's a lousy hypocrite, that's what he is."

I had to agree with her on that point. My dad *wasn't* perfect. He was as self-absorbed as my mother was vicious. His glasses were as thick as ice cubes, and without them he was legally blind. But that was no excuse for him to miss who I was as a person. At least my mother knew me well enough to know which of my buttons to push to get a reaction out of me. He had no clue. None.

Like the night I announced to my family at dinner that I was going to apply to West Point. My dad didn't even bother to lift his eyes from his lumpy mashed potatoes. "No daughter of mine is going into the military" was his only reply. "Only sluts and whores go into the service." His words stung worse than when my mother smacked me across the mouth, so I never brought up West Point again.

But my mother did. She was never one to pass up a bargain, and West Point was a big one. A $350,000 education for nothing. And the only payback—five years in the Army after graduation. Armed with that information, my mother easily convinced my dad that maybe West Point, in spite of all its sluts and whores, would make a wonderful place for his daughter to get an education, after all.

That is, if we ever got there.

I sighed. "That's beside the point, Mom. You wouldn't let go of the steering wheel! What else was he supposed to do?"

"Oh, what good are you? You never take my side." She gave me an ugly look. "If it wasn't for you, we wouldn't even be here. I don't even know why we're wasting our time. You don't belong at West Point. You're not smart enough. Why do you think they waited until the middle of May to accept you?"

I closed my eyes, wishing I could close my ears instead. *Oh, Mom, don't start. Please!* But I knew that once she got going, I couldn't stop her. Nobody could.

"You know why. We *all* do. You don't need a Ph.D. to figure that one out." She sneered at me. "Someone else turned them down. You were their last choice." She turned her back to me. "You'll *never* make it there." She blew her nose into the soggy blue napkin she had clutched in her hand. "We should've just dumped you on a plane. This driving is the pits."

I could feel the rage and hurt frothing up inside me. *I didn't ask you to take me. Do you think I'd ask for this?* I turned away from her, toward the pasture, where a calf nuzzled up to its mother and began to nurse. "So, I'm going to look at the cows, okay?"

"I don't care what you do."

About ten minutes later we were ready to go. Mandie and my dad rescued the glasses from a muddy ditch about a hundred yards behind our car. Then Mandie went back to Danielle Steel, Randy tuned in to Metallica, and we got back on the road.

I closed my eyes. *I can tolerate anything for a few days,* I kept telling myself. *Anything.*

The Corps, bareheaded, salute it
With eyes up, thanking our God—
That we of the Corps are treading
Where they of the Corps have trod—
—CHAPLAIN H. S. SHIPMAN, "THE CORPS"

CHAPTER 2

MONDAY, JUNE 28
9:01 A.M.

MY WATCH SAID 9:01 as we climbed the bleachers of Michie Stadium. The morning was heating up; it was going to be a hot day. A tall cadet stood on a platform below, wearing a white hat, a white short-sleeved shirt, white gloves, gray pants, a red sash wrapped around his waist, a silver saber at his hip, and shiny black shoes.

He briefed the new cadet candidates and their families. I tried to listen to his motivating speech, but my mind was spinning. *I can't believe I'm really here.*

My mother nudged me and said loud enough for the people all around us to hear, "It's a good thing you dumped that ugly boyfriend of yours. Maybe now you can get a cute hunk like that one down there."

What boyfriend? I glared at her. The "ugly boyfriend" she

referred to was nothing more than a guy on my track team who had asked me to the movies. Twice. The second time, he got to experience one of my mother's verbal assaults for dropping me off five minutes late. There wasn't a third time.

"You now have a few minutes to take care of your farewells," the cadet announced. "Afterward, all new cadet candidates will file down the steps, where they will be received by the cadet cadre. While the candidates are in-processing, friends and family are invited to participate in an orientation and a bus tour of West Point. And later this afternoon you will be able to see your candidates once again as they march onto the Plain for the Oath Ceremony. We encourage everyone to attend. Thank you and good luck."

The people around us rose out of their seats. Arms wrapped around bodies. Hands squeezed tissues. Cameras flashed. I stood and looked for my red duffel bag.

My mother started crying. "She's only seventeen, Ted," she told my dad. "She's not ready for this."

My dad cleared his throat and began inspecting his stubby fingernails.

"You're going to be so far away," my mother wailed.

Thank God!

She planted a wet kiss on my cheek and clung to me. Unaccustomed to her embrace, I pulled away. So instead, she began patting the top of my head like I was a five-year-old going off to school for the first time. "I'll write you every day. You know I'll do that, don't you, Andi?"

I nodded and forced down the lump that was forming in my throat. *Don't start crying now, you idiot! Didn't she say only a couple of days ago that she was glad to see you go? You want to leave!*

Mandie hugged me. "Just think—you could be coming with us to Niagara Falls," she whispered. I laughed. "I'll miss you," she said.

"Me too," I whispered back. And I meant it. Out of all the members of my family, she was the only one I hated to leave.

Randy shoved my sister out of the way. "You can always come back home, you know," he said, rolling his eyes. Then he gave me an obligatory hug and reattached his headphones to his ears.

I glanced at my dad. He was now engrossed in picking at a hangnail.

"New Cadet Candidates," said the cadet, "please file down the steps at this time—"

I wiped my hands on my jeans, then picked up my duffel bag and took a long, slow breath. "Well, I guess I'd better go." *Dad?* I bit the inside of my lip and hesitated a moment before turning toward the steps.

"Uh . . . Andi?" my dad said. I turned around. He jiggled the change in his pockets, looking as uncomfortable as a new kid in the lunchroom. I almost felt sorry for him. Almost.

"Good luck," he said, and gave me an awkward hug. "Take care."

"Thanks." I jogged down the white cement steps. I didn't look back.

I followed the other new cadet candidates into a dark tunnel beneath the stadium. A cadet pointed where to go. I looked at him. Our eyes met.

I smiled. "Hi!"

"DON'T SAY HI TO ME, MISS!" he shouted. "What

do I look like, your *boyfriend*? Keep your head and eyes to the front and walk with a sense of purpose!"

I moved quickly past him. *What's his problem?*

"FALL IN DIRECTLY BEHIND THE MAGGOT IN FRONT OF YOU!" bellowed another cadet farther ahead, the tunnel amplifying his already earsplitting volume.

All the new cadet candidates stopped for a second, unsure of what to do.

"MOVE IT!"

We quickly shuffled into a single-file line.

"NEW CADETS," the cadet continued, "YOU WILL KEEP YOUR HEAD AND EYES TO THE FRONT. YOU WILL ADDRESS ALL *MALE* UPPERCLASS CADETS AS 'SIR.' YOU WILL ADDRESS ALL *FEMALE* UPPER-CLASS CADETS AS 'MA'AM.' YOU WILL NOT SPEAK UNLESS SPOKEN TO! DO YOU UNDERSTAND?"

He was answered by a handful of mumbled *yes*es and *yes, sir*s.

"POP OFF!" he hollered.

Pop off? Nobody moved.

"YOU MAGGOTS ARE STUPIDER THAN SOAP SCUM! When you are asked a question, you will respond *immediately* and in a motivated manner. DO I MAKE MYSELF CLEAR?"

"YES, SIR!" we yelled in unison.

"You are no longer little boys and girls. You are new cadets—subhuman maggots, douche bags, grosser than pond water. Not fit to lick the filth from under my grand-mother's toenails! DO YOU UNDERSTAND?"

"YES, SIR!"

"I say again, DO YOU UNDERSTAND?"

"YES, SIR!" I was sure our response shook the stadium's

very foundation and that within seconds hundreds of hysterical parents would come rushing in to see what caused it.

The cadet yelled for us to follow him. The other sub-human maggots and I continued through the tunnel until we reached three more cadets seated at a table, spaced at equal distances from each other. The one in the middle barked, "State your name, Smack."

I froze. *Who, me?* My eyes shot left, then right.

"Yes, you, *Knucklehead*. What is your name?"

I stumbled up to him. "Um, Andi. I mean Andrea. Andrea Davis."

He leaned forward and glared at me, his eyes tiny slits. "YOU WILL ANSWER ALL QUESTIONS IN COMPLETE SENTENCES, *DIRTBAG!*" He leaned back in his chair. "Let's try it again, shall we? What is your name?" He spoke softly, but there was no comfort in his tone.

I swallowed. My spit was thick. "My name is Andrea Davis."

"Sir?" he said.

I hesitated. "Yes, sir. Sir, my name is Andrea Davis, sir."

"NO SANDWICH SIRS!" he screamed. "For morons like you, that means only one 'sir' per sentence!" He rifled through a pile of papers, slammed a tag down in front of me, and roared, "Fill out that tag and attach it to your bag!" I grabbed the pen in front of him and scrawled my name in the appropriate places, but I was shaking so much, I didn't think anyone would be able to read it. Then he dismissed me. I hurried with my bag back into line.

"NEW CADETS!" boomed a voice from my right. My eyes jerked immediately in his direction. "You will have exactly two minutes to relieve yourselves. The female latrine is directly to your rear, and the male latrine is directly to your front. I highly suggest you take this opportunity. Two minutes. MOVE OUT!"

We sprinted in those two directions as if we were fleeing from a burning building. *One thousand one, one thousand two* . . . I sprang into a stall, fumbling with my jeans zipper, my heart pounding and hands shaking. *One thousand thirty-three, one thousand thirty-four* . . . I pulled down my underpants and stared at them in disbelief. *Not today!*

"ONE MINUTE REMAINING!" boomed the cadet.

I started rummaging through my duffel bag. Underwear . . . bras . . . makeup . . . hairbrush . . . alarm clock . . . *Oh, where are they?*

"FORTY-FIVE SECONDS!"

Running shoes . . . toothbrush . . . *Tampons!*

I ripped open the box and grabbed two. . . .

"THIRTY SECONDS!"

The sound of toilets flushing echoed in the tunnel. I added mine to the chorus, jammed the remaining tampon into my pocket, grabbed my bag, and flew out of the bathroom, adrenaline charging through my veins.

"IF YOU'RE NOT BACK IN MY LINE, NEW CADETS, YOU'RE *WRONG!*" A couple of miserable souls straggled to the end of the line. Three white hats descended on them like pigeons on popcorn.

I followed the other new cadets out of the bowels of the stadium and onto a bus. I sank onto a wide, soft seat beside a cute, blond-haired guy wearing a football jersey. Any other time I would have smiled at him. But as the bus pulled away from Michie Stadium, he looked out the window, and I stared at the floor. The bus was so quiet, you could almost hear the sweat squeezing out of our pores.

* * *

The bus stopped in front of a huge, brown brick building. Another cadet was waiting there.

"At this time you will in-process." His voice was loud and confident but lacked the fierceness of the cadets at the stadium. He ordered us to form a single-file line and enter the building.

My eyes took their time adjusting to the dimness as I followed the others down a dark, quiet hallway. Then we entered a huge gym filled with other new cadet candidates and rows and rows of tables. I filled out forms and signed paperwork. I opened an account at the Pentagon Federal Credit Union. I turned in my medical files from my doctor back home. I got my chest, waist, hips, and inseam measured. Then I received my first uniform and was sent into a dingy, but clean, locker room to shed my jeans and T-shirt and don the uniform. A chubby, middle-aged woman guarded the locker-room door.

"Leave your bag after you change," she said.

I didn't talk to the only other girl in the room as I pulled off my clothes and shoved them into my bag. She finished tying her shoes at the same time that I did, and as we stood, I looked at her, and she looked at me. Even though she was about four inches shorter than I, we were mirror images of each other. A white crew-neck undershirt. Long, black athletic shorts with a white "ARMY" emblazoned on the left thigh. Black knee socks. Black shoes. We giggled.

"If my friends could see me now," she said, rolling her eyes.

The woman shook her head and motioned for us to pull the knee socks up to our knees. Then she placed a tiny-beaded metal chain with a card around my neck and pinned two tags, one green and one yellow, connected by a string, to the elastic waistband of my shorts. The tags hung nearly to my knees.

What are these for? I didn't have a chance to ask.

"Go on out the door now, Hon," she said, "and get in the line to get weighed."

A soldier in an Army uniform took my height (67 inches) and weight (121 pounds) and sent me into another line to do pull-ups. More like pull-up. One. Then I got into more lines. I picked up a pair of prescription glasses with brown plastic frames, I got stabbed with syringes, I filled out more forms, and each time, the card around my neck was scanned and a check mark was added to one of my tags. Finally I ended up in another, smaller gym with wooden bleachers lining both sides. A cadet inspected my tags and told me to find my bag and wait in the section of bleachers marked "H."

I eventually spotted my duffel bag and carried it to the bleachers. Three guys were already there, lounging and laughing about three rows up, but I sat down in the first row, alone.

I checked my watch: 10:27. Had only one and a half hours passed since I was sitting in the stadium with my family? *Unbelievable.* I took a deep breath. *Just relax. I think the worst is over.* The past hour hadn't been anything like those first ten minutes. *That must've just been the initiation.* I closed my eyes.

"WHERE DO YOU BOYS THINK YOU ARE, SUMMER CAMP?" bellowed a deep voice, jarring me like a telephone call in the middle of the night. "I WILL NOT TOLERATE ANY *SMOKING* AND *JOKING* IN MY BLEACHERS!" His voice reverberated through the gym, making me feel like he was standing inside my brain. I

★ 17

didn't dare look at the guys in the third row. I didn't have to. I *knew* they were no longer lounging. Or laughing.

The cadet's eyes slowly rolled over the "H" section bleachers and locked with mine. They were blue-gray, the exact color of Lake Michigan on a cloudy day.

"ON YOUR *FEET!*" he roared. We sprang up like jack-in-the-boxes. "Pick up your bags and follow me."

Since I had no bleachers to scramble down, I was the first in line. The cadet was tall and lean and looked like he could have easily stepped off the set of a Hollywood war flick. His uniform shirt was crisp and bright, as was everything else about him.

The Hollywood Hero led us out of the gym and across a huge quadrangle that rang with the sounds of battle—roaring voices and the *BOOM! BOOM! BOOM!* of a beating drum—resounding from the gray granite walls enclosing it. The cadet walked effortlessly, but I had to run to keep up with him.

Once he looked over his shoulder at me and hissed, "Carry yourself in a military manner, Miss. No double-timing in my formation."

Double-timing?

"This is North Area!" he yelled at us as we scampered behind him. "Remember it!"

The Hollywood Hero finally stopped us near a tunnel that went through a building several stories high. I could see green grass on the other side.

"You will enter this sally port," he said, gesturing toward the tunnel, "and report to the Cadet in the Red Sash. You will present arms—salute him." He eyed the four of us with disgust and asked, "Do any of you maggots know which hand to salute with?"

The guy to my left raised his hand and cried out, "I do!"

The cadet lunged toward him and snarled, "YOU ARE NO LONGER IN KINDERGARTEN, MORON! YOU HAVE FOUR RESPONSES, AND FOUR RESPONSES ONLY: 'YES, SIR'; 'NO, SIR'; 'NO EXCUSE, SIR'; AND 'SIR, I DO NOT UNDERSTAND.'" Then he stepped back and yelled, "DO YOU PEA-BRAINED, SCUM-SUCKING, LOW-LIFE GRUB BALLS UNDERSTAND?"

"YES, SIR!"

"Then let's hear it! What are your Four Responses?"

It took us about half a dozen tries to memorize our Four Responses correctly and in order, but when we did, the cadet actually smiled. A Close-Up toothpaste smile. His snow-white, black-visored cap gleamed in the sun and looked like a halo on his head. I smiled back. I couldn't help myself.

I regretted it immediately.

"SMIRK OFF, SMACK!" His spit sprinkled my face, and it suddenly occurred to me that he hadn't used his Close-Up anytime recently. "I'm not your boyfriend, Chucklehead, and I'm not your friend. I'm not your momma, or daddy, or big brother. Save your smiles for the mirror, 'cause that's the only place where they'll be welcome here!"

I could feel my throat tighten and my mouth go dry.

He turned from me and addressed the four of us. "YOU MAGGOTS MAKE ME WANT TO PUKE! MY OLD GRANNY IS MORE TOGETHER THAN YOU WORTHLESS SCUMBAGS! AND SHE'S *DEAD*!"

We all started to shake like a washer on the spin cycle with an uneven load.

"Now, you will report to the Cadet in the Red Sash. You

will salute like *this*." He placed his right hand at the brim of his hat and said, "You will sound off and say, 'Sir, New Cadet X reports to the Cadet in the Red Sash as ordered.' Do you understand?"

"Yes, sir!"

"POST!" he barked.

No one moved.

The cadet blinked. "What are you, a gaggle of half-wits? *Post* means to move with a sense of purpose to your appointed destination. You got that, idiots?"

"YES, SIR!"

"Then POST!"

We hurried toward the sally port and waited in single file for our turn to be called forward by the Cadet in the Red Sash.

I was standing on the dividing line between the sweltering brightness of the quad that the Hollywood Hero had called North Area and the cool dimness of the sally port. A light breeze blew through the tunnel, relieving my sweat-streaked skin.

The person ahead of me turned around. *Another girl!* She had short curly hair, and when she leaned toward me, I could see freckles sprinkled across the bridge of her nose.

"So what do you think?" she whispered.

I shook my head. I had no words to explain what I was thinking.

"So . . ." An upperclass cadet was standing right beside us, his hands on his hips and a smile on his lips. "You two ladies old friends?"

We both relaxed. "No, we just met in line," the girl said.

"Oh, just getting acquainted, huh? How so *very* nice,"

he said. "It looks like you both are in H Company. Maybe you'll be roommates."

We looked at each other and smiled.

"There's only one problem, though, Ladies." I watched his lips as he talked. Saliva, dried and white, stuck to the corners of his mouth. "I'm in H Company, too." Then his smile fell into a hard line, and the hard line changed into a huge oval. "WHY ARE YOU TALKING IN MY LINE?"

Relaxation fled. Muscles stiffened. But somehow we stuttered, "N-n-no excuse, sir!"

He glared at me. I felt as if he could see right through my eyes and down into my soul. "I SAW YOU GAZING AROUND, BONEHEADS!" His face twisted into an angry scowl. "New cadets are not *authorized* to gaze around! Keep your greasy little heads and beady little eyes straight ahead." Then he smirked. "But I'll indulge you with one last luxury." He pointed to his name tag. "LOOK! ADMIRE! MEMORIZE!" Five white letters screamed at us out of their shiny black background: DAILY. "Easy to remember, Ladies. Just think of me as your *Daily* nightmare!" Then he grabbed our tags and read our names out loud: "Davis. Martin." He glared into our faces. "You better remember me, because believe me, I'll remember you!"

Goose bumps sprouted all over my body.

"I DON'T KNOW WHAT YOU THINK THIS PLACE IS, *LADIES*, BUT YOU BETTER LEARN QUICK. THIS AIN'T NO SESAME STREET. THIS IS THE PAIN PALACE. AND IF YOU DON'T LIKE IT, I WILL PERSONALLY ESCORT YOU *OUT THE FRONT GATE!*" And with that, he was gone.

The girl turned around. I kept my eyes fixed on the

back of her head. I did not think of anything until it was my turn on the chopping block.

"DROP YOUR BAG!" the Cadet in the Red Sash roared as I approached him.

I placed my red duffel bag on the ground.

He looked at me as if I were covered in vomit. "You will perform all tasks in a military manner, Miss! Now . . . PICK IT UP!"

I reached down and picked it up.

"DROP YOUR BAG!"

I dropped it—*clunk!*—and winced, thinking of the clarinet inside that my mother made me bring.

"Miss, you will immediately execute at my command. PICK UP YOUR BAG!"

The shouts in the sally port were deafening. I could hear bags dropping to my left and right. I wasn't the only new cadet playing hot potato with my bag.

"Now, New Cadet, drop your bag and report."

I dropped it and shouted, "Sir, uh, New Cadet Davis, um, is reporting . . . I mean, *reports* to the Cadet in the Red Sash on order!" I winced. "*As* ordered." I held my breath, then squeaked, "Sir."

I watched him, waiting for his wrath to erupt. He was taller than anyone in the sally port, I was certain. The features of his face were smooth, almost comforting, like hot chocolate on a snowy day.

"Not bad," he said. "You forgot to salute. Try it again."

I stared at him. *A second chance?*

"I say again, New Cadet, you forgot to salute."

I flung my hand in the direction of my temple, as the Hollywood Hero had shown me, and shouted, "Sir, New Cadet Davis . . . reports . . . to the Cadet in the Red Sash as ordered!"

He nodded and saluted back. "Drop your salute after you see me drop mine, New Cadet." His arm fell to his side, so I copied him.

Simon Says. Kindergarten after all.

He inspected my tags and said, "New Cadet Davis, you are assigned to Cadet Basic Training Company H. On my command you will enter the doorway to my right—your left. Take the stairs to the third floor. There you will report to the First Sergeant of H Company. Do you understand, New Cadet Davis?"

I'd figure it out. "Yes, sir."

"Good. Post!"

I grabbed my bag and took off for the stairwell. *That wasn't so bad!*

"MISS, HALT!"

Oh, no! What now? I stopped and turned around. "Yes, sir!"

"You forgot to salute. Post on back here and try it again."

"Yes, sir!" I retraced my steps, stood in front of him, and dropped my bag at my feet. I raised my shaking right hand to my throbbing temple.

"Did I *tell* you to drop your bag, New Cadet?"

"No, sir." *Way to go, Andi.*

"Initiative is not invited here during Beast, New Cadet."

Beast? Is that what they call this? The name was perfect.

"You'd best do only as you are told." He raised his hand, and as I waited for him to drop it, I could've sworn that his left eyelid fluttered, ever so briefly, before he said, "Pretty weak salute there, New Cadet. POST!" My hand fell with his, and snatching my bag, I fled for the stairs.

Did the Cadet in the Red Sash actually wink at me?

A howl as harsh as the winter wind greeted me as I entered the stairwell. Another cadet. "Neck back, Smack! Take the steps one at a time. Keep your forearms parallel to the ground. At all times when indoors, you will slither along the wall like a snake. I don't want your stinking carcass anywhere near me! And move out! Got that, Smack?"

"Yes, sir!" I yelled, trying to obey these complicated orders while following the stinking carcass ahead of me. Then he tripped on one of the steps, and the weight of the bag slung over his shoulder threw him backward. He grabbed the railing. I shoved my bag into his back to help him stay up.

"WHO'S THAT SPAZZING AROUND IN MY STAIR-WELL?" growled another voice from the first landing above us. I pulled my bag back. The voice's owner, a stocky cadet, looked like a troll who had just crawled out from under some bridge. He bounded down the stairs and bellowed at the sprawled new cadet, "You, Bean Smack! Knucklehead! Trying to take out a classmate?"

"No, sir!"

"PULL YOURSELF TOGETHER, NEW CADET!" he yelled. The new cadet struggled to his feet. "Listen, Bonehead, take the steps *one at a time* and move out in a military manner, keeping your forearms parallel to the ground. And stay on that wall. Now get outa here!"

"Yes, sir!" he answered, and started pounding up the stairs with his arms straight out in front, looking like Frankenstein's monster on a homicidal rampage.

I bit my lip to keep from laughing. *He said* fore*arms, not arms!*

The Troll stepped in front of me. "Are you laughing at

your classmate, Miss? You find this amusing? Do you think you are better than he is?"

"No, sir!"

"Wipe that nasty smirk off your face. You make me sick! Do you actually think that you're going to somehow make it through this place on your own? That you're gonna skate by without making any mistakes? From what I've heard, you've made plenty of mistakes *already*!" He snorted. "You'll probably be the *first* to go. At least this guy here is trying." He thrust his face into mine and whispered, "Personally, Miss, I don't think you've got what it takes to make it here."

His words, so similar to my mother's, cut into me, making me flinch. I swallowed.

"Hell-o! Are you having a brain cramp, or are you just stupid?"

What did he want me to do? "N-no, sir. I—"

"No, you're not having a brain cramp? Or no, you're not stupid?"

I felt trapped. "S-s-sir, I—"

The Troll shook his head with disgust. "Just get your sorry, unmilitary mass out of my AO. POST!"

"Yes, sir!" I yelled. I didn't want to catch any more of the kind of abuse he was dishing out.

He stepped aside to let me pass. I charged up the stairs and made it to the third floor unscathed. On the landing I hesitated. *Now what? Oh—what did the Cadet in the Red Sash say?* I chanced a quick look to my left, then right. Thank God. No cadets were around right then. But the stairwell was anything but quiet. *Come on—left or right?* The door to my left was wide open, so I hurried through it and was confronted with a long hallway. Closed doors lined one side. The other side, the side I was on, was bare. Loud voices filled the hall, coming from a mob at its far end. On instinct, I moved along the wall in the direction of the noise until the mob—a long line of stuttering new cadets—blocked my way. Shouting upperclass cadets swarmed around them like bargain hunters at an after-Christmas sale.

"Stay on that wall!"

"Do not speak unless spoken to!"

"No gazing around! You thinking of buying this place?"

The reason for the traffic jam became clear as the loudest cadet of them all shouted, "Get your beady eyes offa me and memorize that sign, Smacks! Gawk at it like it's your best friend's girlfriend!"

I had a sudden urge to run, to escape this nightmarish place. But where would I go? So I just looked over the heads in front of me at the white sign hanging down from the ceiling in the middle of the hall and mouthed the words spelled out in black letters: "(Salute) Sir, New Cadet _____ reports to the First Sergeant of Hotel Company, Cadet Basic Training, for the first time as ordered."

And then I remembered what the Cadet in the Red Sash had said my next task would be—to report to the First Sergeant of H Company.

A cadet yanked me from my spot on the wall as I was memorizing the sign and shoved me toward a closed door. "Did you understand the sign, Smack?"

"Yes, sir!"

"Good. Knock three times. Wait until the First Sergeant tells you to enter, and report. And leave your bag outside. Got that, Smack?"

"Yes, sir!" *Knock three times. Leave the bag.*

I knocked three times. Knock. Knock. Knock.

"ENTER!" boomed a voice from behind the door.

I opened the door and peeked inside.

"WHO ARE YOU?" screamed the red-faced cadet, with hair the color of peach fuzz, sitting behind a desk. "LITTLE BO-PEEP?" He glared at me from behind gold, wire-framed glasses and hissed, "When I say, 'Enter,' you will walk into the room with a sense of purpose, stop three paces from my desk, and report. NOW GET OUT OF HERE AND TRY IT AGAIN!"

I fled through the door, pulling it shut behind me, and knocked three times again, louder this time.

"ENTER!"

I marched up to his desk, saluted, and yelled, "Sir, New Cadet Davis reports to the First Sergeant of Hotel Company, Cadet Basic Training, for the first time as ordered!" *Whew!*

He stared at me for what seemed like two and a half days. A clock ticked somewhere in the room. My grandparents collected clocks, and when I slept at their house, the clocks all over the house joined together to lull me to sleep with their gentle ticking. The sound didn't fit in this sweltering, inhospitable place.

The First Sergeant finally saluted in slow motion and whispered, "Are you *scared*, New Cadet?"

Am I scared? My stomach was trying to pass for a pretzel and my mouth for a desert. But no way would I tell him that. "No, sir!"

He slowly lifted himself up, slammed his chair against the wall behind him, leaned over the desk, and whispered, "Oh yeah? You sure *look* scared, New Cadet." I felt my lip tremble and bit it quick to make it quit. His eyes narrowed. "Your momma's waiting for you outside. Want to go home?"

That was probably the best thing he could have said to

me. If he had made me a different offer—any other offer—I might have taken him up on it. But the thought of getting back into that blue station wagon, back to 202 Lincoln Drive a quitter, back to my mother's I-told-you-sos—no, anyplace but home. I clenched my fists and shouted, "NO, SIR!"

He studied me thoughtfully. Then he reached under his desk, retrieved a green book, and slammed it on his desk. I jumped.

He snickered, then roared, "SIGN IN, SMACKHEAD! Name. Date. Time. Class."

"Yes, sir." I staggered up to his desk and took his pen.

"Left-handed, huh? That's just another strike against you, Smack."

My hand shook as I began my name. *D, a, scratch, scratch.* I gulped. The pen wouldn't write.

"Get your nasty elbow off my desk, Grub Ball! I don't want your arm hairs touching my desk again!"

I tried again. *Scratch, scratch, scratch.* Nothing.

"WHAT'S YOUR MAJOR MALFUNCTION, BONE-HEAD? YOU TRYING TO GROW A BRAIN?"

"Sir, I . . . this . . . this p-p-pen is, um—" I looked up at him.

His hand shot down, grabbed the pen out of my hand, and threw it against the wall. "YOU ARE TRYING MY PATIENCE, *MISS!*" He slammed another pen down on the desk. "WRITE!"

My shaking fingers formed the correct letters. *Davis, Andrea. June 28, 2004.* I looked at my watch. *11:09.* I could feel his eyes drilling into my head. Class—*2004.*

The First Sergeant spun the book around. Then his head sprang up, fire dancing behind the wire-framed glasses, spreading to his cheeks, his ears, down his neck.

"WHAT?" I had never heard anyone yell so loud in my life. "WHAT IS THAT, *MISS*?" He cursed, making my mother's angry words sound like the sentimental mush on Hallmark cards. He jabbed his finger up and down onto the book until I thought only a hole would remain where my "2004" was written.

He leaned over the desk until his wire-framed face was so close to mine that I could smell his breakfast—eggs and coffee—as he hissed, "Six weeks ago one thousand men and women sat in Michie Stadium, ending four long years of sleepless nights, grueling days, area tours, Cow English, baked scrod, CORs, the IOC, and Juice PRs!"

I bit my lip. *What in the world is he talking about?*

"They gave their sweat, blood, and tears to earn the right to be called the Class of 2004. DO YOU DARE EQUATE YOURSELF TO THEM?"

"N-n-n-no, sir," I croaked, clutching at the fabric of my shorts.

He snatched the pen from off his desk where I had left it and with bold strokes crossed out the "2004" and scrawled "2008" in its place. Then he turned his eyes onto a pile of papers on his desk. "New Cadet Davis, you are in Third Squad, Third Platoon. Room 305. Your squad leader is Cadet Daily."

My body went cold. I remembered Cadet Daily. And he said he'd remember me, too.

The First Sergeant looked at me again and yelled, "WHAT SQUAD, MAGGOT?"

Somehow my vocal cords defrosted enough for me to shout, "Sir, I am in Third Squad, Third Platoon." *Whatever that is.*

The whites of his eyes became my whole world. "Are

you scared *now*, New Cadet?" he whispered.

"NO, SIR!" I shouted, my voice shaking like I had been injected with fifty shots of espresso.

"Only fools don't fear the enemy, New Cadet," he said. "And *I'm* the enemy." My eyes followed his finger to his name tag. The white letters S-T-O-C-K-E-L, etched into the black plastic, seemed to mock me. Cadet Stockel opened his mouth and bellowed, "POST!"

I flew out the door, where the next victim was already waiting.

"Report to your room, New Cadet," I heard some other upperclass cadet say to me, "and deposit your gear. Then report back to the Cadet in the Red Sash. And no gazing around! Do you understand?"

"Yes, sir!" I said. I sped along the bare wall, away from the growing throng of new cadets mouthing the words on the sign. I tried to catch the room numbers out of the corner of my eye as I passed door after closed door on the opposite side of the hall. Random thoughts whipped through my mind. *Sir, I am in Third Squad, Third Platoon. Room 305. The First Sergeant is my enemy. Cadet Daily is my squad leader. The Cadet in the Red Sash winked at me, and I look like I'm scared. I am a dirtbag, a bonehead, a stupid, pea-brained, stinking-carcassed knucklehead. I dared to equate myself to the Class of 2004. I have Four Responses. My name is Davis. I slither like a snake.*

Room 305. I crossed the hall and opened a solid oak door. No locks, no keys. I shut out the clamor of the hallway, dropped my bag, and leaned against the door. I squeezed my eyes shut and took deep breath after deep breath until I finally stopped shaking.

War is hell.
— GENERAL WILLIAM T. SHERMAN,
    WEST POINT CLASS OF 1840

If General Sherman's definition be right,
West Point is war.
— GENERAL GEORGE S. PATTON, JR.,
    WEST POINT CLASS OF 1909 (IN A LETTER WRITTEN
    HOME WHILE HE WAS A PLEBE AT WEST POINT)

CHAPTER 3

MONDAY, JUNE 28
11:13 A.M.

I OPENED MY EYES to four windows and a window ledge over a radiator. Two desks, two vinyl armchairs, and two single beds, completely covered with Army equipment, mirrored each other on opposite sides of the room. A waist-high dresser, two wooden closets, and a sink with two mirrored medicine cabinets above it completed the room.

The name tag DAVIS, stuck on the corner of one desk, drew me to the left-hand side of the room. A piece of paper on the desk told me to take ten minutes to relax and get a drink of water before heading out again. It was signed by Cadet William F. Haywood, H Company Commander. It wasn't exactly a "We hope you enjoy your stay" card with a red-and-white peppermint candy beside it, but it was the only West Point welcome I had gotten today.

The tag on the other desk read QUINN. New Cadet

Quinn. My roommate. She hadn't arrived yet. I wondered what she looked like, where she was from. What her first name was. Would she want to talk to me as much as I wanted to talk to her?

I leaned against the window ledge above the radiator and peered out one of the half-open windows. A green field of closely cropped grass spread before me. Granite buildings bordered the field, their long shadows stretching over the grass like cool fingers. And beyond the buildings, I could make out a faint outline of tree-covered ridges gently curving in the distance—a beautiful contrast to the bright-blue sky. It made me feel better.

I walked over to my bed and stared at all the equipment covering it. Orange pegs, folded canvas, a scratchy dark-green wool blanket, green pouches and straps of all shapes and sizes.

My mouth was parched. I walked over to the sink and slurped out of the faucet, just like I used to do in the bathroom at home in the middle of the night.

My watch said that I had been there nine minutes. I couldn't wait any longer for my roommate to show up. I just knew that somebody was watching my door, hoping that I'd stay a second longer than ten minutes so he'd have an excuse to throw a temper tantrum.

I took a deep breath, grabbed the doorknob, and slithered along the wall to the stairwell.

The stairwell emptied out into the sally port containing the Cadet in the Red Sash. He greeted me with a scowl and said with disgust, "Pretty weak salute, New Cadet. Your next station is Drill." Then he had me join a row of about ten new cadets standing in North Area.

A black cadet faced us. "The position of attention," he

announced as if he were introducing the President. "Keep your head straight, roll your shoulders back. Arms to your side, elbows in, hands loosely cupped."

I squinted, trying to protect my eyes from his white shirt and hat, which reflected the blinding sun pounding down on us.

"Heels together, feet at forty-five degrees. Now assume the position." We rearranged our bodies until we somewhat resembled our teacher.

"For those of you who just joined us," he said, looking right at me, "I am Cadet Black. No pun intended." His lips twitched. "I am going to teach you sorry smacks how to march. When I'm through with you, you will look, act, and perform like soldiers. Got that?"

"YES, SIR!"

"You'll be standing tall and looking good, marching for your mommas and daddies later on today." Cadet Black grinned. "Let's play follow the leader. LEFT FACE!"

When we had all turned left, he yelled, "FORWARD, *MARCH!* With every beat of that drum, your left foot hits the ground, Knuckleheads!"

Now in single file, each of us frantically tried to keep in sync with the persistent *BOOM! BOOM! BOOM!* of the bass drum coming from some corner of North Area—some corner where we weren't allowed to "gaze."

Cadet Black continued to shout in a singsong voice, "LEFT! LEFT! LEFT, RIGHT, LEFT! ON YOUR LEFT!" He marched along to the left of us, shouting out new commands while maneuvering us around other new cadets who were charging through North Area with bulging bags in their arms or marching like we were. He taught us how to mark time, halt, present arms, order arms, and stand at parade rest. He also taught us to "ping"—West Point's version of speed-walking with stiff legs and hands cupped at our sides.

"Learn to love it, Smacks," he said. "That's how you'll get around this place for a year. Pinging *everywhere* you go!"

When we were finished, Cadet Black marked our tags and marched us through another sally port, up some wide granite steps, and into a high-ceilinged, medieval-fortress-like building, which he called Washington Hall. He led us into a huge, dimly lit hall filled with long tables where miserable-looking new cadets were choking down sandwiches and guzzling water. *Lunch.*

He finally stopped at the head of an empty table, set like a table in a classy restaurant with its white linen tablecloth and carefully positioned place settings, and commanded us to sit.

"You see this place, Smacks?" Cadet Black asked. "It's called the mess hall. The place where you'll get to come three times a day to watch the *upperclassmen* eat." He gestured to the plates before us, laid bottoms up, and ordered, "Flip your plates over and pass the food around." He leaned forward and looked at each of us around the table. "You will all drain at least two glasses of water before leaving here. Do I make myself absolutely clear?"

"YES, SIR!"

"Good. Eat up, Smacks. And take a good gaze around this place. Eat and gaze." A smile crept over his face. "This will be the last time you will get to do much of either for a long, long time."

I looked around. I had never eaten in a castle before. Never even been in one, except those I'd imagined while reading Shakespeare in English class. That's exactly what this place looked like—a huge, cavernous castle, complete with exquisite murals and stained-glass windows, gargoyles and statues, flags and banners, stone pillars and balconies, a ceiling at least two stories high, and heavy wooden double doors.

Mess hall. That's what Cadet Black had said this place was called—the "mess hall." The name just didn't fit. Now, if he had walked into my house and said, "This place is called the mess hall," I would have understood. Anybody would. But this incredible place?

I passed the wheat bread and a heaping plate of ham to the new cadet next to me, not bothering to drop any on my plate. My stomach was already full of jumpy intestines. I sipped water and watched my lunch companions eat in silence. I wondered if any of their mothers had taught them how to chew with their mouths closed. I smiled to myself. Mine hadn't.

After lunch Cadet Black marked our tags and sent each of us on a mad shopping spree with two dark-green cloth bags, which looked sort of like Santa sacks minus the toys. We entered building after building and were funneled into line after line, where my bags grew heavy with sheets and towels, uniforms and boots, brown and white undershirts, socks, razors, bars of Dial soap, and Johnson's baby shampoo.

I hauled my bags back to my room and dumped them just inside the doorway, shutting the door with relief. My roommate still hadn't arrived, but I didn't have time to think about it. I wiped my sweaty face on my white T-shirt, slurped out of the sink, and left again to report back to the Cadet in the Red Sash. He snatched my tags and glared at me. His good humor from earlier had disappeared completely.

"Did you get lost between here and the haircut line, Miss?"

Haircut? I resisted the impulse to touch my head. *But I just got it cut last week!* I had wanted it short, easier to deal with. "Sir, I—"

"No excuse, right?" he growled. "Report to the haircut line. POST!"

Before I made it to the short line formed at the edge of the sally port, I heard a cadet with a familiar voice say behind me, "You made it through half a day at West Point walking around in those?"

I turned around. I tried to place him. Tan face. Green eyes. Dark hair, cut real short. *The First Sergeant? No . . .*

The cadet pointed to my shoes with disgust. "Where do you think you are, Miss? Prancing around in some fashion magazine? Preppy and West Point don't go together. This is not the Ivy League. This is the *Un*college."

I looked down at my shoes. I had been so careful to follow the instructions in the admissions packet. It said if you didn't have a pair of black shoes, you could dye a pair black. I had sacrificed my favorite pair that I got from American Eagle—brown boat shoes—meticulously placing masking tape over the shoes' white soles to keep the dye from turning them black, too. They looked practically brand-new. What did I do wrong?

"I'm not having one of *my* smacks be the biggest joke on R-Day."

One of his smacks? My eyes jerked from his face to his name tag. DAILY. The hairs on my arms stood at attention.

"Remember me, Davis?" He leaned closer, peering into my face. "I remember you!" he sneered. "Surprise! I'm your squad leader!" And as he marched me away, he said, "Yes, siree. We're going to have *some* fun this summer, you and me. I can hardly wait."

After fitting me with a pair of new black shoes so ugly that even my mother would have tossed into the Goodwill Dumpster, Cadet Daily said, "Double-time to your room, Davis. Dig White Over Gray out of your barracks bag and get it on." I must have had a clueless look on my face, because he shook his head and said, very slowly and deliberately, like he was talking to someone who was speaking English for the first time, "White Over Gray. That would be a uniform . . . *this* uniform." He pointed to each piece of his uniform. "White shirt. Gray trou. Get it? White *Over* Gray." He tugged on the pieces of gray fabric stuck on each of his shoulders. "Epaulets. Yours are plain gray. No gold stripes or upperclass brass for you," he added, pointing to his shiny gray crests. "Black belt. Gold buckle. Hat." He tapped his with his index finger. "Mine's white. *Yours* is gray. Name tag. And white gloves." He checked his watch. "I'll be by your room to check you off in a while. MOVE OUT!"

Back in the safety of my room I frantically tore into my barracks bags. By the time Cadet Daily knocked on my door, my pants and shirt were on, and I had found my hat and black belt, but no gold buckle. My black shorts and white undershirt were crumpled on the vinyl chair, and the contents of my barracks bags were strewn on the floor from the foot of my bed to the wardrobe closets.

"You need a V-neck T-shirt under your shirt, Davis," he said. "Gold buckle for your belt, gold crest for your hat, your name tag, and white gloves. I'll be back in a minute, and you better have them in your hot little hands." He slammed the door.

I had just thrown the undershirt over my head and was slipping on my shirt when Cadet Daily once again announced his presence with three hard knocks.

"You decent, Davis?"

"Uh—" I started fumbling with the buttons of my shirt. "Yes, sir!"

Cadet Daily banged the door open. Six new cadets, all guys, tripped in behind him.

"These are your squadmates, Davis," Cadet Daily said. He turned to the line of new cadets standing behind him in the position of attention. "Square her away, Third Squad. You've got *five* minutes." He stuck his head back through the doorway. "And keep the door open. At ninety degrees. That's *not* a request. I don't want any hanky panky going on in here!" He disappeared down the hallway.

"We got to keep the door open 'cause there's a girl in here?" asked one of the guys. "Man, that *blows!* With the door hanging wide open and all, that's just askin' for abuse. We might as well have one of us stand out in the hallway, waving those guys right in here."

"Yeah, well, Hickman," said a guy who looked like Jimmy Fallon with a buzz haircut, "we'll be asking for abuse if we don't get her ready by the time Cadet Daily gets back." He looked at me. I was stuffing my shirt into my pants. My undershirt was already soaked, and the wool pants clung to my sweaty legs, making the task nearly impossible. "What do you need?" he asked.

I bit my lip. "Well, my hat"—I pointed an elbow toward the hat at my feet—"needs that gold thing on it. But I can't find it. Or my belt buckle. My gloves are, uh . . ." I looked around the room. "Oh, on my desk. And I need to put my name tag on my shirt." I finished cramming my shirt into my pants and shoved my hand down into my back pocket. "I got it here." I looked at the unhappy faces in front of me. These guys were going to be with me all summer. We were supposed to be a team. And here I was already dragging them down. Not exactly the kind of first impression I wanted to make. I cocked my head to one side and whispered, "Sorry, guys."

"No problem," Jimmy Fallon's lookalike said, gazing around the room. "Looks like your roommate didn't show. We all had ours to help us out." He smiled, offering me his hand to shake. "I'm Christopher Boguslavsky. My friends call me Kit."

"Hi . . . Kit," I said, shaking his hand. "Andi Davis." I was impressed. No one my age had ever shaken my hand before.

"Cool. Uh . . . hey, Cero," he said over his shoulder to a black guy standing near my sink. "Help me find that crest and belt buckle." They started tossing stuff all over the place.

An Asian guy with the name tag PING walked over to me. "You need to pin your name tag on your right pocket," he said, pointing to the pocket that covered my right breast. "Line it up with this seam"— he pointed to the flap— "centered on the button."

I took the clasps off the name tag and tried to stick the plastic pin onto my pocket the way he told me. "Like this?"

He shook his head. "It's crooked. You kind of have to eyeball it." He pulled the name tag off my shirt, his hand brushing against my pocket. "Oh, sorry," he said, his face turning an interesting shade of red.

A guy with sun-bleached hair, a lifeguard tan, and the name tag McGILL stood behind Ping and waved my gloves. "Don't forget these!"

"Thanks." I took the gloves from him and held them between my knees so my hands would be free.

"Found the crest!" Cero yelled, holding it up.

"Great!" Boguslavsky said. He tossed Cero my hat. "Screw it on the hat."

"The name tag needs to go about here," Ping said. He reached his hand toward my pocket again, then pulled it back.

"We only have two minutes left, guys!" shouted a tall guy with dark-brown hair, looking nervously toward the door.

Cero was fumbling with the gold crest and my hat, swearing furiously under his breath.

I looked at Ping. "Hurry up! Just stick that name tag on, then I'll put the claspy things on—"

"Dammits," Ping said.

"What?" I looked at Ping. *Is he mad at me?*

"Quick! Somebody! Throw me the belt!" Boguslavsky yelled.

"Dammits," Ping said. "Those clasps are called 'dammits.' Um, could you, like, unbutton your pocket?"

The guy called Hickman, who had complained about the door being open, tossed Boguslavsky my belt.

"Sure. . . ." I attacked the button.

Boguslavsky jumped over to me and started shoving the belt through the belt loops on my pants. "Hope you don't mind, Andi, but I need to know how long this has to be . . ."

"Uh . . . no. It's okay . . ." I held my stomach in.

"You know, 'cause they're such a pain in the butt." Ping pulled at the flap of my pocket and stuck one end of the name tag into the fabric. "You lose them, they're small, they pinch your fingers." He grinned. "Dammits."

"Hey, watch it," Boguslavsky said. "We've got a lady in the room."

"Oops, sorry," Ping said. "Then again, some people call them 'frogs.'"

"What are you, Ping?" Hickman sneered. "Some kind of walking military manual?" He went to stand behind Ping. "Oh, that's right." He looked around the room. "Y'all, this guy's a sergeant in the U.S. Army!"

"Correction," Ping said, stabbing the flap with the other end of the name tag. "Was a sergeant. Now I'm a knucklehead."

"Anyone got a knife?" Boguslavsky sighed. "Yeah, right. A knife in this place. This thing could wrap twice around her waist. I need to cut—"

"WHAT IS GOING ON IN HERE?" Cadet Daily stomped into the room.

My attendants melted away from me and slid to attention. The half-pinned name tag dangled from my shirt pocket.

"I DON'T KNOW WHAT YOU WEAK, LILY-LIVERED PERVERTS HAVE BEEN DOING WITH THAT FEMALE CLASSMATE OF YOURS, BUT I DO KNOW THAT I GAVE YOU FIVE MINUTES TO SQUARE HER AWAY, THIRD SQUAD! FIVE MINUTES!" He paced back and forth, back and forth in front of the wardrobe closets, kicking my newly issued items out of his path. "I DIDN'T GIVE YOU SIX MINUTES, THIRD SQUAD, AND I DIDN'T GIVE YOU FIVE AND A HALF. I GAVE YOU FIVE. FIVE MEANS FIVE!" He rubbed the back of his neck and continued to pace. "ARE YOU GONNA LEAVE A MINUTE LATE WHEN YOU KNOW THAT ARTILLERY'S COMING INTO YOUR POSITION? ARTILLERY'S ON TIME, ON TARGET. AND YOU'RE DEAD!" Then he stopped and faced us with his hands on his hips. "Time management's everything, Third Squad."

Our chattering teeth and knocking knees applauded appropriately.

4:25 P.M.

Ten minutes later we were standing at attention in North Area among a mass of other new cadets. Nothing shaded us from the blazing sun that beat down on our dripping heads. Cadet Daily had told us that we new cadets weren't wearing our hats to the Oath Ceremony. We were too incompetent to march and wear hats on our heads, he had said. I blinked over and over to keep the sweat out of my eyes.

Cadet Daily's face suddenly appeared an inch from mine. "Davis, you need a haircut! Big time." He looked around my left shoulder, then my right. "You look like a powder puff! Come on." He nudged me out of line. "We have fifteen minutes till first call."

He led me across North Area, dodging pinging beanheads and bellowing cadets. "You're not going to be my problem child, are you, Davis?" He paused. "You show up in some kind of preppy boat shoes, I have to get you shoes. You show up with a poofy hairdo, and I have to take you to get your hair cut. You blab your whole life story to another female waiting to see the Cadet in the Red Sash. You let every guy in your squad put his hands all over you!" He looked at me. "You have no clue what this place is about, do you, Davis?"

I looked at him out of the corner of my eye. "No, sir."

We walked down some stairs into an underground tunnel.

"It's about killing people," he said, his voice echoing in the tunnel.

We walked through a door and into a room with three barber chairs. A Hispanic woman stood with a female cadet, the first upperclass female cadet I had seen all day. The cadet was taller than I and had short blond hair. Her lips twisted into a sort of grimace when she saw me, and turning to the woman beside her, she said, "Looks like you've got yourself another victim, Maria."

Cadet Daily nodded at the female cadet, then looked at Maria. "Do you have time before the parade?"

"No problem," Maria said, selecting a comb from her pocket and motioning me into a chair. "Should only take me five minutes."

Five minutes?

Maria must have seen my eyes, because she spun me away from the mirror before grabbing big chunks of my hair and chopping them off. I watched my sixty-five-dollar haircut, less than a week old, flutter to the floor. When she finished, she turned me around so I could see the result. I'm normally not the kind of person who'll throw a fit if her hair doesn't turn out exactly how she wants it. But when I saw the straight, flat hair cropped close to my head where my short, bouncy bob had been, I could feel my throat tighten and tears form in the corners of my eyes.

"You don't want to be too cute here, Miss," the female cadet said to my reflection. She looked almost triumphant, like Cinderella's stepsisters must have looked after ripping her pretty dress to rags before the ball. The cadet leaned closer, her blue eyes locking with my brown. "Be outstanding," she whispered. "But don't stand out."

The first qualification of a soldier is fortitude under fatigue and privation. Courage is only the second; hardship, poverty, and want are the best school for a soldier.
—NAPOLEON BONAPARTE, THE ART OF WAR, MAXIM LVIII

CHAPTER 4

MONDAY, JUNE 28
5:00 P.M.

A THOUSAND NEW CADETS AND I marched onto the Plain. Standing at attention in perfect rows, we faced our families. About eight hours had passed since we'd last seen them. We'd spent those hours transforming while they'd been busy waiting. I could feel the excitement all around me.

I quickly scanned the crowd for a glimpse of my family, wondering if they'd even bothered to stay. But I didn't spot them. I was actually a little disappointed—I wanted them to see me standing here, to know that I had made it through this day.

Together we raised our right hands and pledged to "support the Constitution of the United States and bear true allegiance to the National Government. . . ." Then, marching in four columns, we moved off the parade field.

Left behind was the cheering, waving, picture-taking throng. Rank after rank marched forward for as far as I could see— down a road, away from the granite buildings, North Area, and the Plain.

Well, that's it. No going back now.

"DRESS IT RIGHT AND COVER DOWN . . ." sang an upperclass cadet, marching to the left of Third Platoon, my platoon. All the members of Third Platoon echoed him, imitating his inflection and volume. Four squads made up Third Platoon; Cadet Daily and the three other squad leaders marched abreast, leading their squads of new cadets behind them. I remembered "dress right" and "cover down" from marching practice earlier in the day. *Stay on line with the guys on your left and right, and directly behind the guy marching in front of you.*

"FORTY INCHES ALL AROUND!" Third Platoon new cadets surrounded me on all sides. I felt as if I were just one bottle among many within a living, breathing Coke crate, rolling down a conveyer belt. And the space between me and any of them—"forty inches all around."

"MOMMA, MOMMA, CAN'T YOU SEE?" The cadet who marched alongside us had a great voice, smooth and soulful. A voice that should've been captured on a CD somewhere, breaking hearts.

"WHAT THIS ARMY'S DONE TO ME!" I peeked at him out of the corner of my eye. *He's the guy who taught us how to march!* The only person who had smiled today, who had joked. *Cadet Black—no pun intended.*

"MISERY, OH, MISERY . . ." Cadet Black sang on, echoing the thoughts of my heart. We followed the companies ahead of us toward a huge brick building crouched near the edge of the Hudson River.

"IS WHAT THIS ARMY IS TO ME!" It felt good to be marching. No thinking. Just marching. Mindlessly repeating back the phrases that Cadet Black shouted out. I could hear the roar of voices in the companies ahead of us, traveling over the warm air. The steady beat of hundreds of feet pounding the pavement in unison—left, right, left, right—relaxed me. I felt my tense muscles start to unwind, like they did a couple of miles into an eight-mile run. . . .

And then I heard her voice.

"Andi? Look, Ted! It's Andi!"

It can't be! I darted a look to my left. And what I saw out of the corner of my eye—my mother, camera in hand, scrambling behind Cadet Black—almost stopped my heart. So they had stayed after all.

"Do you think she can hear me, Ted? Come on, Andi! Look at me! Over here!"

Cadet Black scowled and then barked at us, "Third Platoon! Heads and eyes to the front! One. Two. Three. Four. United States Cadet Corps!"

"Why won't she look at us?"

Please, God, don't let them guess that she's talking to me. I ordered my eyes to stare at the building ahead, which was growing larger with every step. *Don't react. Not at all.*

I could hear her behind us now, her voice growing fainter. "Oh, just shut up, Ted! I only wanted to take her picture, you know. Is that so bad? She could've at least looked at us."

"I USED TO BE A HIGH SCHOOL STUD . . ." Cadet Black sang. I couldn't hear her at all now. But it had taken the entire platoon marching behind us to drown her out.

I tried to relax, to concentrate on keeping in step—but I couldn't stop shaking inside. *How could she have done that to me? What was she thinking?* No other parents had followed the cadets off the field. But then again, my parents were no ordinary parents. I should've expected it. During home track meets my mother had trotted out in front of the starting line just as the starter's gun went off. She had made surprise visits to band concerts and awards ceremonies. She had zipped up and down the aisles during my high school graduation. Every place that I was featured in any way, she and her camera arrived, behaving like a sugar-charged, lollipop-clutching kid in a toy store. And my dad was always in tow, grinding his teeth and looking uncomfortable, but powerless to stop her.

"NOW I'M MARCHING IN THE MUD." Tears settled into my eyes. My throat ached. No other parents had humiliated their new cadet like my parents had humiliated me. I yelled louder, trying to push it all away.

"I USED TO DATE A BEAUTY QUEEN—" My toes rubbed against my new, stiff black shoes. My wool pants clung to the backs of my legs. Clipped hair pricked the skin between my shoulder blades.

"NOW I DATE MY M-16!"

Date my M-16? Weird words, weird people, weird clothes. Suddenly, surrounded by yelling, sweating, White Over Gray—clad kids who only this morning were ordinary teenagers, I felt totally alone.

We reached the building and, one squad at a time, filed inside a huge auditorium. Air-conditioned plushness greeted us. It looked like a fancy concert hall with its rows of crushed-velvet seats. But instead of containing the cultured sounds of an orchestra, the place rocked with loud chanting and stomping feet.

"Fill up this row, Beanheads!" Cadet Daily shouted

at us over the roar. "And keep your skanky bodies off the seats until you are ordered to sit!"

Though every inch of my body whimpered for my seat, I yelled with the others, "WE ARE," (STOMP, STOMP) "HARDCORE!" over and over. "Hardcore H," I guessed then, was H Company's nickname. Our job was to let all the other companies know that we had arrived.

My seat was soft and comfortable when we finally were allowed—no, *ordered*—to sit. The air-conditioning cooled my skin, making me both refreshed and sleepy. This was the only relief any of us had had all day. And Cadet Daily knew it. "Listen up, Knuckleheads! Don't let me catch any of you racking in here. You will *not* be comfortable. That's an order! You will sit at attention." He peered down our row to ensure each of us was listening. "If I see any of you chilling out, I will personally crank up the heat on your sorry maggot bodies! Got it? Instant *dee*-frost!"

So I sat on the edge of my seat and stared at a cadet walking onto the stage at the front of the auditorium.

"I am Cadet Captain Knight, Regimental Commander of Cadet Basic Training," the cadet said. "Otherwise known as King of Beast." His voice lacked the malice that most of the upperclassmen's voices contained, and his welcome was cordial enough, but something about him chilled the room.

"Keep a sense of humor and a high degree of motivation," he told us. He reminded us that we had been selected out of thousands of applicants because each one of us demonstrated that trace of the exceptional intelligence, drive, and leadership ability that marked members of the Corps of Cadets.

"Now, look at the person to your left and right." I looked. New Cadet Ping, the guy who had helped me with my name tag, sat at my left. New Cadet McGill, the guy with the sun-bleached hair and lifeguard tan, sat at my right. "Four years from now, one of you will be gone."

I looked down at my hands in my lap. *Four years.* My feet ached. My eyes burned. My stomach growled. Sweat, dried and crusty, traced my hairline. *Four years of days like this?*

"Most of those won't make it through Cadet Basic Training." He paused. "That's why we call it 'Beast.'"

Will I be the one to leave? I thought of my alternatives. *It's either here or home.* I sat up even straighter on the edge of my soft seat. *No. I will make it. I will.*

7:15 P.M.

The medieval mess hall was filled with noise—of clanging dishes and roaring voices—as if the Crusades were being fought within its very walls. The other new cadets and I sat, by squad, around rectangular tables for ten.

"I am Cadet Black," boomed Cadet Black, sitting at the head of our table. I snapped my head to face him. So did the six other new cadets who had helped me get dressed earlier and were now sitting with me. "No pun intended." His lips twitched. Cadet Daily and another upperclassman flanked his sides. "I am your Table Commandant." Earlier, at lunch, Cadet Black had ignored the new cadets under his charge as they ate. Now he glared steadily at each of us around the table. The overwhelming aroma of roast beef made my empty stomach grumble. I concentrated on breathing in and out of my mouth so I wouldn't have to smell the food.

Cadet Black's eyes rested on me. I hoped it was only because I was sitting opposite him. "I had the pleasure of dining with some of you at lunch."

I rewound my memories from earlier in the day at triple speed. *Did I mess up for him, too?*

"That was then. This is now." He narrowed his eyes. "No more Mr. Nice Guy." Then he began to rattle off orders faster than my mother could hurl dishes. "You will sit at the position of attention at all times. Sit one fist's distance from the table edge, and one fist's distance from the back of the chair. Spread your napkins on your laps, and place your hands on top of the napkins. Position your plate so the West Point crest rests at twelve o'clock. Stare at the crest. *NO GAZING AROUND!*" Once again his eyes traveled around the table, following the contours of our sweaty faces. "YOU GOT THAT, BEANSMACKS?"

"YES, SIR!"

"GOOD. MAKE THE CORRECTION!"

Shaky hands spread linen napkins, fists sandwiched stomachs, and torsos shifted. I stared at my empty plate, my eyes locked on the crest, a black shield superimposed by something that looked like a gold knight's helmet.

"To eat," Cadet Black continued, "pick up your knife and fork. Cut an approximately one-square-inch piece of food. *Big bites are not authorized!* Raise your fork to your mouth. The forearm must be at a ninety-degree angle to the spine, elbow out." He demonstrated. "Then once you've placed the food in your mouth, ground your fork and knife diagonally at the *upper-right-hand* corner of your plate—across the twelve-o'clock and three-o'clock positions. Return to the position of attention with your hands on your lap. Then and only then may you chew and swallow the food. With your mouths closed! DO YOU UNDERSTAND, KNUCKLEHEADS?"

"YES, SIR!"

I don't think I can eat like this! And my defense against the roast beef was wearing thin. *Oh, why didn't I eat lunch today?*

"Davis!" Cadet Daily cut in, yelling down the table at me. "You are the Cold Beverage Corporal."

My heart dropped into my stomach. *The what?*

"Your function in life is to fill all those glasses with ice and a beverage." He pointed to the upside-down glasses lined in neat rows before me. "You will hold up the pitcher of the preferred beverage above your right shoulder, with both hands, like this"—he demonstrated with his plate— "and away from your mouth. I don't want your verminous spit anywhere near my beverage. You will look directly at the Table Com and announce in a command voice, 'Sir, the cold beverage for this meal is—' What's in the pitcher, Davis?"

I peered into one of the two stainless-steel pitchers beside me and yelled, "Sir, water is in the pitcher!"

"No, Bonehead! The *other* pitcher. The one with the *preferred* beverage. What is it?"

I tilted the second pitcher and watched an un-recognizable dark liquid slosh around inside. I racked my brain. *Iced tea? Coke? Grape juice?*

"TODAY, DAVIS. TODAY! WHAT'S IN THE PITCHER?" He pounded the table, making the dishes, silverware, ketchup, salt and pepper shakers—and me— jump. "Immediate Response Please—*IRP!* Morons in the loony bin are quicker than you."

Cadet Black and the other upperclassman sneered down the table and nodded in agreement. I was tired and hungry, and I wanted to cry. Even the mealtime insults I had endured back home were no preparation for West Point's dinner conversation and table etiquette.

Then Cadet Daily said the unbelievable. "Grab a glass and taste it."

I grabbed a glass and shakily poured the liquid. Three sets of upperclass eyes glared down the table at me, daring me to spill it on myself or, worse yet, on the pristine white tablecloth. My squadmates stared dutifully at their crests, probably thanking God, Allah, Buddha, Krishna, and every other higher power they could think of that they hadn't sat in my spot tonight. When I tried to drink, all three upperclassmen jumped out of their seats in rage, roaring corrections and insults at me. My forearm didn't form a ninety-degree angle to my spine. I gulped instead of sipped. I brought my mouth to my glass instead of my glass to my mouth.

I can't even drink right!

Finally, I choked down what tasted like bitter water. And after my fourth attempt of yelling over the din in the mess hall ("We can't hear you, Davis! Try it again! Is that what I told you to say? Do it again!"), I correctly made the announcement, "Sir! The cold beverage for this meal is iced tea. Would anyone not care for iced tea, sir?"

"Just fill all the glasses with ice and water," Cadet Daily said, motioning toward the stainless-steel bowl filled with cylindrical ice cubes. "Three whole ice cubes in each glass. No shrapnel. Do you think you can handle that, Davis?"

"Yes, sir!" I assured him.

"WORK!" Cadet Black bellowed.

I started spooning ice cubes into the glasses.

A mess-hall waiter suddenly appeared, wearing a red coat, white shirt, and black pants. He deposited stainless-steel platters of steaming food—roast beef, wide noodles, and peas with mushrooms—on the table to my left and right before shuffling away.

"Pass that food up here!" Cadet Black growled.

"Boguslavsky!" yelled Cadet Daily, pointing down the long table at Jimmy Fallon's lookalike on my left. "That means you! Function!"

When everyone had a glass of ice water and a plate of food before them, Cadet Black bellowed, "EAT!"

I grabbed my knife and fork and attacked my roast beef, cutting it into minuscule pieces and chomping it down, barely chewing.

"REGIMENT, RISE!" The command from the King of Beast, standing on the balcony in the center of the mess hall, came too quickly.

"ON YOUR FEET!" Cadet Black yelled. Hundreds of chairs pushed away from the tables. I was on my feet with the others, standing at attention and waiting for direction. I snuck a quick look at the table. So much food . . . and all I had managed to get past my lips were three peas, four square-inch pieces of roast beef, and a clump of stuck-together noodles.

Cadet Daily herded us out of the mess hall and into New Cadet Ping's room to teach us the basics—how to fold our clothes and make our beds—West Point style. New Cadet Ping's side of the room was already in perfect order. Along with his own stuff, I noticed, he'd also arranged most of his roommate's. I waited for Cadet Daily to tell us all that Ping was a model new cadet and would be promoted to an upperclassman instantly. Instead, he flipped Ping's mattress upside down onto the floor.

What did he do wrong?

"THE FIRST THING YOU BETTER GET THROUGH YOUR DUMB KNUCKLEHEAD, PING," Cadet Daily bellowed, "IS YOU DON'T DICK ON YOUR CLASSMATES!" He yanked the bleached white sheets and Army-green blanket from under the mattress and tossed them aside. "The objective here is not to make *yourself* look good, New Cadet Ping. This ain't no dog and pony show! This is *West Point*. If you can't hack it, beat it. Go back to being an E-5 in the Army!" Cadet Daily stood nose to nose with Ping, his veins straining against the skin of his neck. "The objective here, New Cadet Ping," Cadet Daily said between clenched teeth, "is to *cooperate* and *graduate*. You got that, Hotshot?"

"Yes, sir!" yelled Ping.

But he had cooperated. He'd helped his roommate out! I thought of how he had helped me with my name tag earlier. *Doesn't cooperate mean help?* But I wasn't sure what anything meant anymore.

Cadet Daily turned from Ping, stepped over the crumpled mound of bedding, and walked over to the dismantled bed. "Get over here, Ping," he snarled. "I'm going to show you miserable maggots how to *properly* make a bed." He eyed Ping with disgust. "And Mr. Combat here"—he flicked the multicolored rectangular pins lined up on Ping's chest—"is going to be my demonstrator." Where Ping had medals, our uniforms were bare—including Cadet Daily's.

When Cadet Daily had finished his step-by-step bed-making class, he smiled. With its tight hospital corners, the bed looked like an olive-drab business envelope. "Now, this is the standard, Third Squad! This bed is so tight, you can bounce a quarter off it." He pulled a quarter out of his pocket and slammed it on the bed. Like a rubber ball, it sprang back into his hand.

Before he could repeat his trick, the door opened and an upperclass cadet stepped inside the room.

"Hey, Daily. Here's the new addition to your squad." The cadet moved aside, and behind him stood a tiny girl with sweaty red hair shaped into a bun. Her eyes, enormous in her face, darted nervously around the room. "New Cadet Bryen. First name, Gabrielle," the cadet announced. "Her roommate decided Woo Poo U wasn't the place for her, so after the parade, when we marched off the Plain, she just kept on going, right into her parents' waiting car." He smiled. "The CO told me to hand her over to you since your female's roommate never showed." He thumped Cadet Daily on the back. "So, Dude, you have the only females in the platoon. Here's your opportunity to excel, my man!"

I bit the inside of my lip. *That's it? Just two girls in the entire platoon? Just me and her?*

After Cadet Daily released us back to our rooms, the first thing Gabrielle did was make her bed. Flawlessly. Then she helped me with mine. "My brother graduated from the Naval Academy two years ago," she said as we crammed my black-and-white-striped mattress into a white mattress cover. "He taught me how to do all this stuff." We heaved the mattress back onto the springs and sat down on the bed to rest. "He just made first lieutenant in the Marines."

I ran my hand along the metal footboard of my bed. I could sense her looking at me, waiting for a response, but I didn't have one. I had no idea what a "first lieutenant" was.

"That's a pretty high rank, you know." She grabbed my pillow and shoved it into a pillowcase. "He told me, 'Gab, keep a sense of humor. It's all a game. Play it the best you can.'" She tossed the pillow on my chair. "I don't know about you, but I've seen nothing, absolutely nothing funny about this place." She untied, then retied her shoe. "All day, all I could think of was my mom and dad." She turned to look at me. "You know what they said to me, right before I left? 'You can always come home, you know!'"

I smiled. "That's exactly what my brother said to me, but he didn't really mean it." *Oh, that sounds really pathetic.* "I mean, he knows I could never do that. You know, go back home." *Okay, you can stop now. You've said enough.* Because I knew myself. If I said one thing more, I'd blurt out my whole life's story, tainting myself forever in her eyes like I'd been tainted in everyone's eyes at school. *This is a new place with new people.* I wanted her to like me. I didn't want her—or anyone—to know what I had left back home.

So I shut my mouth and let her do the talking.

Luckily, Gabrielle was very good at talking, and since she was so engrossed in her own story, I didn't think she'd heard a word I'd said anyway. "They really didn't want me to come here. Oh, they never actually came out and *said* it or anything. But I could just tell." She shrugged. "I guess they were a little disappointed I didn't decide on Penn. They've had this huge college fund set up for me for years." She walked over to her desk and stood on tiptoes to pull the *B.A.G.*—*Barracks Arrangement Guide*—off her bookshelf. She leafed through it and said more to herself than to me, "Yeah. And today I almost took them up on it."

I was glad she hadn't. That would've left me the only female in the platoon.

We both stuffed a barracks bag with three sets of Gym Alpha—West Point's P.T. uniform of gray T-shirts and long black shorts—socks, a swimming suit, towel, and running shoes. We were just about to ping down the hall to the bathroom to arrange our athletic lockers when someone's fist hammered on our door three loud times.

"Enter, sir!" we yelled, and stood in the position of attention, dropping our bags at our feet.

The door flew open and Cadet Daily stomped inside.

"WHAT HAVE YOU LADIES BEEN DOING FOR THE PAST HOUR?" he roared, taking the room in with one ferocious glance. Army equipment still littered the floor. Underwear, socks, undershirts, and toiletries were piled all over the place. "WHAT DO YOU THINK THIS IS, A SIX-WEEK SLUMBER PARTY?" He disappeared and returned seconds later, dragging New Cadet Ping with him. "It is now 2145," Cadet Daily said, looking at his watch. "That gives you exactly fifteen minutes till Lights Out. This room better be squared away by then, Bone-heads." After he was gone, his voice drifted in from the hallway: "And leave the door open ninety degrees when a male is in the room, Davis. I'm keeping an eye on you."

Gabrielle turned to me and raised an eyebrow. I blushed.

"Sorry about this, Ping," I said, happy to change the subject. "You're probably sick of bailing me out again."

He shook his head. "Don't worry, this is my fourth room tonight. I've just finished helping Boguslavsky and McGill next door." He looked around our room. "Theirs was worse than this, believe me. At least you guys know how to fold underwear." Then he grinned. "Plus, you know what they say around here: 'Cooperate and graduate!'"

Up in the morning 'fore the break of day,
I don't like it, no way!
Eat my breakfast too soon,
Hungry again before noon.
—U.S. Army running cadence

CHAPTER 5

Tuesday, 29 June
0530

THE DOOR OPENED with a bang. I shot up in my bed, shaky from adrenaline and lack of sleep. Light from the hallway flooded into the room; it was still dark outside.

"FEET ON THE FLOOR, BONEHEADS!"

I squinted at the silhouette in the doorway. *Cadet Daily.* The overhead lights snapped on and, simultaneously, our metal trash can sailed across the room, crashing against the foot of my bed.

"LET'S GO! ON YOUR FEET! I want you standing tall and looking good, wearing Gym Alpha, outside my room, at 0545. Got that?"

My feet hit the floor, and I scrambled into the position of attention.

"YES, SIR!" Gabrielle and I yelled, trying our best to

sound wide-awake and eager. Cadet Daily left, slamming the door.

I checked my watch: 5:32. I subtracted in my head. *That gives us . . . thirteen minutes.*

We had no alarm clocks—I had turned mine over to Cadet Daily last night. "Don't worry about getting up on time," Cadet Daily had said. "I'll make sure you're awake." He certainly had.

I stumbled to the sink. My exhausted brain buzzed like radio static. Gabrielle and I had spent most of the night scurrying around in the dark with Army flashlights to finish fixing up our room. And now it was immaculate. Too immaculate. Every drawer, shelf, and closet in the room had conformed to the diagrams in the *B.A.G.* Every pair of underwear, socks, and gloves, every undershirt, handkerchief, and bra was folded and positioned accordingly. The uniforms hanging in the wardrobe closets faced left, their hangers canted right. Our combat boots and shoes were lined up along the lengths of our beds, laced with toes pointing to the center of the room. I wasn't used to such orderliness. It made me feel unsettled, somehow. I turned on the water and reached into my medicine cabinet for my toothbrush.

"I am not a morning person," Gabrielle mumbled, joining me at the sink. "I am not a night person. I am a ten A.M. to two P.M. person. The rest of the day, I am worthless. Totally worthless."

I wanted to tell her that I was definitely a night person, that once I made it past midnight, I was good until morning. But I was afraid she'd think I was weird, so I said nothing. The two of us took turns washing our faces, brushing our teeth, and putting in contacts in silence.

Loud music started blasting in the hallway. The theme music from the classic movie *Rocky*. Back home, construction workers used to serenade me with that tune as I ran past them. It had always made me run a little faster and a little better. Now it only made me want to hide.

Gabrielle and I looked at each other. "It sounds like it's coming over the PA system," she said. She stood on her toes and leaned over the sink to remove a tube of lotion from her medicine cabinet. "They probably want to make sure that we're really awake." I watched her put a blob of lotion under each eye and rub it in. "Well, it works. I'm definitely awake."

I pulled on my white socks and running shoes. Last night before he'd left, Ping had told us to wear Gym Alpha to bed, and I was glad we had. Outside our door echoed the tormented cries of the uninformed souls who hadn't and were now catching all kinds of heat as they braved the hallway to retrieve their Gym Alpha from their lockers in the latrines.

The music changed. The eerie theme from another classic movie, that Clint Eastwood Western *The Good, the Bad, and the Ugly*—one of my dad's late-night cable favorites—was playing now. I paced back and forth across the room. I checked my watch. I wasn't about to go out into that hallway of horrors a second before I had to.

Gabrielle was walking in circles near the door, checking her watch and adjusting her bun. Finally she said, "It's 5:42. Think we should go?"

My stomach jumped, but I nodded.

Gabrielle opened the door a crack and peeked outside. "Those guys next door, what're their names again?" she whispered.

"Boguslavsky and McGill."

"Yeah, them. They just left." She turned away from the door and faced me. "Do I look okay?"

Look okay? I hadn't given much thought to my looks. At home I would've never left to go anywhere without a good half hour of "primping," as my mother loved to call it. We had fought many gruesome battles over it. Battles in which my hair straightener was the booty, confiscated and locked away inside my mother's room, and my makeup was the carnage, strewn in broken pieces across the yard. But today, primping just didn't seem that important anymore.

"Well?" Gabrielle asked impatiently. "I don't look fat in these stupid shorts, do I?"

"Fat?" I asked. *At a time like this, who gives a rip if you look fat?* I shook my head. "You're not fat, Gabrielle." I checked my watch again.

"Oh, I always look fat in shorts because I'm so short." She stared up at me. For the first time, I noticed how short she really was. The top of her head barely reached my shoulder. "I had to get a waiver to get in here, you know. I'm only five feet tall." She looked down at her feet and studied her running shoes. "Well, actually, I'm four feet eleven and a half."

"Well, I really didn't notice," I said. She frowned. *What a dumb thing to say.* "I mean, I noticed that you're short, but not *that* short." *Great—that was even worse!* "You look fine, Gab." I checked my watch once more. "Come on! We've got to get out of here! We have one minute."

"Okay." She pulled up her socks. "I'll go first." She charged out into the hallway. I followed, pulling the door closed behind me. She made a sharp right turn, only inches from the wall, and pinged toward Cadet Daily's room. The rest of our squad was already there, lined up with their backs to the wall. Cadet Daily paced before them, yelling something about a "dress off."

Dress off? Who's wearing a dress?

"I was just having a little chat with your illustrious squadmates about dress offs," he snarled at us. He stopped pacing and studied all of us, from head to running-shoed toe. "You maggots are so unmilitary, you make me want to puke!"

Dress offs . . . dress offs. I should know this. Words, uniforms, and names whirled around my brain like snow flurries. Then I remembered. The thing we did yesterday when we got ready for the parade—wrapping our shirts tightly around ourselves and tucking them into our trousers the way people wrap Christmas presents. *But why in the world do we need dress offs to go outside and sweat?*

"You ragbags look like you just crawled out of bed." He looked at his watch and snorted. "We've got to go to formation now. But first let me get one thing through your brainless boneheads." He took a huge breath and roared, "I AM NOT PLEASED WITH YOUR PERFORMANCE THIS MORNING, THIRD SQUAD! YOU BETTER KNOCK YOURSELVES TOGETHER, OR I WILL SEE TO IT THAT YOU'RE GONE COME LUNCH FORMATION! *DO I MAKE MYSELF ABSOLUTELY CLEAR?*"

"YES, SIR!"

"Good. Now, Third Squad—right, *face!*" We turned. "Davis, you're leading. Go down the hall till you get to the stairwell. Don't miss it! Then down the stairs till you reach the sally port, and I'll take it from there. Think you can handle that?"

"Yes, sir!" *To the stairwell. Down the stairs. Into the sally port.* I had done it a million times yesterday, but never with people following me. I sucked in a shaky breath. *Just don't miss the stairs!* The simplest tasks were suddenly impossibly difficult here.

"Good. Third Squad, *move out!*"

I rushed along the wall and made it down the stairs. When we reached the sally port, Cadet Daily led us out toward the Plain, where we had marched for our parents only twelve hours ago. The sun was just beginning to splash color across the sky, and the outlines of the granite buildings were starting to emerge out of the darkness. The air was cool but damp.

"H COMPANY, FALL IN!" yelled an upperclass cadet as we scurried to our places.

In unison four other upperclassmen each bellowed at their platoons.

Cadet Black was one of them. "THIRD PLATOON, FALL IN!" Cadet Daily had told us yesterday that Cadet Black was our Platoon Sergeant. He was the guy whom everyone in Third Platoon, including the squad leaders, would answer to.

"THIRD SQUAD, FALL IN!" Cadet Daily yelled. "Into the position of attention!" We hustled into the spots we had been assigned before Dinner Formation yesterday. The four squads of Third Platoon lined up in four rows, one behind the other, facing Cadet Black. The four squad leaders stood in the far right position, anchoring down their squads. We new cadets stood in height order. In my squad New Cadet Cero, the tallest, stood beside Cadet Daily. Gabrielle, the shortest, was on the far left end. My spot, next to Ping, was somewhere in between.

H Company with its four platoons now formed a giant square, divided into four equal parts—two platoons in the front and two in the back. Two cadets stood facing us at the very front of the formation. One held the guidon—a yellow flag with a black *H*—hanging from a tall staff. The other was our First Sergeant, Cadet Stockel. I recognized his peach-fuzz–covered, wire-framed head. Just the sight of him made my armpits sweat. *Please don't see me.*

Cadet Black saluted his squad leaders as each reported how many new cadets in their squads were present—and how many were not. When all the platoons were ready, First Sergeant Stockel received each platoon's attendance report. Then Cadet Haywood, our Company Commander, walked briskly to the front of our formation. He exchanged salutes with First Sergeant Stockel, who left for the rear.

From my spot tucked inside Third Squad, Third Platoon, I felt my skin tingling as I watched all the precise movements around me. All the squads were straight. All the platoons square. Everything was perfectly organized. It reminded me a little of standing in the center of the football field with my high school marching band during the halftime show. Only this was a hundred times better. Mr. Rodwell, my band director, would've killed for us to look this good.

"RE-PORT!" called a lone cadet from the center of the Plain, his voice drifting toward us across the grassy field.

One by one, the company commanders answered:

"Alpha Company, all accounted for!"

"Bravo Company, all accounted for!"

"Charlie Company, one unaccounted for!"

When it was Cadet Haywood's turn, he saluted and yelled, "Hotel Company, all accounted for!"

"India Company, all accounted for!"

From some distant corner of the Plain a bugle pierced

the morning air, sounding like a call to battle. Then a cannon fired. For one still second all of West Point seemed to hold its breath. Cadet Haywood broke the silence. He shouted at us over his right shoulder, "H COMPANY, PRESENT—"

"PREE-*SENT*—" echoed the platoon sergeants.

"—ARMS!"

And everyone, cadet and new cadet alike, raised their right hands to salute the flag as it climbed the flagpole, formally declaring that June twenty-ninth was a new day.

0615

After marching into North Area, we did stretching exercises and calisthenics to the commands of the bellowing cadets standing on what looked like an oversized collapsible card table. We did repetition after repetition of familiar exercises with new names, like the Side Straddle Hop (jumping jacks) and the Turn and Bend (toe touches), and a few new ones like the Standing Long Sit and the High Jumper. And all the while, upperclassmen circled around us, spewing corrections and insults.

When we finished, First Sergeant Stockel ordered the platoons to line up in reverse height order behind the squad leaders.

"Stretch on your own, Third Platoon," Cadet Black said. "Get ready for the run. I'm setting the pace, and you're gonna get smoked."

I felt the prerace jitters coming on. I stretched my quads and eyed Cadet Black, sizing him up like I did my competitors before a race. *He looks pretty strong.* His legs were long and lean, but muscular—definitely a long-distance runner's legs. I watched the other new cadets twisting and bending around me. *How fast can these guys run?* I bent over at the waist without bending my knees and touched my palms to the ground. I noticed that the other companies in North Area were assembling for the run too.

"What do you have, Davis? Rubber bands for legs?"

I snapped to the position of attention, but Cadet Daily had already passed me on his way to stand at the front of the platoon with the other squad leaders.

"HOTEL COMPANY!" yelled First Sergeant Stockel. "FALL IN!" He waited until we all stood at attention, then shouted, "QUICK TIME, MARCH!" We walked with quick, long strides. I felt more like I was bouncing than marching in my springy running shoes. "LEFT. LEFT. LEFT, RIGHT," he called, his voice amplified three times louder as we marched through a sally port. "DOUBLE TIME—*MARCH!*"

And we were off, trotting at a pace of about eight and a half minutes per mile.

Cadet Black took over the commands for Third Platoon. *"LEFT. LEFT. LEFT, YOUR RIGHT, LE-EFT!"* he called in his singsong voice.

We passed a statue and the Plain on our right. *"A WHOLE LOT OF LEFT! LEFT, YO' RIGHT, LE-EFT!"* On our left stood two mansions, and behind them the brick gymnasium where the bus had dropped us less than twenty-four hours ago.

"WHEN THAT LEFT FOOT HITS THE GROUND, I WANT TO HEAR THAT CLAPPING SOUND!" sang Cadet Black. He ran to the left of our formation, looking at us as he ran.

"Okay, Third Platoon! When I say a phrase, you repeat

it back to me. Loud and in a motivated manner! It'll keep your mind off the running and keep you in step! If you can't hang with the pace, exit the formation! Someone will drop back to police up your sorry carcass!" Then he really let loose. "BUT WE WON'T HAVE ANY FALL-OUTS IN THIS FORMATION. WILL WE, THIRD PLATOON?"

"NO, SIR!" we yelled back.

"*LEFT! LEFT! LEFT, YO' RIGHT, YO' LE-EFT!*" he sang on. I sang back as loudly as I could. I felt great. The pace was too easy, but at least I was running. I felt more relaxed than I had since my dad had driven the Volvo through West Point's gate yesterday morning.

"*LEFT! LEFT! KEEP IT IN STE-EP!*"

Ping was running in front of me. I watched his feet, making sure I stayed in step. He seemed to have good rhythm—he never messed up once. We hung a left. Huge, identical brick houses with enclosed porches and manicured lawns lined the street.

"OKAY, NOW, THIRD PLATOON. LISTEN UP!" yelled Cadet Black. "*C-130 ROLLIN' DOWN THE STRIP—*" he sang.

I echoed his phrase with the other new cadets, having no idea what I was singing about. I accidentally stepped on the back of Ping's shoe. "Sorry," I whispered. *He must think I'm totally uncoordinated.*

"*SIXTY-FOUR TROOPERS ON A ONE-WAY TRIP!*" Cadet Black really did have a great voice. And not too low—I could sing with him.

"*STAND UP, HOOK UP, SHUFFLE TO THE DOOR—*"

Some of the guys in my platoon were struggling with the pace. *I'm barely breathing! They must* really *be out of shape*. And I was surprised to see that the companies ahead of us had already dropped people. New cadets littered the sidewalks beside the road—one here, two or three there—bent over or trotting along, trying to catch their breath. Most of them, I noticed, were girls.

"JUMP RIGHT OUT AND COUNT TO FOUR!"

I looked over Ping's head for Gabrielle. She was hanging in there, her red bun bouncing, behind Cadet Daily. *Just keep it up, Gab. Don't drop out!*

"IF MY 'CHUTE DON'T OPEN WIDE—"

I could hear the loud chanting of the platoons in front of and behind us. *I'd sure hate to live on this street, being woken up at 6:30 in the morning.*

"I'VE GOT A RE-SERVE BY MY SIDE!"

A *"ree-zerve"*? *What's a "ree-zerve"*?

"IF THAT ONE SHOULD FAIL ME, TOO—"

I repeated after him, wondering what came next. It was like listening to a story.

"LOOK OUT BELOW, I'M COMIN' THROUGH!"

A couple of guys made a loud, guttural noise in response: "Hu-ah!" Cadet Black grinned and started singing about two old ladies lying in bed, wanting to be Airborne Rangers, whatever that meant. And after that, something about a granny meeting St. Peter at the Pearly Gates and making him do push-ups.

I was really getting into it now, and so was everyone else. And we were loud, actually having fun repeating these crazy songs. *But what about the people who live on this street? They must hate us!*

I looked at my watch. We had run for nine minutes. Another company, with its gold-and-black guidon leading the way, ran toward us on the other side of the street.

"SOUND OFF, NOW, THIRD PLATOON!" hollered Cadet Black, punching the air with his fist toward the oncoming company, passing by on our left. "LET'S LET INDIA COMPANY KNOW THAT *WE* OWN THIS ROAD! LISTEN UP: *HOLD YOUR NOSE AND BOW YOUR HEAD*—" he sang, and we repeated after him.

"WE ARE PASSING BY THE DEAD!"

Then Cadet Black directed all the insults he could muster at them: "HEY YOU! ON THE LEFT! SICK CALL! LOOKIN' WEAK!" And after every phrase we yelled our loudest. I could see the open mouths of India Company's new cadets as we passed, giving it right back to us. I felt the energy building all around me. It was like being at a pep rally. And suddenly I was proud, proud to be in Third Platoon. We were the loudest and the best. Who cared about the sleeping residents of this street? We *did* own this road!

These boots are made for walkin'
And that's just what they'll do.
If all you're doing is markin' time,
They'll walk all over you.
—U.S. ARMY MARCHING CADENCE

CHAPTER 6

THURSDAY, 1 JULY
1510

WATER STREAMED OUT of the shower heads, drenching me, the seven other new cadets of Third Squad, and Cadet Daily. Wearing a one-piece black Speedo swimsuit and flip-flops, I stood at attention in the shower room of the male latrine. New Cadets Boguslavsky and Ping stood beside me in their black swimming trunks. Gabrielle, on the far side of the shower, was next to New Cadet Cero. The way she pulled at the elastic around her thighs seemed to scream, "I look fat in this stupid suit, don't I?"

"Grab a boot in one hand, your nail brush in the other," Cadet Daily ordered. His voice filled the room, tiled from ceiling to floor. "Cover the boot with saddle soap"—he pointed to the cans at our feet—"and scrub every inch of the boot until all the bluing comes off. Got it?"

"YES, SIR!"

"You've got to get the bluing off so the boots can breathe. The last thing you want on a road march, Third Squad, is waterproof boots. They'll turn your feet into a mess of blisters and you into a haze magnet with crutches." He crossed his arms. "When you finish with the boots, do your low quarters. Understand?"

"YES, SIR!"

"Good. Then, work!"

I'm getting this West Point talk down. After making it through three complete days of new cadet life, I could now understand about half of what was said to me. When Cadet Daily said, "low quarters," I knew that he meant the black shoes worn with White Over Gray—shoes that only a dead person would be caught dead in. I shoved my right hand deep inside one of my combat boots and started scrubbing. Diluted black dye ran from my hands, down my legs, and into the drain.

It hadn't taken me long to learn that the days at West Point varied very little. The routine was already imprinted in my mind:

0530: Wake-up. Reveille and P.T. Formation. P.T. Shower. 0800: Breakfast Formation. Breakfast. Military Skills Training classes. 1300: Lunch Formation. Lunch. Drill Practice on the Plain. More classes. Mass Athletics. Shower. 1800: Dinner Formation. Dinner. Squad Leader Time. Boot- and shoe-polishing time. 2200: Lights Out. Taps. Sleep.

Even the Fourth of July would be no different.

I secretly liked the sameness, though I'd never admit it to anyone. People would think I was crazy to *like* West Point, but here at least life was consistent. Predictable. So different from my life at home.

The pace hadn't let up one bit, though, and that took some getting used to. Every minute was packed with an almost frenzied busyness. I had no time to escape, to get away from everything and just think. Only a scant ten minutes ago, Third Squad had stood on the Plain, clutching M-14 rifles and wearing Battle Dress Uniform Under Arms—fatigues, Army-green pistol belt with a bayonet fastened over the left hip and a quart canteen of water over the right.

Now we were dressed for the pool and scrubbing like washerwomen while Cadet Daily sloshed around us in his flip-flops and swimming trunks, inspecting our work.

As the water continued to spray over me, I realized I was beginning to feel self-conscious in my swimsuit. But not like Gabrielle; I knew I didn't look fat, and wearing a swimsuit didn't bother me. After all, I'd practically lived inside one for the past two summers, lifeguarding at my local YMCA. Standing out and getting noticed was a necessary part of my job then. But now I just wanted to blend in. My problem was, standing here in my black Speedo, surrounded by seven half-naked guys in the shower of the male latrine, I knew I was doing anything but blending in.

I scrubbed the boot harder to erase the thought.

Besides, the only difference that I could see between the male latrine and the female latrine was four urinals. Everything else was laid out exactly the same. The wall of bathroom stalls. The row of sinks. The locker area. The large tiled room, where we stood now, with shower heads all around and no privacy curtains. And everywhere the smell of new cadet–issued Dial soap and Johnson's baby shampoo, mixed with sweat, clung to the damp air.

No difference at all. But I wasn't convinced. Deep down I felt like I didn't really belong here.

"Relax, Knuckleheads!" Cadet Daily's voice disrupted my thoughts. "This is Squad Leader Time." He stopped splish-splashing around and stood in front of Ping, to my left. "Let's get to know each other," he said. "You're first, *Combat*. State your full name, where you're from, what you're famous for, and why you're here. In that order. Do you think you can remember that, Bonehead?"

"Yes, sir," Ping said.

Real relaxing. I bit my lip and globbed more saddle soap on the boot. *I'm next. Great. Famous? I'm not famous for anything. And why am I here? What in the world am I going to say?*

"Sir, my name is George Ping—"

"You're not telling *me*, Knucklehead. I already know everything about you. You're telling your squadmates."

He knows everything about us? About me? I scrubbed harder.

"Yes, sir. I'm George Ping. I just came from the Prep School at Fort Monmouth. Before that I was stationed at Fort Bragg, as a medic with the 82nd Airborne. But originally I'm from Phoenix." Cadet Daily remained in front of Ping, studying him. Ping looked directly at him and said, "And I'm here because I didn't want to be an E-5 in the Army anymore."

"That so?" Cadet Daily smiled. An amused, almost sarcastic smile. "What're you famous for, *Combat*?" He leaned closer. Water from his nose dripped onto Ping's. "How'd you get that Bronze Star, Hotshot? And all those other medals. Steal 'em off some dead guy?"

"Sir, I earned them in Afghanistan."

For a second all scrubbing ceased. I didn't know what a Bronze Star was, but it sure sounded impressive. The lower part of Cadet Daily's face retained the smile, but something like jealousy flashed in his eyes. He stepped back.

"Ping." He spat it more than said it. "I've got a smack named 'Ping.' Unbelievable." He shook his head. "You're going to catch all kinds of heat with a name like that! I almost feel sorry for you, Combat. But don't get your hopes up—*almost* is the operative word. What kind of name is 'Ping,' anyway?"

"Sir, Ping is a Chinese name. In the Fujian dialect of south China, 'Ping' translates to 'soldier,' sir."

"How apropos," Cadet Daily said. Then he turned to me. "Davis, what do you got?"

I stared at the gray water disappearing down the drain, wishing I could follow it. After Ping I had nothing impressive to say. "I'm Andi—short for Andrea—Davis. I'm from Lake Zurich, Illinois. Um, that's a suburb of Chicago. And I'm famous for, um, running, I guess—"

"Running?" Cadet Daily looked interested. "Did you get recruited for track?"

Recruited? I didn't know people got recruited for sports at West Point. I shook my head. "No, sir. But I ran track in high school. Cross country, too."

He turned his green eyes on me. My Speedo suddenly felt awfully skimpy. I tugged at the tongue of my lathered boot. I knew I didn't look much like a runner. Not a long distance runner, anyway. I didn't have the requisite stick legs, and, well, I had too much on top.

Suddenly I heard my mother's voice, speaking to my doctor during an annual checkup: *"With knockers like that, she could be a go-go dancer, couldn't she?"* I squeezed my eyes shut to clear my head. *I'm so glad she's not here now.*

"You any good, Davis?" Cadet Daily asked.

I shrugged. "I guess, sir." *I never went to State.* The

thought just sat there, condemning me. *How good can you be if you never went to State?* I rubbed the toe of my boot with the nail brush. White leather peeked through the lather in places. I had qualified—twice in cross country, and once in the 3000—but had never gone. My mother had seen to that. She hated "that good-for-nothing running."

I chewed the inside of my lip, wondering what to say next.

"You'll wear a hole in your boot scrubbing like that, Davis," Cadet Daily said. I could feel him staring at the crown of my head, waiting. I watched my feet and the bluing running over them. My toes looked funny, tinted gray. "And you came to West Point because . . ." he prompted.

Because one thousand long miles stretched between West Point and home? Because I didn't want to owe my parents anything anymore? But I couldn't tell him—or Third Squad—that. "Sir, I came to West Point because . . . well, um, I'm not exactly sure why." I raised my eyes to his face, and suddenly the words came fast. "But, sir, this girl—a cadet, actually—came to my high school to talk about West Point to anyone who wanted to know about it. That was my junior year. And well, I stopped by her display—it was right in front of the library—and it sounded like something I'd like to do, and I've always liked being outside—"

"If you just want to be outside," Cadet Daily said, annoyed, "join the Peace Corps!"

I had let myself babble, and now he was mad at me. *Way to go, Andi.*

He stepped closer, his green eyes penetrating mine. "If you don't figure out why you're here, Davis, you're never going to stay." He moved on to stand in front of New Cadet Boguslavsky, then turned back to me. "This afternoon, during Mass Athletics, what did you sign up for, Davis?"

★ 75

"Sir, I signed up for softball." I remembered how yesterday afternoon I had surprised myself, hitting a double. That hit had made my day, but I would've traded that play in a second for my running shoes, a long path in the woods, and a big chunk of time—alone.

"Well, I'll make sure you get hooked up with the Women's Cross Country Team. The captain of the team's a personal friend of mine. And tryouts for Corps Squad—" He eyed the faces around the room. "Here's a new vocabulary word for you, Smack Heads. At Woo Poo U, Corps Squad means varsity, NC Double A, Division One." He redirected his attention to me. "Tryouts for Corps Squad are in a couple of weeks."

I might be able to run here! I could've hugged him right there—Speedo suit and all. But, of course, I didn't. "Thank you, sir," I croaked.

"Yeah, well, don't embarrass me, Davis. I better not see you falling out on any runs." He switched his focus onto New Cadet Boguslavsky. "All right, Boguslavsky. You're up."

"Yes, sir. I'm Christopher Scott Boguslavsky, but I go by 'Kit.' And I come from Monongalia County, West Virginia."

"Mono—whatever you said—*County*, Bogus?" Cadet Daily snarled. "We want a city, not a county, Bonehead."

"Yes, sir. I come from a town called Crossroads, close to Morgantown—that's the home of WVU—and down a stretch from Efaw's Knob in Monongalia"—he emphasized every syllable—"County, West Virginia." He had a slight southern accent, one that wove around his words but never quite settled in. "Back home, I'm famous for being the preacher's kid, and I came here because I heard the hunting's good." He smiled. "And, of course, I wanted the challenge."

Cadet Daily crossed his arms and smirked, raising an

eyebrow. "Good answer there, *Bogus*. But guess what?" The top of Cadet Daily's head only reached the bottom of Boguslavsky's chin, so he had to take a step back to get good eye contact. "The hunting's only good for the hunters, Wise Guy. And I've got my sights set on *you*!" He moved along the sloppy line of new cadets, boots, shoes, and saddle soap that stretched across the room. "Mr. Hickman, you're next."

When Hickman opened his mouth, a thick drawl crawled out. "Well, my name is Tommy Hickman from Birmingham, Alabama." He put down his scrubbed boot and picked up the fresh one. "I'm famous for my fastball that got me a 1.02 ERA during my senior year." He paused dramatically, a smug expression on his face. "I'm here because Army Baseball recruited me, and because my dad's a Citadel grad." He stood a little straighter. "*I* want to do better."

There are some people you like immediately. Hickman wasn't one of them.

"You think pretty highly of yourself, Hickman, for being nothing more than a scum-sucking maggot." The smug look on Hickman's face instantly vanished. Cadet Daily moved on. "Okay, Bonehead Bonanno, you're up."

"Yes, sir. My name's Frank Bonanno, and—"

"Whoa, Nellie!" Cadet Daily leaned closer to Bonanno, whose nose nearly touched Cadet Daily between the eyes. "Bonanno, did you shave this morning?"

Bonanno swallowed. "Yes, sir!"

Cadet Daily frowned and closely eyed the condition of Bonanno's face. "I think you need to step a little closer to that razor, Fur Face."

Fur face? From where I stood, two people away, Bonanno's face appeared to have a light haze of stubble in places, but it looked okay to me.

Bonanno swallowed again. "Yes, sir."

"And while you're at it, shave your back. No telling what kind of vermin is hiding in that jungle."

The look on Bonanno's face was one of pure shock. "Y-y-yes, sir," he stammered. The rest of us were staring hard at our boots, trying to keep from laughing out loud. With Cadet Daily around, no subject was sacred.

"Okay, Bonanno, as you were. Finish telling us about yourself."

"Yes, sir." Bonanno had a shapeless nose and bushy eyebrows. And, as Cadet Daily had pointed out, Bonanno *was* a hairy guy. His shorn head seemed mismatched with the rest of his body. "My name's Frank Bonanno, and I'm from Long Island," he said in a voice that I'd only heard taxi drivers in the movies use. "I'm famous for . . . does winning New York State's spelling bee in the third grade count, sir?"

Cadet Daily laughed, then coughed, trying to cover it up. "You're a real go-getter, huh, Bonanno?"

"Yes, sir!"

Cadet Daily shook his head but didn't say anything else, so Bonanno cleared his throat and continued. "Well, when I was in middle school, I was, uh, well, I did some pretty dumb things, so my dad says, 'Son, you've got a choice: military school in high school, or military school in college.' I chose college because, well, frankly, I thought he'd forget about it by the time college rolled around. But he didn't." He cleared his throat again. "So during my junior year my dad took me up here, and I thought, 'Hey, if I've got to go to military school, I ought to go to the best, right?' So, here I am."

"Yeah, just ask Mr. Hickman. The Citadel wasn't good enough for him." Cadet Daily glared at Hickman. "But what Hickman doesn't know, Bonanno, is that West Point might be *too* good for him." He turned, then stopped in mid step. "Listen, Bonanno, don't shave your back, understand? I didn't mean that literally. But *do* pay closer attention to that face. Hairy guys like you need to shave twice a day." He sloshed on. "New Cadet McGill, what do you have for us?"

"My name's Jason McGill, and I'm from Boulder, Colorado." The stubble on his head kept its sun-bleached color even when wet. "I'd like to be famous for winning the Tour de France someday, but for now I guess I'm just famous for having a really cool bike." He laughed loudly— and alone—at his own bad joke. "And I'm here because I didn't get into the Air Force Academy." He laughed again, nervously. "I would've only been two hours from home."

I was wrong. Because of his hair and tan, I had pictured McGill as a California guy who'd spent most of his time on the beach, a surfboard in one hand and a boom box in the other. It made me wonder how the others pictured *me* before I opened my mouth. And, with a sinking feeling, what they thought of me now that I had.

"A zoomie wanna-be." Cadet Daily shook his head. "And a momma's boy. That's a weak combination, McGill. And I've got news for you: If you ain't good enough for the flyboys, you ain't gonna last *here* a week. Might as well start packing now." Then he nodded at the biggest guy in the room, New Cadet Cero. He was about six foot four, all muscle, and black. And he towered a full head and shoulders above Cadet Daily.

Cadet Daily's the shortest guy in our squad, besides New Cadet Ping . . . and Gabrielle. He's only maybe an inch taller than me! Somehow, he had seemed much taller than that.

"Okay," Cadet Daily said, "let's hear it, Big Guy."

For such a big guy Cero had a surprisingly soft voice.

"My name's Phil Cero, and I come from East L.A. I'm not famous for anything, and I'm here because I want to be."

Cero's answer was way too short. Cadet Daily's face became a mask of ice.

"East L.A., eh?" I looked quickly from one face to the other. "You speak any Spanish, *Cero*?"

"Yes, sir. I know a little Spanish."

"Then, I presume, you know the meaning of your last name?"

Cero's Adam's apple moved up, then down. He knew what was coming, and so did I—I understood four years' worth of high school Spanish. "Sir, in the Spanish language 'cero' means 'zero.'"

Cadet Daily slapped his hands together twice in mock applause. "Mr. Zero, famous for nothing. Absolutely nothing. A complete zero." Cero's jaw muscles flexed in, then out. "Hey, Zero, you have a scar under your left eye. Nice touch. Mind telling me how you got it?"

I felt my body tense up. There were some things that people didn't want to share with others. I had a feeling Cero's scar was one of those things, and I felt bad for him.

Cero paused a second, staring back at Cadet Daily.

Cadet Daily took it as a threat. "*IRP!* You need an attitude adjustment, Mister? I'll drop you right here, right now, Big Guy! A little *Leaning Rest* action. Is that what you want?" Cadet Daily's ears, then face, grew crimson as he leaned closer to Cero, his face upturned and eyes blazing.

"No, sir!" Cero said quickly. "Sir, I received the scar during a fight when I was just a kid."

"Just a kid," Cadet Daily repeated, stepping back, his face slowly returning to its normal hue. Then, his eyes still locked with Cero's, he said, "We all know that Ping's been kicking butt and taking names with the 82nd. Why don't you tell the rest of the squad what *you've* been doing since you graduated high school, Zero?"

Cero cleared his throat. "I worked for a couple years after high school, then earned two years toward a bachelor's degree in aerospace engineering at U.C. Davis."

He's already been to college? Why in the world is he here?

"Well, well, well. We've got a bona fide rocket scientist in our midst, Third Squad."

I watched Cero's face as Cadet Daily moved for Gabrielle, his last victim. Whatever feelings and thoughts he had right then were written where nobody could read them.

Unlike Gabrielle, who was hastily rearranging her Speedo as Cadet Daily closed in on her. "Miss Bryen," he said, "last is best. Or so I've heard. Impress us."

She licked her already-damp lips. "I'm Gabrielle Bryen. I go by 'Gab' or 'Gabby.'" She shrugged her shoulders. "Gabrielle is good, too. Actually, I like Gab best, but I'll answer to anything."

"Good, Bryen," he said. "I have a few names in mind, custom-made, for you, too. Go on."

She was babbling, but for some reason, it didn't seem to bother Cadet Daily at all.

"Yes, sir." She continued, "I live, or lived, in Philadelphia. The northwest area of the city, called Chestnut Hill." She tittered nervously. "So, I guess, party at my house after the Army-Navy game!"

"*If* you make it here that long, Miss Bryen," Cadet Daily said.

"That won't change anything, sir," Gabrielle said solidly. "I'll have a party anyway." She glanced at me.

I nodded. *Good comeback!* One thing was for sure,

Gabrielle could talk well on her feet. I wished I were more like her. I could hardly talk at all.

Cadet Daily smiled. He had liked her comeback too.

"I'm famous for being a pretty decent tennis player and for being short. For obvious reasons." She pulled at her elastic again. "I got recruited to play tennis, so that's one reason why I'm here. Another reason—I went to an all-girl school for the past twelve years. I guess I just wanted to see how the other side lives."

Cadet Daily laughed. "Well, Miss Bryen, you picked the place for that."

Why does he keep calling her "Miss Bryen" and me just "Davis"? The skin of my fingers had turned white and seemed to shrink around my bones.

"All right, Third Squad," Cadet Daily said, checking our boots and shoes as he sloshed back to Ping. "It looks like you got most of the bluing off. Put on your boots."

After all our boots were laced, he yelled, "Let's break those boots in real good. Double time in place, Third Squad! *Let's go!* Don't let a little water turn you into a bunch of sniveling wimps! Bring those knees to your chest. Higher! *Higher!*" Our boots slapped the wet tile floor in a rhythmic cadence.

"Okay. Here's what we've got, Third Squad." He paced before us, rubbing the back of his neck. "We've got Mr. Bogus, the Bible-thumping wise guy. Then there's Super-jock Hickman and Shave Your Back Bonanno."

My wet boots were growing heavy, and the floor was slick. *Just don't fall!*

"We have the Zoomie wanna-be, Mr. I-Want-My-Mommy McGill, and the venerable rocket scientist, Mr. Zero. Of course, we mustn't *overlook* our very own Miss Army Tennis, otherwise known as Blueblood Bryen, who needs stilts to reach the doorknob." He had splashed his way down the line. Only Ping and I remained. I pumped my legs up higher and stuck a look onto my face that said, "I'm not tired. Not one bit."

"And finally Mr. Ping, the Combat Soldier, and Oh-Why-Am-I-Here Davis." He stood on the step that led out of the shower. "Cease work!" he yelled. We stopped. Standing on the step, he was taller than any of us.

I think that's how he wants it.

"We have a lot of work to do, Third Squad," he said. "I'm going to spend the next six weeks tearing you down, inch by painful inch, until you don't even remember you were any-body. Then *you'll* spend the next four years building your-selves up to becoming someone again. But not the person you were." He paused, watching our expressions, one by one. "When you go home at Christmas," he whispered, "your parents won't even recognize you." I could sense the panting bodies beside me stiffen. "Here's our squad motto, Third Squad: 'Never surrender!' I want you to brand it into your minds and write it on your hearts. Bury it deep, Third Squad, so that when things get tough—and things will get real tough before I'm through with you—it will be there for you. Never surrender! Let's hear it, Third Squad!"

"Never surrender, sir!" We thundered as the water con-tinued to stream over us.

"LOUDER!"

"NEVER SURRENDER, SIR!"

Cadet Daily smiled, then checked his watch. "Turn off the showers and dry off. I want you standing tall in front of my room in one five minutes, ready for Mass Athletics, wearing Gym Alpha, and holding a filled canteen. Don't be late, Third Squad!"

And then he left.

Hey, hey Captain Jack,
Meet me down by the railroad track.
With those runnin' shoes in my hand,
I'm gonna be a runnin' man.
—U.S. Army running cadence

CHAPTER 7

Monday, 12 July
0550

"ATTENTION ALL CADETS! THERE ARE TEN MINUTES UNTIL ASSEMBLY FOR PHYSICAL TRAINING AND REVEILLE FORMATION. THE UNIFORM IS—GYM ALPHA. TEN MINUTES REMAINING!"

Gabrielle and I stared at each other's reflection in the mirror, our toothbrush-clutching hands momentarily paralyzed. Gabrielle's eyes widened, then bulged, as if some hungry anaconda were slowly coiling itself around her.

"Oh, no!" she yelled, flecks of toothpaste catapulting toward the mirror. "I'm a Minute Caller! I'm supposed to be out there!" She spat into the sink and wiped her mouth on the shoulder of her Gym Alpha. "Where's What's-Her-Name? Oh, why didn't she come by? Why didn't *you* remind me?" She tossed her toothbrush into the sink and scurried for her running shoes.

"Sorry, Gab," I said. "I forgot, too." I chewed on my lip, feeling helpless.

Yesterday First Sergeant Stockel had assigned each new cadet an official duty. I got Laundry Carrier, and Gabrielle got Minute Caller. Later, while Gabrielle and I were putting a final spit shine on our shoes, we had heard a frantic rapping on our door. A female new cadet from Second Platoon, whom I'd never met, burst into our room. She slumped against our door and blew down the front of her shirt before saying a word to us. "I'm Nina Abrams," she said at last. "Since my last name starts with an 'A-b', I get to be the Head Minute Caller this week. Lucky me." She squinted across the room at the names on our shirts.

"I'm a Minute Caller," Gabrielle said, dropping her shoe on her desk. "What do I need to do?"

"Okay. Here's the deal. Your job is to count down the minutes for every formation, starting at ten minutes before. You have to stand under, uh—hold on . . ." She reached into the back pocket of her trousers, pulled out a wilted pad of paper the size of her hand, and flipped through it. Gabrielle glanced at me.

". . . under the clock in the middle of this hallway"—she jabbed the air over her shoulder with her thumb—"wearing the proper uniform for the formation." She ripped a piece of paper out of her notepad and thrust it into Gabrielle's polish-smudged hand. "You have to memorize this tonight."

Gabrielle nodded.

"Tomorrow morning go to your clock, stand at attention facing the clock, and wait. And then at exactly ten minutes to six—because P.T. formation's at six—" She looked at Gabrielle. "You following?"

Gabrielle nodded.

"Give yourself plenty of time to get out there." She looked at her pad again. "Okay, so you're at your clock. At ten till, call that out." She pointed to the piece of paper in Gabrielle's hand. "There'll be two other new cadets at the clocks at either end of the hall. You'll all be yelling this in unison." Nina shoved the notepad back into her pocket. "Try to stay together. Okay?"

Gabrielle nodded again.

"All right." Nina wiped her damp forehead with the back of her hand. "You have to do the same thing at five, four, and three minutes before formation. But don't go back to your room between minutes. Just wait in the hall, facing the clock." She moved closer to Gabrielle and pointed at something on the piece of paper. "When the two-minute bell sounds, yell *this*. It's a little different. Okay? And oh, since the uniform for P.T. is Gym Alpha, you say that *here*." She pointed to the paper again. "Okay?"

Gabrielle stared at the paper and licked her lips.

"After you finish the two-minute call, book it like crazy to formation. If you're late, we *both* get fried. Okay?"

"I think so. I don't . . . I mean . . ."

"First Sergeant Stockel said if there are any screw-ups, he'll chew my butt so bad, I'll get medically discharged." She sighed, then stared at her watch. "It's almost Taps. Look, I'll try to come by here around 0535 tomorrow morning to make sure that you're all squared away. Let's synchronize our watches."

But Nina never showed up, and even though Gabrielle had lain awake whispering her lines after Lights Out, we had both forgotten. I rinsed off Gabrielle's discarded toothbrush and placed it in her medicine cabinet. I hoped she didn't blame me.

"How in the world did we forget?" Gabrielle looked close to tears, and her hands shook as she picked up her shoes. "I could see, maybe, if we overslept. But forget? This really, really sucks, Andi. An *unbelievable* amount."

"I know, Gab. I should've remembered." I began to pace around the room, frenetically straightening and tightening—needing to do something, anything, but stand still. *I'm so lucky.* All I had to do this week as a Laundry Carrier was collect the upperclass cadets' barracks bags of dirty laundry and haul them down to one of the sally ports for pickup. Then later in the week, I'd deliver the cleaned laundry back to the rooms. No way could that be as bad as calling minutes.

"I guess I was so worried about the stupid P.T. test we have this morning that I couldn't think about anything else." *Except for cross country team tryouts this afternoon.* Actually, the two running events had been the only thing on my mind since last night, when Cadet Daily made his final appearance of the day at Lights Out. "Remember, Davis, tomorrow's your big day," he had said. "Tryouts for Corps Squad *and* the P.T. test. Thought you'd like that little piece of information to spice up your dreams tonight." After I was sure Gabrielle was finally asleep, I had crept out of my bed to stretch—trying to psych myself up, trying to visualize my pace, trying to relax. I just *had* to make the team.

"I'm really sorry, Gab." *Please don't be mad at me.* I had just started to believe that maybe she considered me her friend.

"WHERE'S MY MINUTE CALLER?" Some cadet's

voice boomed in the hallway. "OH, MINUTE CALLER! WHEREFORE ART THOU, MINUTE CALLER?"

Gabrielle and I froze. "That sounded like Cadet Aussprung," I whispered, as if the cadet could actually hear me. "The hugest haze in—"

"I *know* who Cadet Aussprung is, Andi." Gabrielle struggled with her shoes, hurling curses at the floor. "I can't get these stupid things on!"

I crouched beside her. "Try untying them, Gab."

"No, Andi! Get my brush!"

Her brush? Brushing hair at a time like this would've been the last thing on my mind, but I rushed back to the sink and grabbed it.

Gabrielle was standing, her shoes now on, pulling up her socks. "Come on! I can't go out there looking like this!"

I tossed her the brush, and she yanked out her bun. Then she raked the brush through her strawberry frizz before twisting her hair back into place. Was she crazy? "Gab, just get *out* there! Don't worry about how you—"

"HO! HO! HO! SOMEONE'S HEAD'S GONNA ROLL!"

"Quick!" she squeaked. "Give me a dress off!"

I sprang behind her, snatched the brush from her, and threw it on her bed so our hands would be free.

"I'm dead. I'm dead. I'm *dead!*" She pulled the waistband of her shorts away from her tailbone. "I'm going to get kicked out, Andi! I just know it."

I grabbed the excess T-shirt fabric from her sides and folded it toward her spine. "Okay . . . now!"

She snapped her waistband back in place. "Why does my last name start with 'B'? Yours starts with 'D.' That's why you didn't get Minute Caller. It's not fair!"

Now she was whining. *Like that helps anything. She*

just needs to shut up and get out there! I did some final tucking. Her T-shirt was wrinkle-free. "Done."

She sprinted out of the room, slamming the door behind her.

I put her brush away and chewed my thumbnail, listening.

"WELL, WELL, WELL! NEW CADET BRYEN! SO GLAD YOU COULD COME TO MY PARTY. BUT, MY, MY, MY. AREN'T WE FASHIONABLY LATE THIS FINE MORNING?" Then silence followed. Silence, that is, except for the quick footsteps of new cadets pinging down the hall and the music of the "Ballad of the Green Berets" blaring over the PA system:

> *Silver wings upon their chests,*
> *These are men, America's best,*
> *One hundred men we'll test today,*
> *But only three win The Green Beret.*

Third Squad had to be standing against the wall in front of Cadet Daily's room at five minutes before formation. I checked my watch. *That gives me one minute, forty-three seconds.* I gave myself a dress off and stared at the doorknob, waiting.

"Attention all cadets!" Gabrielle shouted, battling the Green Berets for superiority of the airwaves. Her voice sounded shaky and thin. "There are . . . six? and a butt minutes until assembly for Physical Training. The uniform is—"

I winced. *Oh, Gab. That's wrong! It's Physical Training* and *Reveille Formation.* Listening to Gabrielle practice last night, I had learned the lines, too.

Doors banged open up and down the hall.

"Cease work, Bonehead!"

"What? Where did Reveille go, Smack?"

"You call that minute calling? I call it a dereliction of duty, Dirtbag!"

My watch said it was time to go. I opened my door to the hostile hallway and peeked around the door frame. Gabrielle stood stiffly against the wall beneath the center clock, attracting upperclass cadets like death draws flies.

"YOU MAKE ME SICK, BRYEN!" I heard Cadet Aussprung roar behind me, feeling guilty as I pinged along the wall away from Gabrielle. "BOWING-TO-THE-PORCELAIN-GOD SICK. IF THERE'S ONE THING THAT CHAPS MY HIDE, MISS, IT'S INCOMPE-TENCE. AND YOU GIVE NEW MEANING TO THE WORD!"

0618

"You know, Andi, he's really hot," Gabrielle whispered to me as we stretched with the other new cadets of H Company.

"What?" I asked, only half listening. We stood inside a huge, drafty building called the Field House. Here we'd soon be doing push-ups and sit-ups for the P.T. test.

"*You* know. Cadet Aussprung. Fourth Squad's squad leader? Cadet Daily's roommate?" She closed her eyes. "The guy with the slate-gray eyes?"

"I *know* who Cadet Aussprung is, Gabrielle."

"He's really gorgeous. *Especially* when he's mad."

"You're really sick. You know that?"

She smiled and bent over to touch her toes.

Cadet Aussprung, the Hollywood Hero. I thought he was cute, too, the first time I saw him. I remembered him leading four other new cadets and me out of the gym and across North Area on the first day of Beast. But the second he'd opened his mouth, any admiration I'd had for him evaporated.

"There are tons of cute guys here. Don't you think, Andi?"

I shrugged. "There are tons of *guys* here, Gabrielle." Guys were just about the last thing I needed to worry about right now. I sat down to stretch my legs.

"Even the new cadets. Some of them are okay, too. And Cadet Daily—"

I looked up. "What about Cadet Daily?"

Gabrielle checked over one shoulder, then the other, to make sure no one could hear her. "He's a *doll*."

A doll? I had never thought about him like that. A prison warden? Yes. An overbearing tyrant? Definitely. A bullying big brother? Maybe. But a doll? Never! It was almost incestuous. I looked at Gabrielle. I just could not figure her out, sometimes.

Cadet Daily suddenly appeared and motioned for Third Squad to huddle around him. "Okay, Third Squad, pair up. I want you two"—he pointed at me and Gabrielle—"to split up."

Gabrielle glanced at me before scooting next to Ping.

Hickman snatched McGill as his partner right away. Bonanno, Boguslavsky, and Cero hesitated, looking at each other.

"Today, Third Squad," Cadet Daily yelled. "Today!"

I felt a twinge of panic inside, just like I used to feel in gym class whenever the kids got to choose teams, fearing

I'd be picked last. *Take a chance, Andi.* I turned to Boguslavsky, the preacher's kid. He'd braved the hallways and the door-open-at-ninety-degrees-when-both-sexes-are-in-the-room policy more than once to polish boots and brass with Gabrielle and me after dinner. Maybe he'd be my partner.

"Uh, hey, guys," Boguslavsky said, nodding at the others. "Go ahead. I'll pair up with Andi." He looked at me. "Okay with you?"

I smiled and nodded, relieved.

"You're gonna count push-ups and sit-ups for your partner and write the number of completed repetitions on the scorecard," Cadet Daily was saying now. He held a stack of narrow cards. "Take one and pass it around. . . ."

"HARDCORE COMPANY, *AT EASE!*" yelled a voice above the low rumble, and a female cadet leaped up onto a P.T. stand at the end of the room. "My name is Cadet Barrington, Hardcore's Athletic Officer, and I will be administering your very first Cadet Physical Fitness Test, otherwise known as the CPFT!"

Hu-ah! and other barbaric grunts erupted in the Field House.

Cadet Barrington smiled. "I'm glad to see that you are motivated. But . . . are you all fired up?"

"FIRED UP, FIRED UP, FIRED UP, *MA'AM!*"

"Okay!" Her skin was so tan that her white socks seemed to glow. "The CPFT is a three-event test, consisting of two minutes of push-ups, two minutes of sit-ups, and a two-mile run. The purpose of this test is to determine your level of fitness during Week 3 of Beast Barracks. In order to pass, you must achieve a minimum score in each event. During the academic year, an actual grade will be attached to your score." She raised an eyebrow. "But today, Hardcore, we're going to do it *just for fun.*"

More war whoops filled the Field House. I whooped, too. It was contagious.

Cadet Barrington had a very feminine voice, but it was loud and carried well. Not shrill or mousey like some of the other female cadets I'd heard. I could tell from her taut face and compact body that she was strong. She looked so confident up on that P.T. stand, I couldn't help but respect her. And the upperclassmen seemed to respect her, too. I hoped that someday I'd have her kind of confidence.

"The first exercise you will perform is the push-up. DEMONSTRATOR, *POST!*" She jumped off the P.T. stand and a stocky male cadet took her place. "Assume a good Leaning Rest position," she continued, as the male cadet got into the push-up position. "Keep your body straight with hands and feet no more than . . ." As she explained with the help of the demonstrator how each push-up must break the horizontal plane, I tuned out. I needed no reminder of how tough push-ups are. I just let the noise pass over me, trying to relax.

"YES, MA'AM!" everyone suddenly shouted. I snapped back to attention.

"Good! Demonstrator, recover!" she cried. The demonstrator jumped to his feet.

"Remember, New Cadets, if your grader determines that you are consistently performing in a substandard manner, he *or she* will order you to discontinue the exercise. Understand?"

"YES, MA'AM!"

"A pretty demanding chick," I heard Hickman whisper to McGill.

"Yeah," McGill whispered back, "but I'd obey her orders anytime."

I rolled my eyes at them. McGill smiled sheepishly. Hickman just studied me with narrowed eyes.

"The next exercise will be the sit-up." Cadet Barrington jumped back onto the table. "During this exercise, your hands must remain at the base of the neck, with fingers interlaced. . . ."

Sit-ups are easy. I can do them all day long. But the push-ups . . . I closed my eyes and took a deep breath, trying to relax.

0643

I blinked away the sunlight as I followed the mass of new cadets out of the Field House.

I felt a tug at my shirt. "Hey! How'd you do?" Gabrielle asked. She shoved her scorecard into my hand before I could answer. "Not bad, huh?" She grinned. "Thank you, tennis!"

I looked at her card—53 push-ups and 79 sit-ups. "*Fifty-three* push-ups?" *How did she do fifty-three push-ups?* I really was a total failure. I was certain nobody in Third Platoon had done fewer push-ups than I had. Probably in the entire company. Even teeny tiny Gabrielle had blown me away. "That's really great!" I said, trying to sound enthusiastic. "Way better than me."

"Really? How many did you do?"

I showed her my card. "Only twenty-two."

"But Andi! You did one hundred and one sit-ups! That's incredible!"

I shrugged.

"No, really. Don't feel bad. Eighteen push-ups pass. And you did twenty-two. That's more than passing. Passing's all that matters, anyway."

"Whatever," I mumbled. *I don't want to "just" pass.*

"I mean, breaking the plane. It's hard to get the hang of that. Even *I* had a hard time."

I stared at her with disbelief. *Thanks a lot, Gabrielle.*

Annoyed, I turned away from her and toward Cadet Barrington, who was now standing beside a huge digital clock and yelling into a bullhorn.

"The two-mile run is on a straight course that doubles back twice to create the length. That means you've got to turn around three times, so watch for the turnaround points." Cadet Barrington pointed down a blacktop road that seemed to run straight into a wooded ridge that curved softly to meet the Hudson River, gently flowing on our right. Over on our left a grassy field surrounded an outdoor track. I wondered if I'd ever get to race on it. *Don't think about that now! Concentrate! You've got to take one race at a time.*

"You will be running by platoons," Cadet Barrington was saying into her bullhorn. "First Platoon will go first, then Second, Third, and Fourth, respectively, set off at five-minute intervals. First Platoon, form up on the start line at this time."

I watched the first group's start until they were nothing but gray, bobbing specks on the black ribbon of road. The next platoon slowly gathered together.

I turned back to Gabrielle. "You know, Gab, I just couldn't figure out what I was doing wrong. Cadet Daily kept yelling, 'No! You're not going down far enough!' or 'No! You're not breaking the horizontal plane!'" I stretched my arms above my head. "I mean, my chest was practically touching the ground, so—"

"Ever think that maybe your chest sticks out a little farther than the average person's? You've got an unfair advantage." She laughed. "Wish *I* had such a liability."

I looked away, embarrassed.

"All right, Third Squad," Cadet Daily said, walking up to us. "Listen up. Second Platoon's about ready to start, so you've got about five minutes before you're up. Remember, you're gonna have three turnaround points on this thing, so stay alert. They're marked with orange cones and upperclassmen, so even knuckleheads like Bonanno won't get confused." He laughed. "Hand over your scorecards now and start moving toward the start line."

When I gave Cadet Daily my card, he tapped the space where my time would be written. "Remember, Davis, I'm expecting great things out of you."

"Yes, sir." After my great push-up score, I was sure he was expecting me to choke on the run.

I jogged over to the start line and picked a spot at the very front. *I've got to have a good start.* I took a deep breath, trying to calm my jittery insides.

"Okay, Third Platoon," Cadet Barrington shouted. "You'll be starting in one minute."

Jason McGill was beside me, bouncing up and down on the balls of his feet and swinging his arms. "What're you shooting for, Davis?"

"I don't know." *I haven't exactly had a chance to train lately, trotting in formation.* I thought about my hollow stomach. *Or eat.* "Under twelve, I hope."

He raised his eyebrows. I couldn't tell if he was impressed or doubtful. "Yeah? For two miles? That's pretty quick."

Cadet Barrington began her ten-second countdown.

I set the stopwatch on my watch. "On the track I usually run about 11:15, but the road's always slower."

"Yeah." Jason nodded like he knew exactly what I was talking about, then set his watch, too. "Mind if I hang with you?"

"Okay, Third Platoon. Ready . . . *Go!*" Cadet Barrington yelled, and I was off, leaving my doubts in the dust. The time for fretting was over.

Five guys blew past me right away. *Just keep it controlled, steady. They're just rabbits.* And as I suspected, less than a minute later one of them faded. Shortly after, I passed another. Then two more, until only one remained. *Don't worry. You have lots of time to catch him. Just relax. Keep him in sight.* Jason stuck right by my side, his breath matching my own. It felt good to finally stretch it out.

I glanced to the right, toward the river. Train tracks bordered the road.

New cadets from the first group approached us from the opposite direction and passed, kicking it in to the finish. The only guy ahead of us from our group was maintaining about a thirty-yard lead on us.

"Let's work together," I said to Jason, "and get that guy."

We passed a compound of cinderblock buildings, surrounded by a chain link fence, on our left. A foul odor settled over the air.

Jason said between breaths, "Nothing like . . . sewage . . . to . . . keep you moving!"

The orange cones, marking the first turnaround, were now visible. The guy ahead of us was just getting to them. I checked my watch: *4:01.* And checked it again as we made the sharp turn around the cones. Two upperclassmen were pointing us back toward the direction where we had just come. *4:12.* I quickly did the math in my head. *He's only got eleven seconds on us.*

When we hit the second turnaround, an upperclassman called out our mile split times. "Five thirty-nine. Five forty. Way to go, Miss! Hey, Mister! You gonna let that *female* beat you?"

Jason and I were slowly gaining on the guy ahead of us. A few stragglers from the previous two platoons filled in the gap. We zigged and zagged around and between them, passing one by one.

After we took the final turnaround, I could feel energy surging through my limbs. *No more turnarounds. It's straight back from here.* I picked up the pace a notch. *Just a little over a half mile to go. Now's the time to start pushing it.*

Jason's breathing grew ragged and uneven, and I felt him drop back. "Go on," he gasped. "Don't . . . wait for . . . me."

"No! Come on, Jason!" I waved my hand forward. "You can do it." I didn't want to leave him.

"No . . . can't hang. . . . Go on . . . just . . . get that . . . guy."

I thought about those twenty-two push-ups. "Passing's all that matters, anyway," Gabrielle had said. I gritted my teeth. *Not for me.* I wasn't going to lose that guy ahead of us. "Keep it up," I said to Jason as I pushed ahead.

The sound of his breath at my side disappeared, and then the rhythm of his feet striking the pavement faded. The rest of the run blurred in my memory. I remember running through the one-mile mark I'd passed earlier and, soon after, flying by the squat buildings with their breath-robbing stench. I remember watching the guy ahead of me grow larger with every step—his dark hair, his sweat-soaked shirt, a black thread hanging from his Gym Alpha shorts, the quarter-sized scab on his left elbow, and finally his Army-issue glasses and the look of surprise as I passed him. And then I remember Cadet Daily jumping up and down, red-faced and openmouthed, the veins in his neck bulging, as I sprinted past the clock. 11:21.

I did it!

I slowed to a jog before I stopped completely, doubled over, my lungs clamoring for air.

"Davis!" I heard Cadet Daily yell. "You kicked some serious booty! Way to go! Oh, yeah! You've earned some Big Bites at breakfast today, Davis!"

I was too beat to smile. "Yes, sir!" I answered, weakly. I could use some food.

"Just *breakfast*, Daily?" I heard another upperclassman ask. "If she were my smack, she'd get Big Bites all week."

"Oh, yeah, Aussprung? Well, you deal with your squad your way, and I'll deal with mine my way. You wonder why you have nothing but lily-livered chuckleheads? It's 'cause you're soft, Aussprung. Way too soft."

But I knew that Cadet Aussprung was anything but soft. His brand of gentleness made every new cadet dart into the nearest latrine whenever he was spotted in the hallway.

"Good job, McGill!" I heard Cadet Daily yell. "All the way in, now!"

I straightened up to watch Jason cross the finish line.

"Eleven fifty-four!" Cadet Daily shouted. "Hu-ah! You see that, Aussprung? Where are *your* smacks? Keep walking, McGill. And take Davis with you. I'd hate to have to haul her carcass back to the barracks." I saw him smirk at Cadet

Aussprung. "Even if she did kick everybody's butt in the *entire* platoon."

Was Cadet Daily actually *proud* of me? I didn't dare hope.

McGill stumbled toward me, and when we both had caught our breath, we walked back to the finish line to watch the rest of Third Squad come in.

"Did you get him?" Jason asked.

"Yeah," I said. And then I smiled. Big. "Yeah, I did."

"Good." He clapped me on the back. "If I'm gonna get smoked by a girl, she'd better be a fast one."

There is no substitute for victory!
—GENERAL DOUGLAS MACARTHUR,
WEST POINT CLASS OF 1903

CHAPTER 8

MONDAY, 12 JULY
1530

"**S**ICK CALL, FALL OUT!" First Sergeant Stockel
kept the scorn out of his voice, but not from his
face as he waited for the handful of new cadets to
step out of their squads and limp to the rear of the formation. Most of them had crutches, so the going was slow.
"TODAY, SICK CALL, TODAY! YOU'RE MOVING LIKE
POND WATER!"

Standing in Third Squad, Third Platoon, I watched the
new cadets hobble past.

Before the P.T. test this morning only two new cadets
had left the sanctuary of their squads for the rear of the
formation. Now there were five. Each of them, because
of sickness or injury, had been put on a medical profile
and was excused from any strenuous training. The two
guys and three girls studied the ground as they moved, I

suspected, to avoid looking at any of us straight in the eye.

New Cadet Offenbacher lagged behind the other four, wincing with every step. As certain as the cannon fired every morning for Reveille, she was among the "walking wounded." The joke being whispered in the latrines was that she had been issued crutches instead of running shoes. After all, no one had actually ever seen her run P.T., and she never went anywhere without them.

"MOVE OUT, MISS 'OFTEN-SLACKER' WITH THE 'PAINS IN THE THIGHS!' WE'RE WAITIN' ON *YOU*!" First Sergeant Stockel bellowed with irritation.

Stifled laughter erupted out of the upperclassmen, up and down the ranks.

Busting on New Cadet Offenbacher had become a favorite upperclassmen's pastime lately. Before lunch this morning H Company had toured the Cadet Chapel, yet another huge Gothic structure that looked like it had been plucked out of medieval Europe. The grueling march to get there took us up one of West Point's steepest hills, but Offenbacher wasn't with us. She and her crutches arrived . . . in a truck.

"She makes me want to puke," I overheard one of the upperclassmen whisper to First Sergeant Stockel. "What's her big medical issue *now*?"

First Sergeant Stockel snorted. "What's not? Last week it was a strained back. Today it's 'pains in the thighs.' Can you say 'sore muscles'? But hey, it's legit—she's got a doctor's signature, so she's got a profile. Miss 'Often-slacker' with the 'pains in the thighs.'"

The upperclassman had gotten a good laugh out of that one. And now, hours later, First Sergeant Stockel decided to share the joke with the rest of the company.

I will never *go on sick call.* I didn't want these people to talk about me the way they talked about Offenbacher. I had had enough of that back home—knowing that the kids whispering on the bus or in the halls at school were laughing at me. Laughing about the one thing I had no power over—my family. And it made me mad that Offenbacher would allow herself to be so weak. *I don't care how bad I'm hurt.* I'd rather put up with any amount of physical discomfort than be the company joke that she was. I almost hated her for it.

"AS YOU WERE, HARDCORE!" yelled First Sergeant Stockel, smirking. "THIS IS A MILITARY FORMATION! All Corps Squad wanna-bes report to Cadet Williams at the entrance of Leyte Sally Port immediately following this formation. All remaining new cadets, fall out into your respective teams for Mass Athletics. . . ."

I sucked in one slow breath. *This is it. By dinner formation, tryouts will be all over. In just a couple of hours I'll be standing right here, knowing if I'm still a wanna-be . . . or not.*

After formation, Gabrielle with her tennis racket, Hickman with his baseball glove, and I with my running shoes hurried over to the other wanna-bes huddling around Cadet Williams in the shade of the sally port.

Not far from us, First Sergeant Stockel was unleashing his wrath on the ragged row of new cadets with crutches. "I will not have a bunch of lame and lazy profile get-overs hiding out in the barracks while the rest of H Company is sweating in the sun!" I heard him yell. "Sick call is not spelled F-U-N. And it is not spelled R-A-C-K. So spread the word, Boneheads. Sick call ain't what it's cracked up to be!"

I noticed something familiar about the girl standing

nearest me, at the end of the row. She had curly brown hair and freckles across her sunburned nose. *I know her. Didn't I talk to her once?*

"You have ten minutes from right now to get yourselves, your crutches, and a barracks bag containing one each: pair of boots and low quarters—"

I know! She's the girl Cadet Daily caught me talking to on the first day of Beast!

"—hat brass and belt buckle, shoe polish and Brasso—"

I stared at the girl again. I remembered how she had smiled at me that first day. Her smile was now long gone as she stood kneading the hand grips of her crutches and watching First Sergeant Stockel. *What happened to her?* I wondered if she was a sick call junkie like Offenbacher. I hoped not.

"—to the Orderly Room and report to the Cadet in Charge of Quarters." First Sergeant Stockel smiled. "And you're in luck, Sick Call, because today the CCQ just happens to be Cadet Aussprung, and I have the utmost confidence that he will keep you gainfully employed for the next hour and a half polishing brass, shining shoes, and memorizing this week's knowledge." First Sergeant Stockel turned to New Cadet Offenbacher. "Like Schofield's Definition of Discipline."

Every week we had definitions and West Point trivia to memorize out of our *Bugle Notes*, the tiny book new cadets were required to carry everywhere. Cadet Daily called it the "Plebe Bible"—a perfect name. Not only did it contain everything we'd have to know as West Point cadets, but it also happened to be about the same size as the pocket New Testament that Kit Boguslavsky always carried in his back pocket.

Gabrielle and I tried to memorize the entire week's knowledge on Sunday nights, quizzing each other while we polished boots and brass, so we wouldn't be scrambling later in the week. Schofield's Definition of Discipline was on page 245 of the book. I already knew it. So did Gabrielle.

First Sergeant Stockel's face had inched closer to Offenbacher's. "Let's hear it, Hopalong. You've had plenty of time to memorize *your* knowledge, skipping out on all that good Army training!"

"Y-y-yes, sir. Sir, Schofield's Definition of Discipline: 'The discipline which makes the soldiers in a free country reliable in battle is not to be gained through harsh treatment. On the contrary—'"

First Sergeant Stockel made a sound like a buzzer. "Cease work, Lamebrain! 'Harsh *and tyrannical* treatment.' You may think you've received some harsh treatment thus far at West Point, Miss Offenbacher, and if it were just up to me, I'd toss a little more *harsh* treatment in your direction. But harsh *and* tyrannical treatment is something altogether different—something you'll never know anything about. Try again!"

She is so pathetic! Her "pains in the thighs" had nothing to do with her brain! The least she could've done was put out the extra effort to know her knowledge cold. Any sympathy I might have had for her vanished. I turned my attention back to the huddle and joined the group of wanna-bes who were holding running shoes.

There I waited with the others, blinking sweat and flies out of my eyes and trying hard to keep from thinking about tryouts.

Finally a black upperclass female loped toward us with enough track team wanna-bes to make a platoon jogging in her wake. "Get on the end and follow me," she called and took off, away from the Plain, down the long hill toward the river, around the grassy field that showcased the track, and into the Field House. Its high ceiling and relative dimness were a haven from the heat. It felt almost like air-conditioning.

"Okay, New Cadets," she said when we were all inside. "Listen up. I'm Allegra Spence, the captain of the Women's Cross Country Team. But you can call me 'Ma'am' for now, all right? If you make the team, I'll be more than happy to drop the formalities, but let's not develop bad habits just yet."

I looked at the mob of tense faces around me. *So many . . .*

She pointed across the track to a medium-height, balding black man wearing civilian clothes—a yellow polo shirt and black warm-up pants—and talking to an Army officer with a mustache. The way he jerked his head back and forth as he talked, I could tell that he was intense. "That's the man you want to impress, New Cadets. Coach Louis Banks, Head Track and Cross Country Coach. You have one chance to show him your stuff, and that's today, so give it all you got."

One chance. I took a deep breath and looked at the floor. *Give it all you got.* The Big Bites of Eggs MacArthur and cottage fried potatoes I'd gotten at breakfast today hadn't come close to filling my stomach. And my tight hamstrings and quads reminded me that only a few hours had elapsed since the P.T. test. Fighting to stay awake during classes on the honor code, hiking up to the Cadet Chapel, and lugging my rifle around during drill practice hadn't helped me get ready for anything but my bed.

"If you were recruited, don't worry. You're on the team"—and she smiled for the first time—"for now." She pointed toward the large group of new cadets sitting apart from everybody else on the far end of the Field House. "Just hang tight over there during tryouts. Afterwards, Coach'll want to talk to you."

I stared. The track recruits sat talking and laughing, looking totally unaware of all the jumping, stretching, and running around them. I even spotted a couple of new cadets sprawled across a high jump mat, asleep.

The mob near the door shrank as Cadet Spence sent us wanna-bes to different areas of the Field House, depending on the event, until only the distance runners remained.

"Okay, guys. I saved the best for last—the ones who go the distance." She paused, taking the thirty or so of us in with one long look. "Wait over there"—she pointed across the length of the track—"and warm up. You'll be nice and close to the latrines. If you're anything like me, you'll need to take care of business before hitting the track." She checked her watch. "We don't have a lot of time to knock this out, so it's going to be 'boom, boom, boom.' A quick mile on the track and that's it. Men under 4:40, women under 5:30. If you can run that, you're on the team. Plain and simple. Any questions?"

Under 5:30? I shook out each leg. *I can run that, maybe, when I'm fresh.* I started chewing on my thumbnail. *What was my mile split this morning—5:39? And I still had a mile to go. I don't know. Maybe . . .* But I knew there were no "maybes" for me. I just *had* to make the team. Running was what had saved me at home, helped me cope. When I was racing on a track or through the woods, I *was* somebody. The medals and trophies I took home told me that, even if no person ever did. Running was the only thing I had. And I felt for a second that if I couldn't be on Corps Squad, I didn't want to stay at West Point.

"Uh, ma'am?" asked a tall, skinny guy on my left. "Are we running in here or outside?"

"Right here." Cadet Spence pointed over her shoulder to the centerpiece of the Field House. "Right on that two-hundred-meter track."

An indoor track? I felt sick. I had never run on an indoor track in my life, had never even seen one up close. I glanced at the others. None of them seemed worried. I rubbed my jagged thumbnail, back and forth, across my upper lip.

How many laps make a mile? It's a two-hundred-meter track, so that makes . . . eight? An indoor track was half the size of an outdoor one. It took a different kind of strategy, a strategy I didn't know. *My mile split this morning was only a 5:39. I'll never be able to knock off nine seconds. Not with all the curves and the short straightaways.*

Cadet Spence looked at her watch again. "Anything else?"

"Yes, ma'am," said a girl behind me. "How many people will make the team? I mean, ma'am, is there a limit?"

"Like I said, if every one of you makes the cutoff times, you all make the team. If none of you do, then no one does. But I will tell you, from past experience, we get very few walk-ons." She shrugged. "That's just the way it goes."

I followed the other distance runners to our spot near the bathrooms and put on my Sauconys from home. I had almost forgotten what a good pair of running shoes felt like. *Probably won't make enough difference to matter. At least if I wore bad shoes, I'd have an excuse.* But I knew that wasn't true. I'd never allow myself an excuse if I failed today. I sat down to stretch my tight, tired legs.

I stared again at the recruits. *How good are they?* I squinted, trying to pick out the skinny ones, especially the girls, who looked fast. *Don't be an idiot. They're all fast. That's why they're there. And I'm sure they've all been to State. Probably Nationals, too.* I sighed. *I don't have a chance.* I grabbed my feet and slowly pulled my body flat against my legs until my face touched my knees. The muscles in my thighs trembled, and I suddenly realized that I was going to throw up.

I got to my feet. As calmly as I could, I jogged over to the bathroom, found a vacant stall, bent over the toilet, and chucked the little bit of shrimp scampi over white rice that I had eaten for lunch into the toilet. Still clutching the sides of the toilet seat, I took deep breaths, trying to relax my churning stomach and my nerves. *It's only one mile. Just five and a half minutes of pain, and it's over. One chance to make the team. Give it everything. You'll spend the rest of your life regretting it if you don't.* I closed my eyes. *Won't survive this place if you can't run.*

I heard a girl's voice, and then the door to the bathroom opened.

"Yeah? That's incredible. New York's a really competitive state, too. I should know—I missed Nationals by thirty-two hundredths of a second in the 800. This girl from Newburgh came out of nowhere and snatched it from me."

I straightened up and wiped my face with toilet paper.

A pair of Nikes walked over to my stall, and their owner, the girl who had been talking, pulled at my door.

"Someone's in here," I said.

"Oops. Sorry," she said, and the Nikes moved away. "But that's okay," she continued, stepping into the stall next to mine. "I'll go someday. Plus I'm hoping to move up to something longer, here. Maybe the 1500."

"Oh," came the other girl's voice for the first time. "Then you're recruited?"

I hesitated, my fingers grasping the latch of my door.

"Yeah. Aren't you?" asked the voice above the Nikes.

"Nope."

"You are kidding! With your times? And qualifying for Nationals? I thought for sure—"

Wonderful. I get to go against girls who went to Nationals. My great victory at the P.T. test didn't seem so great, suddenly. I opened the door and stepped around the waiting girl. She was crouched, tightening the laces on her Asics running shoes.

"Hi," I said, trying to sound casual, and smiled.

She didn't return my greeting, but I could feel her sizing me up as I walked to the sink, her eyes lingering on my shoes.

I felt a prickly feeling rise from the base of my neck to the top of my head. I knew that look. The and-why-are-*you*-alive look the "beautiful people" reserved for me at school. I took a swig of water from the faucet and walked out of the bathroom, feeling cold—and mean.

So you have Asics, Speedy Gonzales. Big deal. My Sauconys are going to kick your Asics' butt.

1729

The door pulled me into my room before I had a chance to turn the knob.

110 ★

"Andi!" Gabrielle screamed, standing in the doorway, on her way to the bathroom in her bathrobe and flip-flops. "You scared me to death!"

"And you almost pulled my arm out of its socket." I walked past her, pulled off my sweat-soaked shirt, and tossed it on my chair. Then I sat down and started unlacing my shoes.

Gabrielle shut the door. "Well?"

I peeled off my socks and wiggled my toes. "Isn't it amazing how much cooler you feel when you take off your shoes?"

"Yeah. Mind-boggling. Come on, Andi! You made the team. Right?"

"How'd you get back so soon?"

"It's not *so* soon. The tennis courts *are* closer to the barracks than the Field House, you know. Plus today was tryouts, remember? *Tryouts?* Since I was recruited, I got to sit in the shade and watch"—she smiled—"sipping Pepsi."

"You dog!"

"And I even snuck one back for my poor, deprived roommate." She walked over to her wardrobe closet and took out a can of tennis balls. "I sacrificed my own property"—she pulled off the lid—"not to mention my very skin if I had gotten caught." A Pepsi can slid out of the canister and into her other hand. "Gorgeous Gray Eyes is on CQ tonight, you know. He was eyeing my tennis balls *very* suspiciously when I passed him in the hall. And all for naught." She tossed the empty canister into the trash can. "But that's okay. One can never drink too much Pepsi. Especially during Beast." She flashed me a saccharine smile, then kissed the Pepsi can. "Of course, if you talk . . ."

I laughed, then picked up one of my sweaty socks and lobbed it at her. "You little sadist." I checked my watch.

"Are you aware that I have to be standing on Daily's wall in eighteen minutes? And that you have to be at your clock in thirteen? And we have a shower to take?"

"Don't bore me with piddly details."

I sighed. "Okay, Gab. We had to run a mile on the indoor track. I've never run on an indoor track. I had to run under 5:30. I've rarely run under 5:30." I dropped my shorts next to my T-shirt and slipped on my flip-flops.

"And? And?"

"And"—I shrugged—"today I did both." I crossed the room, hiding my smile from her, and grabbed my bathrobe out of the closet near the door.

"Yeah!"

I hopped up on the counter of our sink and sat down. And not being able to contain my excitement any longer, I blurted out the details—probably too many details—surprising even myself. "Gab, it really was a miracle! First of all they just sort of put a bunch of us on the track at the same time—many more than you'd ever have in one heat during a track meet. And they ran guys and girls together, which was weird because the guys kept lapping the girls—the guys had to run under 4:40, so they were faster—and it was almost impossible to keep track of which lap each person was on. . . ." I looked at Gabrielle; I hoped I wasn't boring her. "You know, total chaos! So anyway, when I crossed the finish, Coach Banks—that's the Head Coach—was calling off the times. And when I heard '5:28,' I couldn't believe it! You know what I did? I ran right off the track and up to him—the coach—and hugged him!"

"You? No way!"

I nodded. "And I said, 'I did it! I did it!' And he said,

'That's what the clock says.' He was smiling, though. And then I said, 'You won't regret this. I'll work really hard!' And you know what he said? He said, 'You know, Davis, I think I believe that.' I kind of made a fool out of myself, but I was so nervous before, and I didn't think I'd be able to do it, and . . ." I smiled at Gabrielle and held out my hand. "Can I have my Pepsi now?"

Feed 'em up and give 'em hell.
Teach 'em where they are.
Make 'em so mad they'll eat steel . . .
Make 'em hard, but don't break 'em.
—LAURENCE STALLINGS, *WHAT PRICE GLORY?*

CHAPTER 9

FRIDAY, 23 JULY
0633

"DAVIS HAS BEEN BEATING you up all week, gentlemen," Cadet Black said after he formed H Company's Black Group into two squads for our run. "This morning I expect to hear the *rest* of you returning my cadences, too. I'm not fond of duets."

I smiled to myself. P.T. was easily my favorite part of the day. I looked forward to it even more than I did the meals. Since the middle of last week, when Cadet Barrington had divided H Company into three ability groups for the runs, I had had a great time letting everyone in the Black Group know how effortless I found the runs—the runs that most of them struggled to finish—by calling cadences louder than anyone else. And because I was the only girl out of about twenty guys, Cadet Black had had a great time, too, rubbing it in.

"Now, I *know* the pace isn't too fast. Nobody's here by accident. Each and every one of you ran under thirteen minutes on last week's P.T. test. Correct?"

"YES, SIR!"

"Okay, then. A 6:30 pace isn't too fast." He crossed his arms. "So I can't think of a good reason why you're not sounding off. Can you?"

"NO, SIR!"

"You're not like the common riffraff in the Gray Group or the lead butts in the Gold Group. You're the *Black Group*—no pun intended—because you're H Company's top runners. You need a challenge, and it's my job to give it to you.

"Okay. Time to step down from my bully pulpit. Today we're gonna do my famous Chapel Run."

I heard a soft groan sweep through the squads. I remembered our long, hot climb up to the Chapel last week, and I almost groaned myself. It was a tough hill. I'd have to work extra hard to keep up my reputation.

"It'll take us up to the Chapel, past Lusk Reservoir and Michie Stadium. Then down the nice, long hill to Thayer Gate. From there I'll release you to run the last mile back to the barracks on your own." He glanced at me. "As fast as you want. The finish is at Eisenhower Statue. And don't worry about getting lost." He smirked. "Just look for me at your front, Fourth Class, 'cause I'll be there." He stood directly in front of me and said, "No one's gonna beat me to Eisenhower Statue."

I stared at the ground between my feet. It was a challenge. *We'll see about that, sir.*

"Hey, Andi," Boguslavsky whispered behind me. "Take it easy on us mortals, okay?"

I stretched my arms over my head and smiled. I was glad that McGill and Boguslavsky were in the Black Group with me. The looks that I got from some of the other Black Group guys weren't the friendliest at times, especially when we were running up a hill and I was the only one with enough wind for sounding off. But Jason and Kit's presence was comforting. We were the only Third Squad new cadets who were fast enough for H Company's Black Group, and even though I was a girl, I knew that they were glad to have me here. At least they acted like it.

McGill glanced over at Cadet Black, now sitting on the ground and stretching his calves. "You gonna take Cadet Black up on his challenge?"

I pretended innocence. "Challenge?"

He looked back at Cadet Black again. "You know. When he releases us to run back on our own. You gonna smoke him?"

I raised an eyebrow. "We'll see."

0710

Cadet Black had pushed me, *hard*, that last stretch of Thayer Road along the Hudson. But the real race began as soon as the barracks were in sight. As we tore down the corridor of towering granite buildings toward the Plain, I felt myself easing away from him. He fell back one stride. Then two. When Eisenhower Statue was about a hundred yards straight ahead, I knew I had him beat. My body geared up for the final surge.

And then . . . I looked back. Cadet Black was there—a good fifteen feet behind me. Head back, a grimace wringing his face. Legs and arms pumping. Seeing him straining so hard, my desire to beat him dissolved. Instantly. I realized that it was one thing for me to beat my peers. That Cadet Black found amusing; it was a joke we shared. But I wasn't sure he'd be so amused if I beat him, too. I knew a delicate balance exists between impressing someone and threatening someone. And I'd learned a long time ago that threatened people could turn ugly, just like that.

So at the last second I made the decision—I'd save his ego a thrashing. I held myself back, and we finished together.

When we had trotted to a stop, Cadet Black threw back his head and laughed. He raised his right hand and shouted, "Put it here, Davis!" I hid my smile as I returned his high-five. "Man, Davis," he said, walking in circles with his hands behind his head. "You can run! You ever *lose* a race?"

"I just did, sir."

He looked at me knowingly. "Yeah, *right*." Then he shook his head. "You sure are something else, Davis. The Army Team's gonna love you."

I grinned up at him. I couldn't help myself—I felt too good.

He frowned. "Smirk off, Davis! You know better than that!" But as he turned to watch the rest of the Black Group come in, I saw his lips twitch.

It's gonna be a great day!

1405

"WHAT'S THE SPIRIT OF THE BAYONET?"
"TO KILL, SIR!"
From where he stood in the center of the P.T. stand,

an upperclassman with more muscles than Superman glowered down at H Company. Stretched across his biceps and pecs was a yellow T-shirt with a dagger and the word BAYONET emblazoned on its front.

We stood straight and still before him like rows of camouflaged dominoes, our M-16s in our hands. The upperclassman raised his M-16 over his head with one hand as if it were a mere Wiffle ball bat and roared again, "WHAT MAKES THE GRASS GROW?"

"*BLOOD* MAKES THE GRASS GROW, SIR!" we yelled, our voices rising in the heavy air.

"That's right, Hardcore. Thick, red blood makes the grass grow green. You got a motto there, *Hardcore*?"

"YES, SIR!"

"Let's hear it!"

We took in one huge, collective breath before we shouted, "HARDCORE H, BEST BY TEST. WE DON'T CARE WHO'S SECOND BEST. WE'RE ROUGH! WE'RE TOUGH! WE GO ALL NIGHT. WE SHOOT TO KILL WITH ALL OUR MIGHT! DRIVE ON, HARDCORE. DRIVE ON, *SIR*!"

"All right! Today, Hardcore, you're gonna learn the meaning of those motivating words. Fix bayonets!"

"HU-AH!"

I slammed my M-16 on the ground between my feet and, with all the other H Company new cadets, snapped my sheathed bayonet onto the end of my weapon.

Before marching out here to Clinton Field, I'd spent the entire morning cooped up in a silent auditorium with a number 2 pencil, a booklet of multiple-choice questions, and hundreds of other new cadets. And after that, lunch with my hands in my lap and my eyes on my plate. But now that we were finally out here, I was psyched. Yelling and stabbing imaginary bodies and acting crazy was exactly what I needed. Nothing got the blood pumping better than a good session of bayonet drills.

"READY STANCE, MOVE!"

Together, we brought our M-16s diagonally across our chests and stood poised for action with our legs flexed like a quarterback at the line of scrimmage, ready for the ball.

"BUTT STROKE TO THE HEAD, MOVE!"

"HU-AH!" I took a giant step forward and slammed the butt of my weapon upward as if I were smashing an imaginary enemy soldier in the face.

"SLASH SERIES TO THE CHEST, MOVE!"

"HU-AH!" I stepped forward again, slicing the space in front of me diagonally from left to right. Out of the corner of my eye I saw Cadet Daily moving his way down my rank. He leaned into each Third Squad new cadet as he passed, yelling something about blood and guts and killing. The sun poured out of a cloudless sky. Sweat oozed from every pore of my body. My weapon was slick with it. I felt great!

"WHAT'S THE SPIRIT OF THE BAYONET?" the upperclassman bellowed again.

Cadet Daily was getting closer. I gripped my weapon harder and stuck the most murderous, bloodthirsty look on my face that I could muster. *"TO KILL, SIR!"*

"SMASH SERIES TO THE KNEE, MOVE!"

"HU-AH!" As I took out my imaginary opponent's knee with one barbaric stroke of my M-16, I screamed louder than I had all day, hoping Cadet Daily would hear me and be impressed.

Okay, get ready. Here he comes! My heart started to beat faster.

"THRUST!"

"HU-AH!" I lunged forward to skewer my invisible enemy, and—*NO!* My M-16 flew out of my hands and clattered to the ground, just missing the new cadet in the rank in front of me.

Cadet Daily was in my face before I could even move to pick it up. "Davis! What're you doing? Are you spazzing out on me?"

"No, sir!"

"NO?" he roared.

I licked my lips and tasted salt. *So much for impressing him.*

"SMASH SERIES TO THE HEAD, MOVE!" yelled the muscle-bound upperclassman.

I moved for my M-16. "I'm not through with you, Davis! You trying to blow me off?"

I jumped back. "No, sir!" Sweat trickled down my back. I swallowed. My mouth felt dry and pasty, like I'd been sucking on a glue stick.

"Drop!"

I stared at him. *Push-ups? Now? But what about my M-16?* The rest of H Company were now bashing the air with the butts of their weapons and screaming for blood. Except me.

"I said, 'Drop,' Davis! Now, *move!*"

New cadets everywhere were stealing sidelong glances at us. I knelt in the grass and got into the Leaning Rest. The muscles in my arms quivered.

The commands came fast and furious from the P.T. stand, and battle cries ripped from the throats of my classmates in a frenzied response.

Cadet Daily bent over me and shouted above the noise.

"Low crawl over to your weapon and secure it. And don't take all day! MOVE OUT!"

Low crawl? Here? In front of everyone? But I had to obey. I plunged to the ground and slithered on my elbows and knees over the ten feet of grass to my weapon as fast as I could. I was mortified. I had become more than just a distraction; I was a one-woman vaudeville show with Cadet Daily as director, producer, choreographer, and prop man. And right now I hated him for it. It reminded me of the times my mother had humiliated me in front of my team-mates after track practice, barging into the girls' locker room and calling me names that prison guards reserved for their worst inmates, because I had made her wait for me in the parking lot a few minutes longer than we had arranged.

I crawled back to Cadet Daily, dragging my M-16, and stopped at his feet.

"Now get back into the Leaning Rest and knock 'em out till I get tired!" he shouted. "Hold on to your weapon at all times, Davis. And after each repetition I want to hear, 'I will not drop my weapon!' Execute!"

I hesitated, staring at my M-16. *How in the world can I hold my weapon* and *do push-ups?*

"Today, Davis, today! I told you to do push-ups on your weapon, not *kiss* it!"

I wound the sling around one hand and then the other, pulling my weapon to lie over both. Then I lowered my chest toward the ground and pushed myself back up. "I will not drop my weapon."

"Louder! And get your gut off the ground!"

I did another push-up, trying hard not to sag. "I will not drop my weapon!" I clenched my teeth. *Jerk! It's not like I did it on purpose or something.*

"WHIRL!" commanded Mr. Muscles from the P.T. stand.

"I will not drop my weapon!"

I kept squeezing out push-ups, one by one, gasping and grunting and trying to ignore all the slashing and stabbing around me. The grass beneath me grew slippery with my sweat, and my arms became so tired, I could barely go down at all.

"On your feet," Cadet Daily said at last. "I'm tired, Davis. Tired of watching your miserable carcass writhing around on the ground."

I sank to my knees, then staggered to my feet, using my M-16 as a crutch.

"Treat your weapon like a boyfriend, Davis. Respect it, care for it, develop a meaningful relationship with it." I felt my face burn, but not from the sun overhead. I didn't know the first thing about how to treat a guy. And he probably knew it, too. "Never abuse it. It may save your life someday. Be faithful to it, and it'll be faithful to you."

Cadet Daily turned around, and I resumed the Ready Stance.

"BUTT STROKE TO THE GROIN, MOVE!"

I gritted my teeth, and taking a giant step forward, I drove the butt of my weapon upward with one particular enemy soldier in mind. "HU-AH!"

1520

When bayonet drills were over, Cadet Daily gave us thirty minutes of free time. Well, sort of. We were to use the time to turn in our M-16s, check our mail, change into fresh brown T-shirts and spit-shined boots, drink a canteen of water, write a letter home, and get into Battle Dress Under Arms—pistol belt, bayonet, full canteen, white gloves, and M-14 rifles, cleaned—for drill. Any time remaining after accomplishing all that would be considered our free time.

A few minutes after we had turned our M-16s in to the weapons room and had visited the mailroom, Gabrielle and I were at our desks, sitting in fresh brown T-shirts, and chugging water from our canteens.

"I'm so hot!" Gabrielle said between gulps. "I can't stop sweating. This T-shirt is almost as soaked as the one I just took off. And look!" She walked over to me and lifted the bangs away from her forehead. "I'm breaking out all over the place! I have more red on my face than on the top of my head!"

"It's not that bad, Gab." I put my drained canteen on my desk and started fanning myself with my four pieces of mail. Gabrielle exaggerated everything.

"Easy for you to say." She yanked her bun out of her hair and sank back into her chair. "You don't have any. You sweat like a beast but never get zits. It's not fair."

Talking about my looks made me uncomfortable; it reminded me of my mother. She loved to comment on my looks, too, but never in a remotely positive way. I changed the subject. "So, did you get any mail?"

"Yeah. A letter from my mom and dad, and one from Sherry." She smiled, holding it up. "I've told you about Sherry, haven't I? My best friend?"

"Yeah." I felt a little stab of pain. *What about me?* I glanced over at Gabrielle. She had already ripped open the envelope and was reading the letter with a huge grin on her face, raking her fingers through her damp hair. I turned away and looked at the four letters in my hand, feeling stupid. *Of course you're not Gabrielle's best friend.* I knew that those few nights we managed to stay awake after Taps, whispering about home and guys and West Point fears, couldn't compete with years of friendship. Years full of slumber parties and shopping trips, phone calls that lasted half the night, and ditching class to just hang out—things I never did. Life in my house was totally incompatible with having a best friend, so I never had one.

Gabrielle giggled and slid the letter into the top drawer of her desk. "Sherry's great. She writes the best letters. She's getting ready to leave for school at the University of Pennsylvania. But it's not like she's going *away* away. I mean, she lives just a few streets from me in Philadelphia, you know."

"Yeah, I remember. You told me—"

"We had it all planned, Sherry and me. We were going to be roommates, I was going to play tennis for Penn, and—"

I nodded. "Oh, yeah. You got recruited there, too." I started picking at one of my envelopes. Listening to her talk about Sherry made me feel strange inside, but I couldn't name the emotion. I felt insignificant and intimidated and a little bit jealous, all mixed together.

"You'll just have to meet her sometime, Andi. You'd love her."

I sorted through my letters. Two from my mom, one from my sister, and one from a credit card company with big print on the outside saying I was preapproved for a $3,000 credit limit.

Gabrielle pulled her second letter from its envelope. "Sherry might be coming up with my parents at the end of the summer. You know, that day Cadet Daily told us about? After Beast, when we can spend the whole day with our parents?"

"Yeah? Maybe I can meet her then." I had no idea if my own parents were going to come. I wasn't even sure if I wanted them to. But there was one thing I *did* know: Just the thought of introducing them to Gabrielle made me sweat. I pulled out the letter from my mom, the one with the oldest postmark.

Dear Andi,

Finally you wrote. We are making up our minds if we should come all the way to West Point at the end of the summer. It is 1000 miles, you know. When you never bother to write, it doesn't make me feel like we should bother to come. Next week is Randy's birthday. He will be thirteen. A teenager already. We are going to have a nice party for him, but only family. I don't want any of his bratty friends around.

That ugly, skinny boy from your running team came over the other day, the one that asked you on dates but you were smart enough to avoid like the plague. He came over to hear how you are doing. He's a nice boy, but nothing special. You should find one of those West Point boys. They are a much higher caliber and smarter, too. You wrote that you made the running team. That's crazy. You won't have time for running in college! You don't even get a grade for it, do you? But you never listen. You'll run yourself right out of West Point. You'll see. And for what? You should join the band. We spent all

that money on that clarinet and all those years
of lessons. That would be more productive than
running, that's for sure.

Do you eat and sleep enough? Write, okay?
It's not easy when your kids go away. I told you I'd
write to you every day, didn't I? And I have kept
that promise. How many other mothers write every
day?

Love, Mom

I didn't know which I wanted to do more—scream or
cry. *What did you expect? Something nice and encouraging?*
I looked back in the envelope for a note from my dad.
Nothing. *Typical.* I dumped the letter in the trash can and
stashed my mother's second one in my desk without opening it. Then I opened the letter from my sister.

Dear Andi,

Congrats on making the cross country team!
Mom thought it was stupid, and Dad said nothing
as usual, but I think it's great!! I can't wait to tell
Coach Wolf. He'll be so excited!

Things are about the same as always. I went to
the library almost every day this week. It's too hot
to stay in the house (Mom won't run the a/c when
Dad's at work). Plus Mom's been in a really bad
mood ever since we got back from West Point. I
think it's 'cause you're gone. But you know me,
I just stay out of her way.

Five more weeks till school and counting.

I know you have enough junk to worry about,
but I thought you should know that last week Dad

*moved all the stuff out of your room and put it
down in the basement. I guess since you're not
living here anymore, he figured he'd use your room
for an office. He said when you come home for
Christmas, you can sleep on the couch downstairs
(unless he's on it, of course!). Anyway, when they
were moving your stuff, Mom found one of your
diaries and, of course, read it. Then ripped it up in
a million pieces. I guess she didn't like how she was
portrayed in it? So it's gone. So are all your race
trophies. I was able to hide the one you won at
Sectionals last year, though, before she got to it.
   Your boss from the Y called and asked how
you're doing. That's about all the excitement from
here. Miss you.*

Love, Amanda

I laid my head down on my desk. *Could this day get any
worse?* I walked over to the trash can and shredded the
letter. Then I walked back to my desk, yanked open the
top drawer, grabbed the unopened letter from my mother,
returned to the trash can, and shredded it, too.

Gabrielle was watching me. "Do you always destroy
your letters?"

I shrugged and started putting on my boots. I didn't
feel like talking right now—to her or anyone.

I could actually feel the silence in the room. Gabrielle
finished lacing her boots, then walked over to her wardrobe closet and started rummaging around. "Uh, Andi,"
she finally said, "I'm going to fill my canteen with the cold
water from the drinking fountain. You know how I hate
tepid water. If you want, I'll fill yours, too."

I quickly wiped any trace of tears out of the corners of my eyes and looked at her over my shoulder. "Thanks, Gab. My canteen's on my desk." I smiled a little. "I still have to write that letter home." That was the last thing I wanted to do, but it was an order, and Cadet Daily would check. I knew my nose was red; it always got red when I tried not to cry.

But Gabrielle didn't notice, or pretended not to. She snapped her pistol belt around her waist and got my canteen from my desk. "We only have like"—she checked her watch—"four minutes to be on Daily's wall, you know."

"Yeah. I'll keep the letter short and sweet." *Real short.* When Gabrielle had left, I pulled a piece of paper and a matching envelope from my box of West Point–issued stationery, grabbed a pen, and scribbled:

> *Dear everyone,*
> *I'm still here.*
>
> > *Love, Andi*

1705

"Davis, what is your major malfunction?" Once again, Cadet Daily stood inches from my face. I stared at the gold West Point crest on his black plastic helmet, so I wouldn't have to look in his eyes. "The rest of Third Squad is squared away. Look at me, Davis, when I'm talking to you!"

"Yes, sir!" I stared at his green eyes and chewed on the inside of my lip, trying to think of pleasant things.

"You *like* being the weak link in the chain, Davis?"

"No, sir," I croaked.

Third Squad had spent the past hour roasting under

128 ★

the afternoon sun while practicing the Manual of Arms—
a series of complicated movements with M-14s, done in
perfect unison and snappy precision. Movements tricky
enough for right-handed new cadets to master, but almost
impossible for someone left-handed, like me. I might as
well have been manipulating the M-14 with my feet, as
coordinated as I felt.

Cadet Daily stepped away from me and rubbed the
back of his neck. The black helmet on his head and the
saber hanging from his waist reflected the blazing sun
overhead as he paced before us.

"As you know, Third Squad, Drill Competition is next
week. As you also know, Third Squad, H Company has won
the Cadet Basic Training Drill Streamer Award for the past
three years. We intend to continue our tradition of excel-
lence. I will not, I repeat, WILL NOT allow my squad to
hold H Company back. H Company has a reputation to
protect. Do I make myself clear, Third Squad?"

"YES, SIR!"

"And I will not, read my lips, WILL NOT allow any
bonehead to make Third Squad look bad. *I* have a reputation to protect." He glared at me. "Do I make myself clear,
Davis?"

"Yes, sir!"

He stepped in front of me. "Glad to hear it. Continue
to rest in place, Third Squad, while I give Davis here a little
of my *undivided* attention. DAVIS, ATTEN-*TION!*"

I snapped to attention, holding my rifle flush against
my right leg and my left arm at my side.

Cadet Daily moved closer, silently studying my face.
I held my breath, the pulse in my temples pounding out
the seconds. Finally he dropped his gaze to my feet. "Why

isn't the butt of your weapon in line with the toe of your boot?"

"No excuse, sir!"

"Make the correction. This is basic stuff, Davis!"

"Yes, sir." I looked down at my feet. *It's only off a half inch! What's his problem?*

"Attention to detail, Davis. Sloppy soldiers get troops killed. RIGHT SHOULDER, ARMS!"

Right Shoulder Arms—from the ground to your shoulder in four steps. I can do this! I took a deep breath. *One thousand one.* I snapped the M-14 up and across my body with my right hand. At the same time, I crossed my left arm under my right, catching the center of the rifle. *One thousand two.* I jerked my right hand, uncrossing my arms, to hold the butt of the rifle in the palm in my hand. *So far, so good. Now for the hard part—one thousand three.* I flipped the M-14 around ninety degrees and winced, anticipating the barrel slamming into my right shoulder. With my left hand, I guided the rifle farther up my shoulder . . .

"CEASE WORK, DAVIS! You will keep all inappropriate facial contortions to yourself. You are a military machine. You are not paid to feel." His eyes left my face. "AND WHAT IS *THAT*?" He pointed to my left hand. "The fingers of your left hand should be extended and joined, with your palm facing your body. Like a salute, Davis. Easy stuff. And the first joint of your index finger should be touching the rear of the receiver group."

The what? What's he talking about? My throat was aching, throbbing, feeling like it would burst. *Don't cry, don't cry, don't cry!*

"Now look at your weapon, Davis."

I directed my eyes downward.

"It's canted. No, not merely canted, Davis. It's practically lying flat against your chest! The movement's called Right *Shoulder* Arms for a reason!"

The brown wood of the handguard and the black steel of the barrel blurred into the camouflage pattern of my shirt. I blinked.

"This is unacceptable, Davis! ORDER, ARMS!"

I shakily brought my weapon back down to my side.

"Do it again, Davis. RIGHT SHOULDER, ARMS!"

Cadet Daily stopped me before I even got the rifle halfway across my body. "ORDER, ARMS! DO IT AGAIN!"

Over and over he shouted those two commands—Right Shoulder Arms and Order Arms. With my every mistake, he grew more incensed, and with his every correction, I became more flustered, until his face was red and my body shook.

"WHAT IS YOUR PROBLEM, DAVIS? I've been holding your hand for the past ten minutes, taking you *by the numbers* through something you should already know by now, and all I have to show for it is a migraine headache and a squad of thirsty boneheads!" He put his hands on his hips and said with disgust, "What do you have to say for yourself, Davis?"

My lips were trembling. I pressed them together and swallowed. "No excuse, sir."

"That's right, Davis. There *is* no excuse for your pitiful performance today." Then, barely above a whisper he snarled, "Well, *I* have something to say. I'm profoundly disappointed in you, Davis."

His words opened wounds that a bayonet never could. I took a deep breath, trying to quell my frustration and shame, rage and pain from exploding all over my face. *Tell him about being left-handed! Then he'll understand this isn't my fault and take it back!*

"Sir, may I make a statement?" I blurted.

"What?" he snapped.

"Sir, I'm left-handed."

"WHAT DID YOU SAY, DAVIS?"

It had been exactly the *wrong* thing to say, but I'd said it. I couldn't take it back, now. "Sir." My voice caught. "I s-said, 'I'm l-left h-handed.'"

Silence. Silence. And more silence. Finally Cadet Daily spoke with terrifying calmness. "Third Squad, atten-*tion*! Be on my wall ten minutes before dinner formation. This training session is over." Then he opened his mouth and roared, "POST!"

In unison, Third Squad, with New Cadet Cero leading the way, scurried in single file for the nearest sally port and pounded up the stairs. Gabrielle was in front of me. In my hurry to get to my room, I was afraid I'd plow right over her.

And then I heard his voice, filling the stairwell. "YOU'RE HISTORY, DAVIS!"

He bounded up the stairs, two steps at a time.

"WHAT ABOUT IT, DAVIS? READY TO KISS THIS PLACE GOOD-BYE?"

He shadowed me. Up the flight of stairs, across the landing, then up the next.

What was I thinking? I had opened my big mouth and brought this on myself.

"WANNA PACK YOUR BAGS AND CALL HOME TO YOUR MOMMA?"

I clenched my teeth and willed my eyes to stare dead ahead. *Do not look at him!* But I could see him out of the corner of my eye—his twisted lips, and his red face, and those stupid, bulging veins.

"YOU CAN TELL HER YOU COULDN'T HACK WEST POINT BECAUSE YOU'RE *LEFT-HANDED*!"

I had now reached the third floor and my hallway. I checked the room numbers. 311 . . . 310 . . . Gabrielle was moving out, along the wall in front of me as if she were trying to keep Cadet Daily's rage from engulfing her, too.

"Poor, poor New Cadet Davis," he whined in a mocking voice. "Being left-handed is just so *unfair*! And to think—*Napoleon* was left-handed, *too!*" I could feel his breath on my face, he was so close. "Make my day, Davis. Let's see some big, fat, salty tears."

309, 308 . . . *Shut up! Shut up! Shut up!*

"Too proud to cry, Davis? Is that it? Come on. Prove what everyone already thinks about you—"

307 . . . 306 . . . *Faster, Gab!*

"—That you're *weak*, Davis, and you don't got what it takes to make it here!"

I felt like I had been shocked with 1,000 volts. It was Cadet Daily's voice, but my mother's words. *That's not true! I do have what it takes! I do! You don't know anything about me!* I felt that stubborn, crybaby lump again, throbbing so hard in my throat that my teeth ached.

305! Gabrielle darted across the hall for our room.

Bang! She flung the door open and scurried inside. Seconds later, I crossed the threshold and . . .

BANG! I slammed the door behind me.

Gabrielle gasped. I looked back at her with horror. *Did I really do that?* I was dead.

BOOM!

The door flew back open, sending our trash can rattling

across the floor and leaving a trail of shredded paper behind. Cadet Daily filled the doorway.

"Enter, sir!" Gabrielle squeaked in a voice an octave higher than normal.

"I already have," he said between clenched teeth, his eyes boring into me. "Miss Bryen," he hissed, barely above a whisper, "post. I want to talk to Davis. Alone."

"Yes, sir!" She placed her M-14 in our weapons rack and bolted out the door.

The latrine. That's where I would go. It's a great place to hide.

Cadet Daily stared at me. I tried to stare back just as furiously, but my vision was blurred. And my lips were trembling so violently that no amount of lip biting could stop them.

Then his expression softened. "Sit down, Davis," he said, nodding toward my bed.

That trace of compassion was enough to break the little resolve I had left. I collapsed onto my bed and those big, fat, salty tears that Cadet Daily had hoped for came— fast with gasping sobs. He walked slowly toward me, took my rifle from my hands, and put it in its slot in the weapons rack. Then he pulled my chair over to the side of my bed and sat down, facing me.

"All right, Davis. What's up?"

"Sir . . . I . . . don't want . . . to . . . be . . . here," I said between sobs. There, I'd said it. Now everyone would be happy—Cadet Daily, my mother . . . especially my mother.

"Yes, you do, Davis."

"No, sir . . . I don't," I gasped.

"Homesick?"

I shook my head from side to side. "No . . . sir . . . It's . . . too *much* . . . like home."

Cadet Daily stood up. He walked to my window and looked outside, rubbing the back of his neck.

Calm down. Calm down. You look like a fool.

Still looking out the window, Cadet Daily said, "That's fine, Davis. Leave. And every day for the rest of your life, you'll look in the mirror and hate yourself." He spun around and his anger was back. "Listen to me, Davis. Four years from now, worthless trash like Miss Offenbacher will march into Michie Stadium, collect her diploma from the President of the United States, and become a second lieu-tenant in the United States Army. And where will you be? One insignificant name among thousands on a list of grad-uates from some no-name institution? Is that what you want, Davis? Knowing what you *could've* been?"

"But . . . sir . . . I c-can't do . . . *anything* . . . right here." I let out a huge, involuntary sob. "I'm the weak . . . link in . . . the chain."

He turned away from me and faced the window again to let me cry.

"I—I'm not . . . crying because . . . I'm sad or . . . anything . . . sir. I . . . j-just hate . . . it when . . . I can't do . . . something . . . right."

"Don't worry about it, Davis. No one leaves this place without crying at least once."

I sniffed. "You said . . . that I . . . don't have . . . w-what . . . it takes. . . . And . . . everybody . . . thinks so."

"I don't think that, Davis," Cadet Daily said, now lean-ing against the window ledge.

"But . . . you s-said . . . that you were . . . disappointed in me."

"I was!" He stomped away from the window and sat back down in the chair. "You were sloppy and unmotivated.

That's not typical Davis behavior. Yeah, I was disappointed in you." He pulled off his white gloves and shoved them into his black plastic helmet. "Look, Davis. *I* think you have what it takes. I *know* you're head and shoulders above most of your knucklehead classmates in H Company. I wouldn't waste my time with you if I didn't think so. I'd dog your butt until you broke, then FedEx the pieces to your front door. But *you*, Miss Andrea Davis from Lake Zurich, Illinois, *you* have to believe that you have what it takes."

I wiped my tears on the white gloves that I clutched in my hands. Nobody had ever told me I had *anything* before. I was always stupid and ugly and ungrateful. I sniffed again and tugged at the tag on the inside of my glove. Size 4.

"You *have* the raw materials—brains, talent, drive. But that's not enough to make it through this place. A thousand kids walked through Thayer Gate four weeks ago, with the same stuff that you have. But guess what? Not all of them are here today! And you know why? Because this place is hard, Davis. It takes more than a high SAT score and a varsity letter. It takes self-discipline. Not the rules that West Point puts on you, but the rules you put on *yourself.* That's what character is all about. Slamming doors when you're mad isn't self-discipline. Making excuses for poor performance, even when they're true, isn't self-discipline. Feeling sorry for yourself isn't self-discipline."

"Yes, sir." I started to feel a little better. This place, I realized, wasn't anything like home. Here, all the name calling and yelling had a purpose, a purpose aimed to give us character, not to hurt us.

"I can't imagine you being a quitter, Davis. But if that's what you want, I can't make you stay. But I can make you think about it." He checked his watch and stood up, his helmet under his arm. "All right. 'Nuff said. Police up your roommate. You've got twenty minutes to be on my wall in White Over Gray." Then he smiled, and it wasn't a nasty smile. "Drive on, Hardcore."

I watched him walk out my door, feeling as if a fifty-pound ruck had been lifted off my back. The day I'd leave West Point would be the day I collected my diploma from the President of the United States. I had no other choice, and I found that fact strangely comforting. I opened my mouth and yelled, "NEVER SURRENDER, SIR!"

"That's right, Davis," I heard Cadet Daily answer from somewhere in the hallway. "*Never* surrender."

Here we go again.
Same old stuff again.
Walkin' down the avenue,
In a column, two by two.
One more week and we'll be through.
I'll be glad and so will you.
—U.S. ARMY MARCHING CADENCE

CHAPTER 10

MONDAY, 2 AUGUST
0510

THE SKY WAS BLACK, the air foggy and damp, and the morning much too early for the boom from the Reveille cannon. H Company was silent, except for the muffled clink of equipment as we trudged through West Point's sleeping streets, up the hill past the Cadet Chapel, behind Michie Stadium, and into the woods. Marching in columns, two by two, like the long animal procession to Noah's Ark, we resembled odd, prehistoric creatures ourselves. Wearing Kevlar helmets and web gear, and slightly hunched from the weight of our rucks, we gripped our M-16s and moved toward our destination, Lake Frederick. In about four hours we'd be twelve miles from the only home we'd known since the beginning of Beast, five weeks ago.

I was thinking of nothing in particular as I marched,

but I had a lot on my mind. I thought about what Cadet Daily had told us yesterday. "I've got you for one more week, Third Squad," he had said. "After that, you're on your own."

On your own. It was a scary thought. I couldn't imagine life at West Point without Third Squad. I'd gotten used to the routine, to my squadmates' and Cadet Daily's constant presence. I didn't feel ready, not yet.

I thought about what I'd feel like a week from now, marching back from Lake Frederick, with Beast finally behind me. I wouldn't be a new cadet anymore; I'd be a plebe. An accepted member of the United States Corps of Cadets. All the cadets from the upper three classes would be back from summer training then and, as Cadet Daily had put it, would be "ready and waiting to steal your lunch money."

Then I thought about what Cadet Daily said we'd do this week at Lake Frederick—throw hand grenades and practice tactics, run obstacle courses and sleep in tents, get gassed and read maps. "All the skills you've learned in Beast," Cadet Daily had said, "are gonna come together at Lake Frederick. All the drill and ceremony, honor classes, rifle marksmanship, bayonet drills, P.T., discipline, and attention to detail we've been pounding into you, day and night, all summer long, is going to make sense. At Lake Frederick, Third Squad, we're gonna make *warriors* out of you!"

I tried not to think about the muscles in the back of my neck that ached from the weight of my ruck. Everything I owned was either packed in that ruck, worn on my body, or locked inside H Company's trunk room in MacArthur Barracks' basement.

I thought about room 305, how it had looked when I'd closed my door that morning. The room was bare, the beds stripped down to their black-and-white-striped mattresses, the drawers and closets empty. A slight breeze had been blowing through the open windows, but we had left nothing on the shelves or desktops for the wind to carry away. In a week we'd return, but room 305 would no longer be ours; it would house other people's uniforms and books. No scrap of paper, not even a whiff of Gabrielle's baby powder, would remain to prove that we had ever lived there.

We stopped only three times, and then just long enough to refill our canteens and have Cadet Daily check our feet for blisters. We changed our socks and then moved on, plodding up long, rocky hills, across meadows, and over trails through thick woods. Along the way we passed a few new cadets who had fallen by the wayside.

Better watch your step. The last thing I wanted was to be numbered among the "walking wounded" and loaded onto a truck to finish out the ruck march, in my eyes, a failure.

My fingers grew numb, and my arms ached from holding my weapon across my chest as I marched. Dust covered my boots, my M-16, and everything else that wasn't slimy with sweat. My Kevlar's chin strap tasted like soggy pretzels with too much salt.

Finally we came out of the woods and into a huge, flat, grassy space. New cadets from I Company—the company that had been marching ahead of us—were scurrying around and erecting canvas pup tents into rows.

"Here we are, Third Squad," I heard Cadet Daily say. "Welcome to Lake Frederick."

My heart sank. The village of little tents and campfires

encircling a silvery lake that I had envisioned faded into the dusty, olive-drab shanty-town reality that I saw. And then some voice from inside me with a tone amazingly like Cadet Daily's said: *This ain't no Girl Scout camp, Davis. You're in the Army now.* I smiled to myself.

"Okay, Third Squad," Cadet Daily said. "You get to take a short break while we wait for the stragglers to arrive. Cadet Aussprung and I just got tasked to help police them up. We don't want any Hardcore boneheads left wandering around out there, lost and crying for their mommas. By the way, Third Squad, I want to commend you on your outstanding effort. You all made it. You lived up to our motto—"

"NEVER SURRENDER, SIR!" we yelled.

Cadet Daily smiled. "That's right, Third Squad. *Never* surrender."

"Push-ups!" screamed Cero.

Push-ups? Now? I thought of my exhausted, aching body. *He's got to be joking.*

Cero dropped to the ground. "Motivational push-ups, Third Squad! PUSH-UPS!"

"PUSH-UPS!" Third Squad roared in unison, dropping to the ground to push out a few, rucks and all. This ruck march hadn't kicked *our* butts!

"Okay, Third Squad, okay!" Cadet Daily was laughing. "Cease work!" He waited for us to stumble to our feet. "Now, listen up. Ground your gear—"

We grunted a collective sigh of relief and moved to dump the burdens off our backs.

"Hold up, Third Squad! Did I give the command to move?" His smile was gone. "Never assume anything, you got that? You know what happens when you assume?" He looked us over, one at a time. "It's all contained in the word, Third Squad. It's all contained in the word. Now—you will ground your gear, remove your Kevlars, and take off your boots. Make sure you drink at least one full canteen of water, then refill it at the water buffaloes. Over there." He pointed toward a small hill about a hundred yards away where the camouflaged portable water tanks stood. "And remember—keep your weapons secured at all times, Third Squad. When I get back, I'll inspect your feet. Fall out!"

I stumbled forward as I dropped my ruck.

Kit laughed. "I guess that's what happens, Andi, when your ruck weighs half your weight."

"What about when it's half your *height*?" Gabrielle said, flinging her ruck to the ground. "I look like a stupid turtle with this thing on!"

"Hey, don't let Daily hear that, Gab. He's into nicknames, remember?" Kit dumped his ruck, too. Then he started massaging his right shoulder with his left hand. "Whew. Thought we'd never stop. This kind of walking's brutal on the ol' shoulders."

I took off my helmet, tossed it on top of my ruck, and ran my fingers through the damp mop on my head. "They're really going to let us rest. Thank God."

"What? The Iron Woman is actually tired?" Kit asked, smiling. "Unbelievable."

My BDU shirt was soaked, and the brown T-shirt under it clung to my back. I pulled the wet fabric off my skin and squinted at him. "Oh! Did I say I was tired?"

Jason McGill dumped his stuff next to mine and winced. "Man, my feet are killing me. I'm afraid to take my boots off and see the damage." He pulled out a canteen and swore. "Empty." He looked at the water buffaloes up on the hill, then back down at the empty canteen in his hand. "Great."

"Here, Jason. Catch." Gabrielle tossed him hers.

"Thanks, Gab. But don't you need—"

"Are you kidding?" Gabrielle plopped down on the ground. "I've drunk so much water on this stupid ruck march, I'm about to wet my pants. Life's rough for us females, you know. All you guys have to do is go behind a tree, whip it out, and—"

"I'm glad you know so much about the male anatomy, Gab," Kit said, laughing. "But you can spare us the details. We already know all about the benefits."

Gabrielle's face turned a shade darker than her hair, and she started to talk fast. "If I have to drink another sip of that water, I'll gag. You know, one thing I can't stand is tepid water. Especially tepid *tap* water. Makes me want to puke!"

"What did you expect, Bryen?" Hickman tossed his helmet on the ground next to her and sat down on it. "Pellegrino on ice?"

"That would be great, Hickman. But actually, I prefer Perrier. Chilled with a twist of lime. You got some?"

I laughed and sat down between Jason and Kit. Cero was sprawled on the ground across from me. He was leaning against his ruck with his boots off, eyes closed, and an open canteen lying on his chest. I smiled as I worked on taking off my boots.

Here I was, just sitting around with these guys, relaxing and joking around like a normal person. I used to watch the kids in the lunchroom or in the hallways between class periods do it, wondering what it would feel like to really be part of a group. Not just someone watching from the sidelines, hanging on the fringes. Now I knew, and it felt great.

Jason pulled off his socks and whistled under his breath. "Not good." His toes, the outsides of his feet, and his heels were bloody and raw. And almost half his toenails were black.

My feet started to throb sympathetically. "Jason!"

"Yeah, I know. If Daily sees them, that's it. Profile for me, for sure." He hung his head, looking at his mangled feet. "McGill and Often-slacker, two peas in a pod."

"Hey," said Hickman, "speaking of that Often-slacker chick, Davis and Bryen, y'all did good today. Congrats."

I looked at Hickman, then quickly dropped my eyes. Was that a compliment? Or an insult? It was hard to tell with Hickman. I'd just let it pass.

But Gabrielle was glaring at him. "And what exactly do you mean by putting the phrase 'speaking of Often-slacker' in the same sentence with Andi and me?"

"What do *you* mean, Bryen? Don't tell me you haven't noticed. I mean, you're all three *females*. Right?" Hickman looked around at the rest of us, nodding his head.

Gabrielle pulled off her socks and wiggled her toes. "I resent the comparison. Hardly a compliment, thank you very much."

I didn't like the direction that the conversation was going either. But I liked the hostility even less. "He didn't mean anything by it, Gab," I whispered.

Hickman narrowed his eyes. "Well, to be honest, Bryen, I didn't think y'all'd be able to hang."

"You didn't think that Andi could hang?" She looked over at me. For support, I think.

At home, I'd always get pulled into my parents' fights. I didn't want it happening here, too. I didn't want to have to pick sides. So I said nothing. *Let's just drop this conversation. Please!*

Hickman shrugged. "Yeah. Humping twelve miles with a pack on your back's a lot different than running twelve miles, you know. Ruck marching takes lots of upper body strength. Girls just aren't made for that kind of stuff."

"*What?*" Gabrielle looked at me again.

I wanted to disappear.

Kit stretched his legs out in front of him and leaned back against his ruck. "Well, Hickman, there's one thing you've failed to take into account. We don't have just *ordinary* girls here," he said in his slow, easy way. "They're Third Squad caliber, same as you and me. You can't just look at *girl* or *guy*, Hickman. You've got to look at the individual." He smiled at me. "And Andi and Gab can hold their own with any guy."

Jason nodded. "Yeah, where've you been all summer, Hickman?"

Those two are great! I'd always heard that actions spoke louder than words when it came to self-promotion. But right then, the words coming from Kit and Jason spoke louder than any action we could've done. And I was grateful for it.

Hickman flexed his jaw muscles. "Hey! What're you guys jumping all over me for? Man! I just said they did good, didn't I?" Then, suddenly, he smirked. He pointed toward the wood line where the H Company stragglers were making their way over to us. "Just look over there. What do you see?" He crossed his arms. "'Nuff said. End of story."

We looked. Most of the stragglers were females, with a few recruited, overweight football players mixed in.

The scene sickened me. Those women dragged down the rest of us girls—like Gabrielle and me—who worked hard to prove we could be as tough as the guys. That we belonged here. They made Hickman's smugness seem justified.

I could physically feel myself hardening against them. Repelling them.

"Facts are facts, guys," I heard Hickman say, his voice heavy with self-satisfaction. "And I'm entitled to my opinion."

"Then keep it to yourself." We all turned toward the voice. One of Cero's eyes was opened, staring at Hickman. "You're cutting into my rack time, pal. And I like my beauty sleep." Then he yawned and slowly rolled to his side with his back to Hickman.

Bonanno suddenly stood up. "Hey, uh, how abouts I fill up some canteens? I'll make a run to the water buffalo. All this argumenting's getting on my nerves."

"I'm with you on that one, Bonanno," Kit said. "Let me give you a hand." He got to his feet and started collecting canteens. "Hey, where'd Ping go?"

Hickman was chewing on a long blade of grass. "He's over there." He waved his hand toward where Fourth Squad was sitting. "Bein' a hero. Fixin' up some guy's feet."

I looked at Jason. "Hey! Why didn't we think of that? Ping used to be a medic, right? I bet he can fix you up. Hey!" I called after Kit and Bonanno, already on their way to the water buffaloes with their arms full of canteens. "Stop by Fourth Squad and tell Ping to hurry back, will you?"

A couple of minutes later Ping was jogging back over to

us with his weapon slung across his back and a camou-flaged pouch in his hand.

"What's up, McGill?" he asked. "Bogus and Bonanno said your feet look like ground beef."

"Yeah," Jason said, "raw ground beef."

Ping squatted in front of Jason and held the feet in his hands, gently turning them this way and that. He blew out slowly. "You ain't kidding, buddy." He shook his head. "You finished the march on *these*?"

Jason nodded.

Ping shook his head again. Without another word he opened his pouch and got right to work with razors, disin-fectant, foot powder, and moleskin, his hands working fast to mend Jason's feet.

"Okay, Boneheads!" Cadet Daily yelled, making his way back to us. "Mission accomplished, Third Squad. We're gonna hold formation in about five minutes, so let's get a quick look at your piggies—" He stopped abruptly and looked at the feet in Ping's hands. "What did you do, McGill? Step on a land mine?"

"I've got them under control, sir," Ping said without looking up. "As long as he keeps them dry, he shouldn't have to go on profile."

Jason nodded. "Sir, they don't hurt that bad. Really. They look worse than they are. I don't want a profile, sir."

Cadet Daily folded his arms across his chest and watched Ping finish. "Well, *Combat*," he finally said, "I'm glad to see you putting that Combat Medical Badge to good use, for once. Besides looking pretty on your uni-form, of course." He paused. "I know this ain't brain surgery, Ping. But I'm counting on you to keep McGill, here, healthy. You hear?"

"Yes, sir."

"It'll be my butt if he gets gangrene or something and has to get his feet whacked off." Then he moved on to inspect the rest of our feet.

After First Sergeant Stockel held a formation to make sure that all of H Company had made it to Lake Frederick, he drove our guidon into the ground. "This is your standard, Hotel Company. Your rallying point. Erect your shelters in line with it. Look for it if you become disoriented. And whenever you see it, remember that you are Hardcore Company, the most motivated, high-speed, low-drag, combat-ready company in Beast!"

I only half listened as he turned us over to our platoon sergeants; my eyes were on the guidon. With no wind, it hung limp from the top of its staff, this year's drill streamer dangling below it. All those evenings that I'd spent practicing the Manual of Arms had paid off. I had mastered the movements, and Hardcore had won the competition. One glimpse of it should remind me that I hadn't held my company back. But now Hickman's opinion was gnawing at me, my small victory tainted. I had a lot more work to do.

Cadet Black released the platoon, one squad at a time. Shouldering our rucks, we followed Cadet Daily past the line of half-erected tents to our squad's area.

"Okay, listen up," Cadet Daily said. "As we've done before, roommates will be tentmates." He designated which piece of ground each pair would occupy. "Remember to leave a couple of feet between tents, and cover down on India Company." He nodded at the rows of tents that were already up behind us. "We want Tent City 'dress right, dress.' Just like a formation."

"Tent City?" Gabrielle whispered to me. "How imaginative."

"The sooner we knock this out, the sooner you can rest! Remember—no sags, no wrinkles. Third Squad, fall out!"

"NEVER SURRENDER, SIR!"

Gabrielle and I dragged ourselves over to our spot. Just like in the barracks, Jason and Kit were our neighbors. They were dropping their gear on our left. A few feet on our right, two guys from Second Squad had just finished snapping their shelter halves together and were spreading the butterfly-shaped canvas on the grass. One of the guys nodded at us. Gabrielle smiled back. I looked away.

I stripped myself of all my gear and stretched my arms over my head. New cadet voices in relaxed conversation mixed with the *clink-clank* of entrenching tools hammering tent pegs into the ground and spread, row by row, over the grassy field. Another new cadet company emerged from the woods, marching in double file behind G Company's guidon.

I glanced at Gabrielle. Her fingers were working in frantic motions, smoothing and adjusting her sweaty but somehow still frizzy hair. Then she opened one of her ammo pouches, fished out some Chap Stick, and ran it over her lips. *Gabrielle—always worried about her looks. Even after a twelve-mile ruck march.* I rolled my eyes and started digging around in my ruck.

I pulled out my tent poles, tent pegs, and shelter half. After fitting the poles together, I started unwinding the rope from around my tent pegs.

I stole glances at Kit and Jason as they worked, mirroring everything they did. By now, putting up tents wasn't anything new to us. We had practiced setting them up during Squad Leader Time several times, and had even bivouacked once—on the rifle range the night before we fired our M-16s. But Gabrielle and I still hadn't been able to erect a habitable tent on our own. We understood what we were supposed to do. But somehow our tent always ended up looking like we had thrown a blanket over a broken-down, swaybacked mule.

When we had pounded the last tent peg into the ground, Gabrielle and I stood back to inspect our work. It looked only slightly better than our previous attempts.

Gabrielle tossed her entrenching tool on the ground. "Oh, forget it! This sucks. I'm gonna get help."

"No, wait a minute, Gab. I think I know what's wrong." I really wanted us to figure this out on our own. I walked over to the left side of the tent. "Look. We just have to pull these tent pegs out here and move them—"

"Great. Let's let Ping do it." She looked down the line of Third Squad tents. "His tent's up, and he's just sitting there, talking to Hickman—"

Hickman. I thought about what Kit and Jason had said to Hickman earlier. They'd gone out on a limb for us. We owed this to them, if not to ourselves. "We really don't need Ping's help, Gab."

"Are you kidding? As soon as Cadet Daily sees this thing, you know what he's going to do. He'll haze us, and then he'll yell at the top of his lungs so the whole world can hear." She deepened her voice to mimic Cadet Daily's. "'Hey, Ping! I got a mission for you! Bryen and Davis's tent needs some CPR! Let's put that Combat Medical Badge to good use.' I, for one, would like to avoid that." She leaned closer to me and whispered, "Especially with Nathan

Monroe right next door. I want him to think I'm squared away."

I frowned. "Gab, what are you talking about?"

"You know, Andi. Nathan Monroe." She jerked her head toward the Second Squad tent next to ours. "The big guy? With the golden hair and baby-blue eyes? He has the cutest dimples when he smiles."

Gab definitely had her priorities. But they weren't mine.

New Cadet Monroe was the new cadet who stood directly in front of me in Second Squad at least three times every day in formation. I could describe the shape of his head and knew that he needed a haircut at the end of each week because stubble always grew down the back of his neck by Friday. But I didn't know his first name, had no idea what color his eyes were, and had never made him smile.

"He was recruited for football. A quarterback, Andi. And he's from San Antonio, Texas, and he's really nice and—I told you all about him. Remember? The day we fired our M-16s. He was in the foxhole next to me."

She was really starting to irritate me now. "Well anyway, Cadet Daily won't need to haze us this time, Gab. We're going to get this tent right, all by ourselves."

"Why do it ourselves when Ping can do it better? And faster."

"Because I hate to always have him do our work for us, that's why! I don't want to be . . . the weak link in the chain." I got down on my hands and knees and yanked out a tent peg. "Where'd I put my e-tool?" I sat up and looked around. "You see it, Gab?"

"Weak link in the chain?" Then she snorted. "Oh, I get it. Hickman's little remark is getting to you, huh?" She put her hands on her hips and glared at me. "That's ridiculous! We pull our weight, Andi. Everyone, even Hickman, said we—"

I looked up at her. "Oh, yeah? Well, I don't call getting someone to bail us out all the time 'pulling our weight.'"

"But Ping doesn't mind, Andi! He likes—"

"Well, *I* mind. Okay? So pass me your e-tool? Please?" Standing up to her was hard. It would've been easier to just get Ping. I put out my hand; it was shaking.

But Gabrielle didn't notice. She had crossed her arms and closed her eyes. "Plus it's not bailing us out. It's called 'cooperate and graduate.' Ever hear of that? It's one of Cadet Daily's most favorite things to say."

I dropped my hand. "Yeah. '*Cooperate* and graduate,' Gab. Not '*get over* and graduate.'"

"You're so funny, I forgot to laugh."

Couldn't she see that getting the guys to do things for us all the time wasn't really that different from falling out of runs or ruck marches? That every time we did it, we became weaker in their eyes, and soon they'd despise us like they despised Offenbacher? Well, I wasn't going to play that game.

"Your e-tool, Gabrielle?" *Great, now my voice is shaking*.

Gabrielle huffed but tossed me her e-tool. "I just don't understand you, Andi. You're acting really weird, you know that? What are you trying to prove, anyway?"

I didn't answer her. Instead, I uprooted the other two tent pegs on that side of the tent and worked on stretching the canvas as tightly as I could.

"There you go, not saying anything," Gabrielle said. "As usual."

She was right; I knew I hardly ever said anything. But now I wanted to. I wanted to scream, "You wouldn't understand! You don't have to prove anything. You can go home to your mom and dad and your debutante balls anytime you want. You don't have to belong here. But I do . . . because I've never belonged anywhere!" But I just couldn't do it. It was better—safer—to say nothing. I'd said way too much already, and now she was mad at me. I pounded the tent pegs back into the ground. I took a deep breath and sat back on my heels. "There."

Gabrielle was watching me, her arms crossed again. "There, nothing. The rest of Third Squad is already done. So we're the weak link in the chain whether Ping helps us or not."

I ignored her and walked to the other side of the tent. "Oh—there's my e-tool."

"Good. Give mine back."

"Hey, Andi," I heard Kit's voice behind me. "Why don't you try angling the tent pegs toward your tent instead of up and down. You know, at about 45 degrees? It'll give you some more pull."

I heard Gabrielle snort again. I nodded at Kit, resigned. "Oh, that's right. Ping did that the last time he—"

"And try moving that one up some," he said, pointing to the peg holding down the tent's front right corner. "See? So it's even with the other side? And that should do it."

"Yeah. That makes sense—"

"Shh!" Gabrielle hissed. "Andi wants no free advice, Kit. She likes doing things the hard, stupid way."

Kit gave me a look that said, "What's up with her?" I just shrugged my shoulders. Kit rolled his eyes and walked the few feet back to his tent and unrolled his bedroll, mumbling something about rather living on a rooftop than being around a contentious woman.

And somehow I felt better. For some reason, I didn't mind Kit's kind of help. Maybe because he'd been so laid back about it, just sort of offering it up to us like I'd seen him do with some of the Third Squad guys on occasion. Or, maybe more importantly, because he let *us* do the work. He didn't wave us aside and fix things himself while we just stood there. He didn't assume—or better yet, make me feel—that I was incompetent.

After Gabrielle and I fixed all six tent pegs around the tent, we stepped back. "Well, Kit?" I called over to him. "What do you think? Better?"

Kit gave us a thumbs-up.

"So I guess we just need to tighten the ropes at the front," I said, thinking out loud. "And hopefully that should be it."

"I'll do it," Gabrielle said, pushing past me. We watched as she slowly pulled on the rope, causing the front tent pole to tilt forward. Like magic, the sag in the middle disappeared.

I could tell that Gabrielle was trying hard not to smile as she held a tent peg in one hand and looped the rope around it with the other. "Mind pounding in the peg, Andi? I can't do everything, you know."

"No problem, Gab." I grabbed an e-tool and started hammering.

"You hit my hands, girl, and you're—"

"You've just got to trust me, Gab."

"I do," she mumbled.

When we were done, our tent looked perfect. I put my

hands on my hips and smiled. "It really looks good. Huh, Gab? No sags. No wrinkles."

Gabrielle bent over and rummaged around in her ruck. Then she stood up and held out two sticks of wilted Extra spearmint gum. "A piece?" She raised an eyebrow. "For peace?"

I laughed and looked over both shoulders to make sure no upperclassman was around. "Where in the world did you get that?"

She gave me a secret sort of smile. Then she shoved one of the pieces into my hand and whispered, "Just chew carefully."

I have a fine incipient case of split personality,
The masculine lined up against the feminine.
This is no place for the feminine.
—DICKEY CHAPELLE, WOMAN WAR CORRESPONDENT
(KILLED WHILE COVERING THE VIETNAM WAR)

CHAPTER 11

THURSDAY, 5 AUGUST
0045

SIMULATED BOMBS SCREECHED through the air and white lights flashed, then hovered like spotlights over the woods we'd soon enter. We should have been snuggled inside our sleeping bags. But instead, we sat shivering on metal bleachers and watching the starless sky spit drizzle, the water beading on our ponchos and rolling off. With camouflaged faces and vacant stares, we looked like veteran troops as we waited out the minutes until it was Third Squad's time to go out on our first night patrol.

Finally, Cadet Daily stood up. He tossed Cero a roll of green duct tape. "Pass that around, Zero. Tape everything metal, Third Squad—flashlights, M-16 straps, LCE suspenders—and anything else that makes noise. Including your mouths, if necessary." He tossed a wad of olive-green cord to Ping. "That is what we call dummy cord, Third

Squad, invented especially for knuckleheads like you. Go ahead, Combat. Help them tie their weapons to their bodies. Leave only about three feet of slack, max. I don't want to spend the few hours of rack time we'll have left tonight beating the bushes for an M-16 that was lost in the dark. Now get hot. We're moving out in a few."

After Cadet Daily had inspected our tape and tie jobs, he formed us into a single-file line with Kit in the front and Ping in the rear. "Remember, Third Squad," Cadet Daily said, "this is a tactical patrol. As soon as we move out, noise and light discipline will be enforced. That means no talking and no flashlights. Tonight realism is the name of the game. You got that?"

"YES, SIR!"

"I'll be on point, and Ping, you'll bring up the rear. Remember—no crowding. Keep your intervals, about two paces between men." He pointed at the two fluorescent squares on the back of Kit's helmet. "Keep the 'cat eyes' on the back of the helmet in front of you in sight at all times, Third Squad, and you'll be good to go. I won't tolerate any weak excuses from anyone who wanders off. Understand?"

"YES, SIR!"

"Now, for all the noise out here. When you hear a whistle and seconds later an explosion, that's 'incoming'—you hit the dirt. When you hear a pop and seconds later you see bright light flooding an area, that's an 'illumination flare'— you freeze. This ain't rocket science, Third Squad. Just use your heads. Stay alert, stay alive. That's what it's all about. Now let's move out."

We followed Cadet Daily into the woods, peering into the blackness, silent as snakes. The rain had softened the earth, muffling our movement. Even after my eyes adjusted to the dark, I could barely make out the shapes of the trees enclosing us. I held my weapon out in front and pointed it toward the trees, watching for any sudden movement. Years of running cross country had taught me to make split-second decisions about footing. But now, unable to see the ground, I chose each step carefully, feeling with the toes of my boots for rocks or tree roots—anything that could trip me up. And I watched the cat eyes, piercing the darkness from the back of Hickman's Kevlar moving directly in front of me.

My imagination quickly took over. I was creeping through the jungles of Vietnam, or the forests of eastern Europe. The enemy was out there, waiting, watching. Maybe somewhere someone had a round chambered in his weapon that was destined to rip through my body, ending everything in a second. I felt my pulse speed up, but I wasn't afraid. I concentrated on keeping my breathing quiet, my footsteps soundless. I was ready for anything.

A whistle screamed overhead. *Incoming!* The explosion crashed as we dove for the dirt. Then we silently got to our feet and moved on, only to hug the muddy ground again and again.

Just after we started down a long hill, a new shrieking sound came from behind me and shattered the silence. "My knee! My knee! Oh, my knee!"

Gabrielle!

Cadet Daily appeared instantly. "What's going on?" he hissed in a voice that only barely passed for a whisper. He crouched beside Gabrielle, who was now a crumpled, moaning heap, rocking back and forth in the mud and clutching her knee. "Bryen?"

"Sir, I tripped. My knee . . ." She made a move to stand,

but only ended up crying out again. "Something's broken, sir. I just know it. It hurts so *bad!*"

Ping had slipped up the line and was kneeling beside Gabrielle, his hands already examining her knee. I stood beside them, wishing I could do something to help. *Poor Gab!*

"Keep it down, Bryen." Cadet Daily leaned closer to Gabrielle. "You've gotta suffer silently. Understand? You're compromising our position."

The rest of Third Squad pressed closer, trying to get a look at our first real casualty.

Ping tapped Cadet Daily on the shoulder and whispered into his ear. I strained my ears to hear Ping's words over Gabrielle's whimpering. ". . . knee's intact . . . sir . . . nothing's broken . . . badly bruised . . ."

Badly bruised? I stared back at Gabrielle, confused. *That's it?*

Cadet Daily turned back to Gabrielle. "Listen to me, Bryen. You've gotta suck it up, understand? You are jeopardizing the safety of every member in this squad. In combat, soldiers are shot, and they don't make a sound."

"Yeah," I heard Hickman whisper beside me. "And all she did was fall down. Give me a break."

The darkness could hide the disgust on Hickman's face, but not in his voice.

I chewed on my lip. I couldn't completely disagree with him. Why couldn't Gabrielle just stop blubbering? A wave of irritation surged up inside me. *Doesn't she have any pride?* I stepped away from her and moved closer to Hickman, hoping the subtle gesture would distance me from Gabrielle in the eyes of the squad. I wanted to show them that I was disgusted by her unmilitary reaction, too.

Immediately, I felt guilty. Disloyal. Gabrielle was my roommate. My friend.

I heard a *pop* overhead, and instantly we were blanketed with white light. Nobody moved until the light melted into the dark.

"The enemy knows our location," Cadet Daily said. "We've got to move. *Now.*"

In that instant I understood. Gabrielle had been wrong; pain or no pain, she should have been quiet, she should have kept it in. This was about something bigger than loyalty or friendship. This was about life and death.

I saw Ping help Gabrielle to her feet. "Just lean on me, Gab," I heard him whisper. "You'll be okay."

But still . . . shouldn't *I* have done something?

I moved aside to let them pass ahead of me, and as I followed behind Third Squad in the dark, one thought plagued me: Gabrielle was hurt, and I had deserted her.

0525

Sounds faded in and out around me, muffled and murky at first, as if I were floating in a pool of water just below its surface. Then, gradually, the sounds became louder, sharper—people talking, the snaps of tent flaps popping open, sleeping bags unzipping, equipment clinking. I slowly became aware of the hard ground under my body and the musty fabric of my sleeping bag. My body was warm, but my nose was cold. Something moved against me, then groaned.

I opened my eyes. Light filtered through the canvas of the tent that enclosed Gabrielle and me like two larvae in a canvas cocoon. *Morning already?* I rolled over and squinted at my watch—5:27—then closed my eyes again.

It was already morning when we went to bed last night. My limbs felt heavy, tired, like they'd been injected with some kind of drug. *Got to get up . . . need to get dressed . . . before Daily . . . gets . . . here.* And I slipped back into the no-man's-land between wakefulness and sleep.

"RISE AND SHINE, MAGGOTS! IT'S A GOOD MORNING TO DIE!"

The tent shook and my eyes snapped open.

Cadet Daily!

We both shot up into a seated position of attention, our legs still bound by our sleeping bags.

"I want a verbal confirmation that you're conscious. Bryen! Davis! You up?"

"Yes, sir!"

"Good. You got exactly twenty-two minutes to police up yourselves and your area before Reveille. I was generous, Ladies—I gave you seven extra minutes of La La Land 'cause of our late night. Don't make me regret it."

"Yes, sir!"

"How's that knee, Bryen?"

"Fine, sir."

"I'll check it before we move out to training." He moved away, and I heard him repeat his morning greeting to Kit and Jason next door. "RISE AND SHINE, MAGGOTS. IT'S A GOOD MORNING TO DIE!"

A good morning to die? And then, with a jolt in my gut, I remembered. *We're getting gassed today!* We were going to practice what it felt like to die.

Gabrielle sank back into her sleeping bag and moaned. "Three and a half hours of sleep. They'd never think of letting us sleep in for once."

"Hey, Cadet Daily gave us seven extra minutes, Gab."

Gabrielle snorted and covered her head with her sleeping bag.

I fumbled with the zipper of my sleeping bag with shaky hands, swollen from lack of sleep. Then I untangled the sling of my M-16 from around my leg and laid the weapon, warm from my body, on the ground between Gabrielle and me.

Okay—I've got to find my glasses. No contacts allowed today—Cadet Daily said. I started feeling around my side of the tent for my glasses. *All right—where are they?*

"Come on, Gab." I prodded the mound inside the sleeping bag beside me with my foot. "Get up."

"Okay, okay! I'm moving." She squirmed out of her sleeping bag and looked at me. "Your boyfriend drool on you last night?" she asked, pointing at my left thigh.

"What?" I leaned over to inspect it. My nose had just about touched my thigh before I saw what she was pointing at. "Oh . . . *this*?" I licked my thumb and tried rubbing the grimy streak off my thigh. "I guess I didn't wipe off my M-16 good enough when we got back last night. It was really muddy out there, huh?"

Gabrielle didn't answer.

I sensed she didn't want to talk about last night. I could understand that; I wasn't so sure last night had been one of my better moments, either. I worked quickly to fill the silence. "I'll tell you what"—I nodded toward my M-16— "I'm really sick of sleeping with this thing."

"No complaints, Andi. You know what Cadet Daily says: 'It's the only boyfriend you've got right now.'"

Every night that we'd been out here, Cadet Daily had reminded us to guard our weapons well. "You don't have a girlfriend anymore," he'd say. "'Cause Jody's got her." Then he'd smirk at Gabrielle and me. "And you ain't got no boyfriend, either. So, Third Squad, when you go to bed tonight, cuddle your M-16 and consider yourselves lucky."

The subject always bothered me. It made me feel both uncomfortable and inadequate. I didn't want Cadet Daily thinking that I'd sleep with a boyfriend . . . even if I had one. And I didn't like him broadcasting the fact that I was a female. I'd rather have him—and the rest of the squad— think of me as just another one of the guys.

I nodded, then pulled socks out of my ruck and wormed my feet into them. The tent was silent once again. Suffocatingly silent. I knew we'd have to talk about last night eventually. Last night wasn't going to leave on its own. I took a deep breath and plunged right in. "So Gab, how's your knee this morning . . . really?"

Gabrielle tugged at a string on her sleeping bag and shrugged.

"It looked bad last night." I waited for her to say something.

She continued to groom her sleeping bag.

"Is it still swollen?"

"Does it *look* swollen?" she snapped back.

I'd said the wrong thing, and now I had to fix it. "I can't tell, Gab. I took out my contacts last night, so *everything* looks swollen." I laughed, hoping she'd laugh, too. But she didn't. "Are you going to see the medic today? Or—"

"I'm not going on profile, if that's what you're getting at. So don't get your hopes up, Super Troop."

My hopes up? Super Troop? I watched her bend her knee up, then down. *What did she mean by that?* Did she really think I was glad that she got hurt? Or was she insinuating something else? This wasn't like Gabrielle;

she always said exactly what was on her mind.

But . . . wasn't she right? Wouldn't the whole incident—Gabrielle's accident and her yelling—actually end up benefiting me in a twisted sort of way? Didn't it make me look that much better—more "hu-ah"—in comparison? And wasn't that what I'd wanted all along? To have the guys think of me as one of them and not some wimpy female in disguise?

I felt miserable. These thoughts were taking me to a place I didn't want to go, shaping me into the kind of friend that I'd never want to be.

"Besides," Gabrielle was saying, "Ping said he'd look at my knee before breakfast, and he's better than any worthless company medic, anyway." Then she looked at me and sighed. "I—I guess I made a real idiot out of myself last night, huh?"

I didn't exactly know how to answer that question. I had been both embarrassed for her and angry at her last night. And rightly so—if we'd really been in combat, Third Squad could've gotten wiped out because of her. But I couldn't tell her that. She was my friend, and I didn't want to make her feel bad.

"Well . . ." I stammered. "You *were* hurt, and well, it's over now and it was only practice—"

"*You* wouldn't have yelled."

I didn't like the way she'd said that, accusingly. And I didn't like the way she was looking at me, studying me. It made me nervous; I needed something to do. I got on my hands and knees and felt down the length of my sleeping bag, searching for a lump that might be my glasses. "That's not necessarily true. I mean, if I were really hurt—"

"My knee got bruised, Andi. Not broken, not blown

out, not anything. Just bruised." She crawled over to her ruck at the foot of our tent. "And everybody knows it."

"But that doesn't mean it didn't hurt, Gab. Sometimes bruises hurt more than breaks." There, that was a true statement, one that I hoped would make her feel better. After all, I'd had twisted ankles and shin splints that had kept me from running before.

"Whatever." She dug into her ruck, her back toward me. "I almost wish I were debilitated for life. At least then I'd be justified a little for last night." One of her hands left her ruck and moved up to her face. "After all, all I did was 'fall down.'"

I closed my eyes. *So, she heard Hickman.* "Gab, I—"

"Let's just drop it, okay?"

"Okay." The silence was so strong now that it seemed to be squeezing the musty air between us. I cleared my throat. "Hey, uh, are my glasses on your side? I can't find them."

"Correction, Andi. You mean 'Tactical Eye Devices,' right?" She wiped her face on her T-shirt. "What for?"

"Because I need them to see, Gab. Why else?" I laughed nervously, grateful to be talking about something else. "Come on, do you see them? I'm totally blind."

"But you wear contacts. So what's the big deal?" She pulled out her BDU pants and crawled back onto her sleeping bag. "You didn't lose a contact, did you?"

"No—"

"Well, that's a relief." She lay down on her back and started wiggling into her pants.

"Gab! We're not supposed to wear contacts today. Remember? Because we're getting gassed?" My stomach twitched, thinking about the day ahead of us. *Don't think about that now.* I pulled out my BDU pants and lay down on my sleeping bag next to her. "Remember what Cadet Daily said? 'Tear gas and contacts don't mix.'"

"Well, I'm wearing mine, anyway. The gas can't be that bad." She jammed her brown T-shirt into her pants. "Plus, I think it's stupid that we can't wear our civilian glasses. I mean, what's the big deal?" She jabbed me with her elbows as she worked on the buttons of her fly. "Wearing TEDs is just another big haze."

"Well, I guess it's because they want us all to look the same, and—"

"Tactical Eye Devices. What's so tactical about them, anyway? They're ugly." She sat up and started weaving her BDU belt through her belt loops. "Around here 'tactical' and 'ugly' seem to be synonymous: If you wanna be 'hu-ah!' you gotta look gross. It should be a cadence." She stabbed the end of her belt through the buckle like she was thrusting her bayonet into the enemy. "No way am I going to wear TEDs in public. And neither should you, Andi. Who's going to know if you wear contacts or if you don't? Don't be such a duty dog." She pulled her brush out of her ruck and ran it through her hair. "I may be a wimp, but at least I won't be an ugly one."

I glanced at Gabrielle and chewed on the inside of my lip. I'd said something wrong again. I just wanted to do the right thing and stay out of trouble. I wasn't a risk taker like Gabrielle. She was always testing the boundaries here— talking at unauthorized times, sneaking food back from the mess hall under her hat, chewing the sticks of gum her friends enclosed in her letters, wearing the faintest shade of lipstick to dinner when no makeup was allowed, and now blowing off Cadet Daily's instructions to not wear contacts. Maybe my need to play by the rules was what was annoying her. I sat up and pulled my ruck onto my lap. *I've sure started some winner conversations this morning.*

"TEDs aren't that bad," I said, trying to turn the focus off of me. "Kit wears them, and he looks okay."

"Kit's a guy, Andi." She pulled out fresh socks and jammed her feet into them. "The Army didn't have femininity or style in mind, believe me, when they created TEDs." She pulled the drawstrings on her ruck. "So, you dressed? I'm going to open the flaps. It smells like moth balls in here."

Gabrielle was right. The Army-issue glasses *were* ugly. Even more ugly, if it were possible, than our low quarters. The only people whom I had ever seen wear glasses so hideous in the real world were geeks in the movies . . . and my dad.

TEDs—what a perfect name. Not only would my dad have paid money for the thick, brown plastic frames, but he shared the name—Ted. Just then, thinking of my dad wearing his way-out-of-style glasses, almost made me feel sorry for him. It suddenly struck me how pathetically out of touch he really was. Maybe he was just incapable of understanding that things like encouraging letters or having a bedroom to come home to might be important to me. I mean, anyone who would walk into LensCrafters and actually choose that style of glasses out of so many . . .

I sighed. "Okay, Gab. You win. TEDs *are* ugly."

But Gabrielle wasn't listening. She was staring at the snapped tent flaps, thinking. "You know, Andi, I can't believe I never thought about it before, but if you put Kit in a pair of tiny wire-frame glasses—dark brown with a touch of gold, maybe?—he'd be a pretty cute guy. You know, the intellectual type." She smiled to herself as she ripped open the flaps and stumbled outside. Cooler air and light flooded into our tent.

"The grass is dry, Andi. You'd never guess we spent half the night in the rain."

I tossed my ruck, boots, and canteen outside the tent before crawling out myself. Then I sat down beside Gabrielle, just outside the opening of our tent, to pull on my boots.

"Howdy, neighbors. And how are you on this fine morning?"

I squinted in the direction of the voice. Two blurs were sitting in front of Kit and Jason's tent next door.

"Awake," Gabrielle answered without looking up, quickly twisting her hair into a bun.

"Glad you're off to a good start," Kit said. "How's the knee?"

"It still works."

Hoping to come up with something other than Gabrielle's knee to talk about, I put my other foot into its boot and found the new topic in the bottom. "My TEDs!" I yelled, exaggerating my surprise, and nudged Gabrielle. "See? Right where I'd be sure to find them. Mystery solved." I smiled at her then, hoping she'd smile back and break the tension. But all she did was shrug, uninterested.

I quickly stuck my TEDs on my face and looked back at Kit and Jason, now in focus, sitting cross-legged and dressed like us in brown T-shirts and BDU pants. "Hey, guys. Nice to . . . see you."

Kit and Jason had shaving cream smeared on their faces and a canteen cup on the ground between them. Kit dipped his razor into the cup and felt around his face with his fingertips. "I didn't know you wore glasses, Andi. Interesting."

"That bad, huh?" I grabbed my toothbrush out of my ruck and squeezed toothpaste on the bristles.

"That's an understatement." Gabrielle watched me as I

brushed my teeth. "Try using water. You'll never get the scum off your teeth brushing dry."

I smiled again at Gabrielle, my mouth full of foam. "Thanks, Mom."

"I didn't say that you looked bad, Andi—" Kit said.

"Of course not," Gabrielle muttered. "She *never* looks bad."

Now what? Her snide remarks were really starting to worry me. She seemed to resent my very presence—and since we'd left the tent, it was getting worse. Every single thing I said or did just brought on another jab. I stopped brushing and stared at Gabrielle. *Okay, just don't let it get to you.* She was having a bad day because she'd had a bad night. But she'd get over it. Eventually. I'd just have to ride it out.

"—I said 'interesting,'" Kit was saying. "And, anyway, from what Cadet Daily said yesterday, it won't matter what we look like after we hit the gas tent."

"Yeah," Jason said. "In a couple of hours we're gonna be slobbering all over ourselves and twitching like roaches that got hit with Raid." He limped over to his tent. "Everyone will be nasty. With a capital 'N.'"

"Thanks for the graphic description," Gabrielle said.

Kit grinned. "TEDs will just add to the charm."

I spit around the corner of my tent and rinsed my mouth with water from a canteen.

Gabrielle stared at the toothpaste foam on the ground. "I guess we know which side of the tent you're tightening."

I ignored Gabrielle and went back to lacing my boots. "How're your feet, Jason?"

"They're okay—they only hurt when I first put my boots on." He suddenly got a strange smile on his face, then ducked into his tent before hobbling over to us. "Gab, you act like you rolled out of the wrong side of the rack this morning. So I have a little something for you. To, uh, you know, cheer you up."

Gabrielle smiled up at him. "You do?"

"Sure." He scooped something out of his pocket and sprinkled it into her open hand.

Gabrielle looked down and screamed, flinging Jason's gift on the ground. "Toenails! Nasty, bloody, disgusting toenails! You are such a child!" She scowled back at Jason, who was laughing and returning Kit's high-five. "How old are you guys, anyway? Ten?" She poured water over her hands. "Why didn't you do that to Andi? Oh, wait, let me guess—it's 'Let's Pick on Gab Day,' today. Right?"

Jason shrugged. "Andi wouldn't have screamed, Gab. She's, you know, too tough for that." He got a sick look on his face then, realizing too late what he had said. "Sorry, Gab. I didn't mean . . . about . . . well, you know—"

Gabrielle's face froze. Mine burned. Any other time his compliment would have made my day, but right now it was probably the worst thing he could've said. I didn't want praise this way, not at Gabrielle's expense. And right then I made up my mind: The next time praise came my way, I'd be standing on my own merit, not on someone else's misfortune.

"LET'S MOVE, THIRD SQUAD!" I heard Cadet Daily yell as he stomped toward us. "Tighten down those tents! Get into the proper uniform! Come on—you ain't the Rag Bag Brigade! Let's go! Reveille's in two minutes, and you're behind the power curve!"

We jumped to our feet and scrambled in different directions—throwing bodies into BDU shirts, grabbing weapons, hammering tent pegs, strapping on gas mask pouches, and covering heads with BDU caps.

And the discomfort of the moment was forgotten.

Gas! GAS! Quick, boys!—An ecstasy of fumbling,
Fitting the clumsy helmets just in time;
But someone still was yelling out and stumbling,
And flound'ring like a man in fire or lime.
—WILFRED OWEN, "DULCE ET DECORUM EST"

CHAPTER 12

THURSDAY, 5 AUGUST
0810

AFTER BREAKFAST FOUR bus-sized Army trucks were lined up to haul H Company to the gas tent. Cadet Black was standing at the rear of one of them. "Get your motivated selves up to this deuce-and-a-half, Third Platoon, and mount up," Cadet Black yelled. "It's a good morning to die!"

"These guys are real original," Gabrielle whispered. "If I hear that one more time—"

"Hey, you know the deal," Ping whispered back. "Repetition aids learning."

I clutched my barracks bag, containing my MOPP suit, and said nothing. They seemed so casual about this; I couldn't even pretend to be.

"Two lines, Third Platoon! First and Second Squads, on the left side. Third and Fourth, on the right. Move out!"

We double-timed to the rear of the truck and stood, close together, in line. Mixed into the odor of sweaty bodies and morning breath was the smell of diesel and dirt that clung to the huge piece of canvas, forming the truck's sides and roof behind its cab.

I hope the gas isn't as bad as this stench! I'd like to put my mask on now.

We clambered aboard one after the other. Two long benches faced each other from either side of the truck. I squeezed next to Jason, placing the butt of my weapon and barracks bag on the floor between my feet. Ping took the spot on my left. I listened to the new cadets from First and Second Squads, sitting on the other bench across from me.

"This is gonna suck."

"Naw. Cops use tear gas all the time."

"Is that all it is? Tear gas?"

"Well, I'm not breathing it. I'm holding my breath."

"Yeah? So, what's gonna keep it out of your eyes?"

When all of Third Platoon was inside, Cadet Black slammed the tailgate shut. The motor started up, and we were off.

The truck bounced over the surface of the road and jerked whenever the driver shifted gears, causing us to rock against each other like passengers on a crowded subway car. The roar of the motor, our dreaded destination, and insufficient sleep created an overwhelming combination. New cadets started nodding off, their chins resting on their chests. Soon the grits that I had eaten for breakfast settled in my stomach, and resting the bill of my Kevlar on the muzzle of my weapon, I, too, fell asleep.

The truck jerked to a halt, and I awoke with a start.

Cadet Black opened the tailgate and hustled us out of the truck and into a clearing of sun-fried grass surrounded by trees. Standing in the far corner of the clearing, a large tent waited.

The gas tent. The grits in my stomach became one hard lump.

"Okay, H Company," First Sergeant Stockel said, after we were all seated in a semicircle around him in the grass, "listen up. Today is the culmination of all that NBC training you've had this summer, and especially the skills you learned yesterday. Today you will understand *why* we had you out here yesterday running between stations in the woods, wearing your MOPP suits in ninety-nine-degree heat, looking like packs of camouflaged Darth Vaders."

Laughter rippled around the semicircle.

But First Sergeant Stockel didn't smile. "After today, Hardcore, NBC will mean more to you than some TV network that broadcasts sitcoms and soap operas. After today, Hardcore, *Nuclear*, *Biological*, and *Chemical* warfare will be permanently etched in your minds. Today, Hardcore, is a day that, I hope, you will file away in your hard drives as one of your worst"—he scanned the semicircle with narrowed eyes behind wire-framed glasses—"and your best. Worst because you will see what havoc relatively harmless gas can do to your body. And best because you will gain confidence in your equipment. Today your MOPP suit and protective mask will become something more to you than a bad Halloween costume."

All was quiet around the semicircle.

I chewed on my thumbnail and glanced over at the tent at the far end of the site. Two upperclassmen in MOPP suits and gas masks emerged and walked toward one of the deuce-and-a-halfs. And then a humvee with a red cross painted on its sides pulled into the site. I looked at Ping.

He grinned at me and mouthed the word, "Medics."

It sure boosted my confidence to see them here.

Before First Sergeant Stockel broke the company down into squads for the training, he told us what to expect. First, our squad leaders would test us on donning our MOPP suits and gas masks, and then the moment we'd all been dreading would come—we'd file through the gas tent and take one deep breath.

Cadet Daily collected us from the semicircle and led us to a copse of trees in a far corner of the training site, then remained standing while he had us sit on the ground around him.

"Eloquent speech out of Cadet Stockel," Cadet Daily said. "Reminded me of myself. Hope you took it to heart." He paced back and forth before us, rubbing the back of his neck. "Okay, Third Squad. Let's get that blood pumping through your cerebral tissue. What does the acronym MOPP stand for?" He stopped in front of Kit. "Bogus?"

"Sir, MOPP stands for Mission-Oriented Protective Posture."

"All right! You knuckleheads are more awake than you look. And what about MOPP levels—why do we have them? Zero, you're up."

Cero paused a moment before he spoke. "Sir, the MOPP levels determine what equipment soldiers must wear, depending on the chemical threat. Sir, there are five MOPP levels—Zero through Four. Sir, the MOPP equipment consists of—"

Cadet Daily put his hand up. "Cease work there, Motivated Trooper. You're getting ahead of me." He turned to

Gabrielle and smirked. "Why don't you finish where Zero left off, Miss Bryen?"

Gabrielle's head shot up. She'd been nodding off. "Sir, I do not understand."

"Zoning out there, Bryen?" Cadet Daily shook his head. "Stay alert, stay alive, soldier. Dig her out, Hickman."

Hickman imitated Cadet Daily's smirk. And with the voice of a bored state trooper from somewhere south of the Mason-Dixon Line, he said, "Sir, the MOPP equipment consists of an overgarment—jacket and trousers—overboots and gloves, and an M-40 series protective mask with hood."

Cadet Daily crouched until he and Hickman locked eyes. "Smirk off, Hickman! I don't know who you think you are, pal. But you are *not that person!*" He leaned closer and said through clenched teeth, "You got a problem coming to the aid of your squadmate here?" He pointed at Gabrielle.

"No, sir," Hickman answered quickly.

Yes! I knew Gabrielle *should've* been more alert, but Hickman's attitude sucked. And now Cadet Daily let the whole squad know it.

Cadet Daily slowly rose to his feet. "I didn't think so, Hickman. Moving right along." He stepped past me. Phew. "Bonanno, let's just cut to the chase. What's MOPP Four? Because that's what you'll be wearing today." He looked at his watch. "And don't take all day."

Bonanno nodded. "Yes, sir. Sir, MOPP Four is when you wear all your MOPP gear because you know you've been gassed."

"That was inelegant, Bonanno. But accurate. Now, Third Squad—ON YOUR FEET!"

We jumped to our feet.

I knew what was coming next. *Okay . . . get ready.* Like

a gunslinger about to go for his six-shooter, I inched my left hand up my thigh and toward the gas mask pouch on my hip.

"You know the drill!" Cadet Daily yelled. "You have nine seconds to don and clear your protective masks. Gas! Gas! Gas!"

I took in a gulp of air, released my chin strap . . .

"CEASE WORK!" Cadet Daily roared. "HOLD IT RIGHT THERE, THIRD SQUAD!"

I froze, my hand still on my helmet's chin strap.

"A number of you No-Go'd before you even got your masks out of your carriers! What did you do this morning, Third Squad? O.D. on stupid juice?" His eyes lingered on each of us as they traveled around the circle. "The *last* thing you want to do, Third Squad, is suck in a huge amount of air when someone signals 'Gas!' You stop breathing. Period. Do you hear me? Because if you don't, you might *never* get your mask out of its carrier. And you'll be nothing but a blue hunk of twitching human flesh, waiting to be crammed into a body bag." He paused, rubbing the back of his neck. "I'm not being melodramatic, Third Squad. You are training for combat. And when the smoke from the battlefield has lifted and the carnage is revealed, you will find yourself in either one of two states: alive"—he looked up at us—"or dead. And a dead lieutenant isn't much use to his troops."

Dead. I tried to picture myself dead on some faraway battlefield with other dead all around me. And surprisingly, the thought didn't really scare me much. I only hoped that my death wouldn't be caused by some stupid thing that I did. I'd want the minister at my funeral to say I'd been brave. I wondered how my family would feel when the military bugler played Taps. Would my mother cry?

"All right, Third Squad." Cadet Daily clapped his hands together. "As you were."

I noticed that my fingers were still clutching my chin strap. I slowly lowered my hand to my side.

"Let's do it right this time. You've got nine seconds." Cadet Daily yelled again, "Gas! Gas! Gas!"

This time I held my breath, released my chin strap, and dropped my Kevlar to the ground with the others. With my left hand I yanked open my gas mask pouch, pulled the mask out with my right . . .

"SEVEN SECONDS!"

I held the rubber facepiece with both hands, checked the hood and harness—*Okay, hood hanging down, harness up*—I opened the facepiece wide, jammed my chin into the chin pocket, pulled the harness up over my head . . .

"FIVE!"

What's going on? The mask wouldn't fit. I struggled with the elastic harness, but the mask was too tight. Something pressed hard against my cheekbones. I yanked the mask off my face and looked inside. *Nothing.* My hands shook. *Oh—what's wrong?*

"THREE!"

I glanced at the others. Some were still clearing their masks, but everyone was wearing them—except me.

"TWO. . . . ONE. . . . CEASE WORK!"

We snapped our hands to our sides.

The hood from my mask, which was still in my hand, dangled in the dirt.

Cadet Daily slowly made his way around the circle, checking masks. "Go!" meant "pass," and "No-Go!" meant "fail," and so far, he was giving out all "Go's." Then he stopped in front of me.

"One of these smacks is not like the others," he sang softly. "One of these smacks just doesn't belong." He leaned closer and whispered, "You forgot to remove your glasses, Davis."

I winced. *I am such an idiot!* That's *what was wrong*. I'd been so used to wearing contacts, I'd forgotten I was wearing TEDs.

"When I tested you on this yesterday, Davis, you got a 'Go.' Right?"

"Yes, sir."

"So I assume that the only reason that you failed to do something as elementary as removing your glasses today was because you had contacts in yesterday. Correct?"

"Yes, sir." I stared at the place between his eyebrows. *Calm down! It's just a stupid mistake. So you aren't perfect. It's not the end of the world.*

"So, continuing with this line of reasoning, Davis, since you were not accustomed to removing your glasses when donning your mask today, you forgot. In other words, you had a major brain cramp, correct?"

"Y-yes, sir." I bit the inside of my lip and braced myself for the coming explosion.

He stared at me for a long time. "Okay, Davis," he finally said. "Put your mask back in the carrier. Let me check the rest of these guys, and then I'll retest you. All right?"

"Yes, sir." I almost smiled.

As he walked away, he said, "Just make sure you put your inserts in right, or you won't get a good seal. And you'll be a 'No-Go' again."

Inserts? "Yes, sir," I squeaked, my brain working double time. *What in the world are inserts? Think!*

"All clear!" Cadet Daily yelled. Everyone, except me,

tore off their masks and wiped their sweaty faces on their sleeves. "Return your masks to your carriers and your Kevlars to your heads. In a few minutes I'll give the signal for gas again. This time you're gonna don *all* your MOPP gear. This is the standard, Third Squad: You must go from MOPP Zero to Four in eight minutes. You will don your masks first, then the rest of your gear, in this order: trousers, jacket, boots, gloves. Got it?"

"YES, SIR!"

I folded the hood around the mask and stuffed it inside my carrier. *MOPP Four, eight minutes. Mask. Trousers. Jacket. Boots. Gloves. Got it.*

"Make sure everything is snapped, zipped, and tied, or you'll 'No-Go.' I know putting your mask on first will make life difficult, Third Squad. But hey, that's the way it'll be when the balloon goes up, so get used to it." He checked his watch. "I highly suggest you organize your gear on the ground in front of you. You've got three minutes—WORK!"

I emptied my barracks bag and worked on arranging my MOPP gear on the ground—gloves under boots, under jacket, under trousers.

Cadet Daily stood over me. "Davis," he said quietly. "Listen. I'm just gonna retest you on your mask at the same time I test these other guys on MOPP Four. After you don your mask—if you pass—continue on with the rest of your MOPP gear. With everybody else. Understand?"

I looked up at him, relieved. "Yes, sir."

He nodded and walked away.

Cadet Daily can be pretty cool. Sometimes. Maybe nobody even noticed that I No-Go'd. It *was* pretty hard to see out of the masks. I chewed on the inside of my lip, watching the others stack their gear in neat piles. *But I've* got *to find out about those inserts.* I just couldn't No-Go again. Not after Cadet Daily had cut me that break. I glanced at Hickman on my right, then at Bonanno on my left. Between the two of them, I figured Hickman would be more likely to know. *Oh, why couldn't Kit be next to me? Or Ping?* I closed my eyes. *Oh, well. You gotta do what you gotta do.* I turned to Hickman and whispered, "Hey, Tommy?"

"Yeah?"

"Hey, do you have any idea what 'inserts' are? Do they have something to do with the filters?"

Hickman stopped stacking his MOPP gear and stared at me. "So you 'No-Go'd.'" It was a statement, not a question.

I made my pile neater. "Well . . . yeah. I, um, sort of forgot to take off my glasses when I donned my mask." *You didn't have to tell him that!*

Hickman sighed. "Look, Davis. If you got issued TEDs, you got issued inserts. People that need glasses put prescription inserts into their masks so when they take off their glasses and put *on* their masks, they can see." He shook his head. "They went over all this yesterday."

"Oh." I managed a fake laugh. "Well, I guess I really didn't pay attention since I normally wear contacts—"

Hickman did not look interested.

"So . . . inserts are those weird-looking glasses things with the wires on the ends that came with my TEDs, huh?"

Before my lips had finished forming the words, I had already figured out the answer to my question. And I cringed inside. I'd packed away those weird-looking glasses things with the wires on the ends in MacArthur Barracks' basement with the rest of my stuff. *What an idiot!* I had thought they were a replacement set of lenses for my TEDs in case the originals ever broke.

Hickman shrugged. "I have no idea what they look like, Andi. I don't need glasses."

I smiled, trying to play the whole thing off as if it were no big deal. "Well, thanks for the info." I turned away from him and gnawed on my fingernails, one after the other. *What am I going to do? I can't see without glasses . . . or inserts! Oh—Gabrielle was right! I should've worn my contacts! Cadet Daily's going to kill me. . . .*

"Gas! Gas! Gas!" Cadet Daily suddenly yelled. He was moving toward me.

Oh, well. It's a good morning to die.

"Eight minutes, Third Squad." Cadet Daily nodded at me. "Starting . . . now."

Here goes. I held my breath and dropped my Kevlar to the ground. *Glasses . . .* I pulled off my TEDs and shoved them into the cargo pocket of my pants. The world was now a blur of browns and greens. I reached for my gas mask . . .

Okay, just act like you can see, and he'll never guess you don't have inserts.

"Seven seconds . . ."

Somehow, by the time Cadet Daily said, "Cease work, Davis," the nine seconds were spent, and I had donned and cleared my mask. Cadet Daily moved closer and checked it. Then he thumped me on the top of my head. "You're a 'Go,' Davis. Drive on."

I did it! Thank God! I pulled the hood over my head. Then I unbuckled my LCE and shrugged it off, letting it drop to the ground. I stumbled to my pile of MOPP gear and snatched what I hoped were trousers off the top, holding them close to my face. *Pants! So far, so good.* I struggled to get them over my combat boots. *Now—the jacket.* Sweat trickled down my neck, and steam from my face fogged my mask, further blurring my vision. I took my time with the jacket, making sure that I didn't mismatch the snaps. By the time I finished, I felt like I was standing in a sauna dressed in a triple-thick sweatsuit with a plastic bag over my head.

"YOU'RE AT FOUR MINUTES, THIRD SQUAD," Cadet Daily yelled.

Now—the overboots. I bent over, hard to do with so much on, and, like a drunk trying to fit a key into a lock, I fumbled to get those floppy, one-size-fits-all rubber boots over my combat boots. Lacing the overboots was even worse: looping the laces through this eyelet and back through that one, inside to outside, letting my fingers do the seeing since my eyes couldn't.

"THIRTY SECONDS REMAINING!"

Only thirty seconds? I looked up. I didn't see much movement in the haze. *Great. Is everyone done already?*

I dropped to my hands and knees, groping the ground for my gloves. *Oh—come on! Where are they?* Squinting didn't help. *Okay—just calm down. You'll find them. . . .*

My fingertips touched rubber. *Yes!* I scrambled to my feet and pulled the gloves over my hands. Then I slapped my Kevlar on my head. *Done!*

"Five . . . four . . . three . . . two . . . one . . . CEASE WORK!" Cadet Daily yelled. "Okay, Third Squad, let's see how you did." Cadet Daily traveled around the circle until he reached me. "I think I'll start with you, Davis." He looked me over, from foot to head, then stepped behind me. "May I touch you?"

Something's wrong. "Yes, sir!" I yelled through my mask. *Please don't say I'm a No-Go again. Please.*

I felt him tugging at the bottom of my MOPP jacket. "You failed to snap one of the three snaps that connect your jacket to your trousers."

I wanted to clobber myself. *Idiot!*

"But I'm a reasonable guy, Davis, so I'm gonna make a deal with you. You make the correction in five seconds, since you had five seconds to spare, and you're a Go. If you don't . . ." He smacked his lips. "I guess Third Squad will get to see your encore performance of"—he now stood facing me—"blindman's buff."

He knows. He definitely knows. I was thankful for my mask just then. I held my breath. *Okay, go ahead. Haze me. I deserve it.*

"Make the correction."

I stood there, shocked that he had shown me mercy for the second time today.

"Who are you, Davis? Helen Keller? I said, 'Make the correction!'"

"Yes, sir!" I found the snaps along the back hem of my jacket and made the correction before he changed his mind.

When I looked up, Cadet Daily was gone. He had moved on to Hickman and, I was amused to hear, was correcting him for the same mistake that I had made.

After he had inspected each of us, Cadet Daily said, "Okay, Third Squad. Let's get those pores opened up and those lungs cranking. I want you to get the full benefit of today's training. Double-time in place. Ready . . . *begin!*"

He made us run in place. He led us through fifty repetitions of the Side Straddle Hop. He made us run in place. He dropped us for push-ups. He made us run in place.

"Bring those knees to your chest, Third Squad! What's

the matter? You stay up all night or something? Put a little pep in your step!"

Pep in my step? I felt like I was slogging through wet concrete up to my waist. And I was unbelievably hot.

"Looks like Third Platoon's 'in the door,' Third Squad," Cadet Daily said, pointing across the site toward the tent. "See? First Squad's going in . . . right . . . *now!*"

I peered out of my mask's fogged-over eyepieces, seeing nothing.

"And Second Squad's standing by. It's time for you to join the fray. Put on your LCEs and line up behind Hickman. Then double-time over to the tent. QUICKLY!"

I felt the ground around me with my feet for my LCE until I kicked it. I snatched it up and jumped behind Hickman. I fumbled with my LCE, untwisting its suspenders and snapping its buckle, and tried to catch my breath as the rest of Third Squad pushed and stumbled their way into a single-file line.

"What are you waiting for, Hickman?" Cadet Daily yelled. "An engraved invitation? Move out!"

I jogged behind Hickman, squinting at the ground; its browns and greens rushed under my feet like a treadmill. *Just don't trip. Keep moving, but whatever you do, just don't trip!*

I heard a lot of yelling as we neared the olive-drab blur that was the tent. I squinted. On one side I could make out a line of new cadets shuffling in. On the other side new cadets staggered out, their masks in their hands and their arms flailing. Upperclassmen holding—*canteens?*—had formed a sort of corridor just outside the exit, greeting the new cadets with faces full of water as they burst outside.

"Come on! Keep the line moving, New Cadets!"

"Oh, yeah! It's a good day to be a soldier! HU-AH!"

The scene wasn't a pleasant one. *I don't want to do this.*

"Veer to the left of the tent, Boneheads!" yelled an upperclassman. "And double-time in a circle. I don't want you resting while you wait!"

Hickman curved us to the left, and soon Third Squad was trotting around and around like circus elephants.

"Keep moving, New Cadets!" the upperclassman yelled.

I tripped along behind Hickman for what seemed like forever.

"Okay . . . *you!*" The upperclassman grabbed my arm and shoved me toward the tent. "Go on inside. The rest of you, follow him."

Follow him? For a moment I was confused. *He did mean for* me *to go in first, didn't he?* Then I realized— MOPP suits made us sexless.

I stepped forward and batted the canvas with my hands. *Oh—come on! Where's that stupid door flap?*

A Third Squad member banged into me from behind, and I was inside. I blinked, trying to adjust the little sight I had to the dimness. My chest rose and fell, and my ears filled with the sound of my own breath. *Well, this is it—no turning back now.*

"Don't just stand there, Dip Wad!"

I snapped my head in the direction of another blur— an upperclassman, standing in the center of the tent. He was dressed in MOPP Four, waving me in.

I stumbled forward, running my rubber-gloved hand along the wall of the tent to guide me. The rest of Third Squad crept inside like they were expecting a ghost to pop out at them.

"Hustle it up, New Cadets! What are you waiting for?

Christmas? Let's go! My old granny moves faster then you!"

I took cautious, shallow breaths. *Okay. This isn't going to be that bad. It's really hot in here, but—*

"Welcome to my humble abode, New Cadets," the upperclassman said. His voice came out slightly muffled through his mask, as if he were speaking with a hand clamped over his mouth. "Anyone feel a burning sensation? Or smell something like burned rubber being shoved up your nose?" He paused. "No? Good. Looks like everyone has a good seal. Believe me, you'd know it, otherwise."

I took another breath. *No burning. No smell. Good seal. Relax. This isn't so bad. . . .*

"Now, when I say, 'All clear,' you will remove your masks . . ."

I squinted over at the exit, judging the distance. *Okay, just hold your breath till he says we can go. You can swim the length of a fifty-meter pool without coming up for air. You can do this.*

". . . and immediately begin reciting the national anthem, starting with the second verse—loud and in a motivated manner."

The national anthem? Reciting it wasn't a problem— I knew it. It had been part of Week Two's knowledge. Reciting while holding my breath, however, *was* a problem. But I'd do it. Somehow . . .

"For those of you who got hippopotamus lungs and think you can hold out on me, think again. I'm a very patriotic guy—I *love* the national anthem. So if you make it through the second verse, keep on going and recite the *first* verse. 'Cause your only ticket outa here's that coughin' sound. Understand?"

I was going to have to breathe the stuff.

"YES, SIR!"

He paused. I waited with the others. One breath . . . two breaths . . . three breaths . . .

"ALL CLEAR!"

I gulped, filling my lungs with air, then pulled off my mask. The fiery slap that hit my face almost made me suck in again.

Together we started to chant the second verse of the national anthem at triple speed: "Oh, thus be it ever when free men shall stand Between their loved homes and wild war's desolation; Bless'd with vict'ry and peace—"

My face burned and itched like it did whenever I'd come into my warm house after running in a subzero wind chill. But much worse. Suddenly someone tall doubled over, then whipped around for the exit. *Was that Kit? Gone already?*

". . . may the heav'n-rescued land Praise the pow'r that hath made and . . ."

Another fled.

". . . preserv'd us a nation! Then conquer we must, when our cause it is just . . ."

Another bolted. The smallest person in the tent— *Gabrielle*—staggered after him, clawing at her eyes.

Don't look! I squeezed my eyes shut—they were starting to tear. Snot leaked out of my nose, ran down my chin . . . *Hold on!* I really did not want to breathe that stuff.

". . . And this be our motto: 'in God is our trust!' And the star-spangled banner . . ."

I opened my eyes. Besides the upperclassman, only one other person and I remained. He was huge. *Cero?* I was reaching my limit; my air was almost gone.

". . . in triumph shall wave . . ."

I clenched my fists. Blood pounded against the inside of my skull.

". . . O'er the land of the free and the home . . ."

No! I had taken a breath during the natural pause of the verse, just like I would've if I'd been singing. Dry, scratchy air, like super-concentrated car exhaust, rushed in. Mucus spewed out. I sucked in again. *I'm drowning! No—my throat's on fire!* I wasn't in an Army tent, I was in an airtight phone booth with a thousand chopped onions. I scrambled for the exit and, waving my arms wildly in front of me, found the opening in the canvas.

". . . of the brave." Cero had finished the verse. Alone.

Sunlight and cold water struck my eyes simultaneously. Shouting faces hovered above me. Hands pushed me forward. Water drenched my hair, my face, my neck.

"Keep moving forward, Davis!"

"You're doing okay!"

"No stalling! Someone's right behind you!"

More snot than I ever imagined my body could produce covered my face and MOPP suit. Thick lines of drool hung from my mouth to my waist. No sunburn, not even the one I got on my first day of lifeguarding two summers ago, had ever fried my face like this. I bent over and coughed until I was sure that I'd see foamy chunks of lung fly out of my mouth.

Someone's hand came down on my shoulder, hard.

I reeled around. *Cero.* His eyes were red. His face, covered with slime. His MOPP jacket dripped water and goo.

"Davis! Just wanted to say . . ." He turned away from me and spewed mucus out of his mouth. "I just wanted to say . . . I'm glad you left when you did. . . . I couldn't . . ." He started coughing, then cleared his throat and spat again. ". . . hold out . . . much longer." He wiped his nose on his sleeve. "Man! That stings! That MOPP suit really . . . soaked up that stuff."

I shook my head. "Hold out . . . much . . . longer?" My words came out in wheezy gasps.

"Yeah." He held his mask under his arm and peeled off his gloves. "I just wanted . . . to be the last guy . . . out of the tent, that's all." He paused to take three raspy breaths. "You know, to really . . . experience the stuff."

"*Experience* the stuff, Cero?" I shook my head again. "Not me! I just didn't want to *inhale*, that's why *I* stayed in so long." I coughed, then swallowed. Coughed, then swallowed. And finally spat. "Procrastination, I guess."

"Man, I thought you guys would never come outa that fiery furnace!" I turned around. Kit was standing behind me, a canteen in his hand. "I was starting to think you were doing a Shadrach, Meshach, and Abednego."

"A *what*?" I squinted at Kit and started coughing again. "Kit, sometimes . . . I think . . . you belong . . . on another planet . . . or something." I wiped my mouth on my shoulder. *Ouch!* My lips burned like I'd smeared them with Tabasco sauce.

Kit winked. "What can I say? I'm just a pilgrim traveling through. Here." He handed me his canteen. "You look like you need a drink."

I took a swig, swishing the water around my mouth before I swallowed. "Sorry, but I think the gas has affected both your brains, guys."

"Me?" Kit wheezed a laugh. "I wasn't in there long enough, Andi. I took my obligatory breath, and I was outa there. I figured, why prolong the misery? But this guy"—he pointed at Cero—"just admitted that he *wanted* to experience the gas. Now tell me who's killed some serious brain cells!"

Cero opened his mouth to say something, then just smiled and shook his head.

"You've got a point there, Kit." I reached down between my MOPP pants and my BDU trousers, feeling for the cargo pocket that held my glasses.

"All I can say is you guys are way more 'hu-ah' than me," Kit said.

Cero shrugged. "'Hu-ah' probably isn't the right word, Bogus." He glanced at me. "I'm speaking for myself, of course. Sentimental would be more accurate, I think."

"Sentimental?" Kit and I said together.

I slid my TEDs on my face. *Finally—I've got my eyes back!*

Cero frowned. "Okay, now I do sound like my brain's been affected. Forget I mentioned it." He scanned the packs of slime-covered, hacking new cadets who were milling around all over the training site. "I don't know about you guys, but I'm ready to shed these threads. Where's Third Squad at?"

"I'm the guy to ask," Kit said. "I just came from there to police you two up." Then he looked at me. "And I'll tell you what, Andi—Gab's one unhappy camper right now."

I felt my heart speed up. "Why? What happened? She's okay, isn't she?"

"Oh, she's *okay*," Kit said. "But she wore her contacts today and—"

"She lost them."

Kit nodded. I shook my head. *Poor Gab!* These past twenty-four hours had been rough ones for her.

As we made our way over to Third Squad, Kit said,

"Okay, Cero. I'm not letting you off the hook. You just can't say something like 'CS gas makes me feel sentimental' and drop it."

Cero flexed his jaw and stared straight ahead.

I nudged him. "Yeah, that's right, Cero. There's nothing *sentimental* about coughing your guts out!"

Cero slowed his steps, then stopped completely. His eyes bounced between my face and Kit's. "Look, guys," he finally said. "It's no enigma, okay? It's just that, well, tear gas and my family go way back, that's all." He glared at us. "It's not a joke, guys."

Kit stared back at him. "You see us laughing, Cero?"

Cero stared at the toe of his boot, kicking a stone that was stuck in the dirt. "Look, when my grandma was about my age, she got a good dose of tear gas. My uncle, too. Same age, same town, twenty-seven years later. End of story."

"Oh! So they were in the Army, too?" I don't know why exactly, but I regretted the question the second I asked it. I started pulling off my gloves to give me something to do.

"Not exactly. Not unless," Cero said, dropping his voice as if he were talking more to himself than to me, "you think the color of your skin is some sort of uniform." Then he looked at us, his eyes guarded. "No, during the Watts riots, 1965, and the Rodney King riots, 1992. Respectively." He crossed his arms. "L.A.'s the place to be if you wanna get gassed."

I didn't know how to respond to that, and apparently neither did Kit, because we said nothing together.

"Nope, my family's no fan of the Army," Cero said. "Or West Point, for that matter." He shook his head and laughed softly. "Definitely not West Point." He let out a long, tired breath. "My grandma's the toughest lady you'll ever meet. She raised me and my brothers when my mom took off. But back when she was my age, she had two passions—antiwar protests and civil rights. And she's never let them go. For as long as I remember, she's combined the two in hating the military." He paused. "Her first husband was K.I.A. in Vietnam."

Killed in Action. "Sorry . . ." I chewed on my thumbnail. It tasted like burned rubber.

"Yeah." Cero stooped down to pick up the stone he'd been working out of the dirt all this time, then tossed it from one hand to the other, one hand to the other. "She's always going around saying stuff like 'Vietnam was the black man's war' and quoting Dr. Martin Luther King, Jr." He clenched his fist over the stone and closed his eyes. Lines creased his forehead. "'We have been repeatedly faced with the cruel irony of watching Negro and white boys on TV screens as they kill and die together in brutal solidarity, realizing that they would never live on the same block in Detroit.'" He opened his eyes. "Pretty good, huh? Yeah, my grandma has his speeches memorized like preachers know the Gospels." He shrugged, his eyes wary again. "But hey—this means nothing to you guys. You don't want to hear this."

I looked back at the tent. Mass pandemonium still encircled it. "No, Cero! It's really great. 'Cause today you got to carry out the family tradition. It didn't happen during a riot"—I nodded at the tent—"exactly. But it is the sixth week of Beast, you know. That should count for something!" I smiled, hoping that this time I had said the right thing.

A little spark flashed in his eyes, and I knew I had.

"That's right," Kit said. "You got your own square on the ol' family quilt, now."

What a cool thing to say!

"Yeah." Cero turned toward Kit, a grin creeping across his face. "Yeah. 'A square on my ol' family quilt.' Hey, that's good, Bogus. I like that." He paused, scratching the side of his face. "You know, I haven't written my grandma all summer, except when Cadet Daily told us to, of course. But now I think I've got something to write home about. Something she can relate to. Maybe she'll finally see that, well, we all have our causes." He chucked the stone toward the woods. "Mine's making it through this place. East L.A. ain't gonna be my cage."

We watched the stone sail through the air, then hit a branch before bouncing off the leaves as it dropped to the ground.

"Well, Cero," I said, "when you write her, tell her about us." I nodded my head toward Kit. "Tell her that we live on the same hallway as you. Okay?"

"I will." He nodded. "I want her to know that." Cero clapped us both across the back. "Thanks, guys." Then he squared his shoulders and the hardness was back in his eyes—just like that. "'Nuff said. Let's hook up with Third Squad. They're waitin' on us!"

As I sat with Third Squad in the copse of trees, peeling off my soggy MOPP suit and listening to Gabrielle's requiem for her lost contact lenses, I felt like a real human being for the first time all summer. For a few minutes Cero had cracked open his onyx exterior and let me see inside.

And I realized that I wasn't the only one with a quilt square to stitch.

Our doubts are traitors,
And make us lose the good we oft might win,
By fearing to attempt.
—WILLIAM SHAKESPEARE, *MEASURE FOR MEASURE*

CHAPTER 13

SATURDAY, 7 AUGUST
1250

"DON'T TELL ME," Gabrielle said. "That's lunch."

I pulled my eyes away from "Scott's Fixed Opinion" in my *Bugle Notes* and followed Gabrielle's gaze. Cadet Daily was at the rear of one of the deuce-and-a-halfs parked near the entrance of the site, pulling brown plastic packages out of a box.

"Yep," Ping said. "Good old MREs. The perfect midday snack."

"Good old MREs." Gabrielle made a face and, with one practiced jab of her index finger, stopped her TEDs from sliding down her nose. "Meals Ready to Eat. Three lies in one."

Most of Third Squad laughed.

Gabrielle smiled, obviously proud of her joke. "And I thought there was an honor code around here."

"Hey," Kit said. "Food is food, Gab. They actually let us eat, out here at Lake Frederick, so whatever they throw my way, I'm eating. I'll take quantity over quality every time."

Cero yawned, looking at Gabrielle out of one half-opened eye. "All I've got to say, Bryen, is out here, there's no more inch-sized bites, 'order arms,' or sitting at attention. No room inspections and no drill. And that's good enough for me." He scooted back a few feet and leaned against a tree trunk. "All we've got to do all day is run around in the woods, then chill out at night—play cards, go swimming, hang out, rack." He tipped his Kevlar over his eyes. "I'll tell you what, life at Lake Frederick is *good*."

"Yeah, life is good *now*," Jason said. "But in a few days, we'll be back to the ol' same old same old."

Cadet Daily arrived, tossing each of us an MRE. "Okay, Third Squad—chow's here. And no sniveling about what you get," he said. "I ain't your maître d'."

My MRE landed in my lap. I shoved my *Bugle Notes* into my back pocket and flipped the package over to read what was to be my lunch. Stamped onto the industrial-strength plastic was: MEAL NO. 8. HAM SLICE.

Ham slice? Well, it can't be any worse than the stuff my mother pops out of a can and serves at Christmas.

Cadet Daily looked at his watch. "You boneheads have about twenty minutes to scarf down those MREs before the first obstacle of the Leader Reaction Course." He pointed down the dirt road in the middle of the woods. Off to the right, high walls of corrugated aluminum loomed, sandwiching each obstacle and hiding it from our view. "We'll get to see how you guys work as a team. And there are eight obstacles—just enough for each of you to get a turn being the leader."

Each of us will be the leader? I ran my finger along the edge of my MRE.

"I'll be evaluating each leader's reaction—hence the name, Leader Reaction Course—as he"—Cadet Daily paused, glancing at Gabrielle and me—"or she assesses the situation, comes up with a plan to clear the obstacle, and motivates the squad to execute the plan. This is gonna be a good time, Third Squad. So eat up. I'll be back in a few."

Come up with a plan? That everyone has to follow? I looked at the Third Squad members around me. *What if I can't figure out what to do? Or they think my plan is stupid?*

I knew one thing about myself: I'd much rather be part of a group, taking orders. Not giving them. And I'd always been that way. My mother used to sneer at me and say, "You are such a follower. You never think on your own. You'd walk right off a ten-story building if someone told you to." I hated hearing it. But even worse was admitting that she was right.

I bit on the inside of my lip as I tore a hole in the tough plastic package and reached inside for the lumpy vacuum-packed packets: Ham Slice with Natural Juices . . . Potatoes au Gratin . . . Accessory Packet . . . Crackers . . . Cheese Spread . . . Brownie, Chocolate Covered . . .

"Anybody wanna trade?" Bonanno held up his MRE. "Chicken with Rice. I had it yesterday. It was pretty good if you use the Tabasco sauce."

"And if you like coagulated chicken grease," Gabrielle said. "No thanks. But here, take mine—Spaghetti with Meat and Sauce." She tossed Bonanno her unopened MRE.

"Spaghetti? Really?" Bonanno snatched the MRE out of the air. "You're the best, Bryen."

"I know. But I have my motives: I'd rather not eat than

waste thirty-five hundred calories on manufactured vomit."

Hickman snorted. "Blue Blood Bryen doesn't like MREs. What a surprise." He spat on the ground. "Since they're designed to sustain *soldiers in combat*."

Gabrielle took a swig of water from her canteen. "And your point, exactly, *Hick*"—she paused to emphasize the first syllable—"man?"

But Hickman didn't get a chance to expound; Cadet Daily was back. "Sorry to cut it short, Third Squad, but your feast is over."

We grabbed our gear and followed Cadet Daily down the dirt road to the first obstacle. Behind the first aluminum wall a huge upperclassman in a yellow T-shirt and BDU pants greeted us. "Welcome to the LRC," he said. "I'm Cadet Sabo, and I will be the safety observer for this obstacle." He extended his sun-browned, muscled arm toward a wooden wall about twelve feet high and eight feet wide that slanted away from us and was set in the middle of a sawdust pit. Except for the red areas running down its outside edges and along its bottom third, the wall was painted gray. A rope attached to the top of the wall dangled halfway down.

Gabrielle pulled my sleeve. "That's the guy from bayonet training," she whispered. "He's hotter close up than from far away. Cadet Sabo—he's no Monet."

I frowned at her. *What is she talking about? And why is she talking?*

"You know, Andi, some guys are—'Monets.' They look better from a distance."

"Do you ladies have something you'd like to share?" The upperclassman, Cadet Sabo, glowered at us. "Expertise on the LRC, perhaps?" The rest of Third Squad turned to look at us. "Maybe *you'd* like to take this block of instruction?"

"No, sir!"

I glanced at Cadet Daily, leaning against the corrugated aluminum. The most prominent part of his body was his red face, turning redder.

Cadet Sabo nodded. "Then I suggest you keep your mind on the task at hand. As I was . . ."

I glared at Gabrielle. *Thanks a lot!* The last thing I wanted right now was to bring attention to myself. That was about the quickest way to becoming the leader first—annoy the guy in charge.

". . . this is the scenario. You've been taking heavy fire from enemy snipers in your area of operations and have requested close-air support. Your mission is to get your squad and supplies safely across this river, represented by this sawdust pit here." Cadet Sabo waved his hand toward the pit filled with coarse sawdust behind him. "In an estimated thirteen minutes those air strikes are gonna come fast and furious, pummeling this riverbank. That gives you a *maximum* of thirteen minutes to be safely on the other side of the river. Now, this river has an immediate thirty-five-foot dropoff from its banks. In addition the enemy has laid a narrow minefield along the edge of the water"— Cadet Sabo pointed to the red-painted piping that encircled the pit—"as you can see here." Making a big deal of stepping over the red piping, he walked through the sawdust until he reached the gray slanted wall and leaned against it. "You must use this partially constructed bridge to cross the river. However, be advised: The bridge is also booby-trapped." He ran his hand down the outside edge of the wall. "Anything painted red is mined. That means whatever touches red blows up. If a person touches it, he dies. If your equipment hits it, it's lost. And if anything—equipment or personnel—falls into the *water*," he said, stomping back to us through the sawdust, "it sinks. Plain and simple. Only *I* walk on water, people. Now, direct your attention to the partition behind you."

A wooden crate, rope, and plastic barrel were stacked against the corrugated aluminum. "Those are your supplies: an ammo box, a twenty-six-foot rope, and a fuel barrel. They must make it across the river with you. You may use any or all of this equipment to assist you in breaching the obstacle. But hint: Something that looks helpful may be a distractor in disguise. Now, direct your beady eyes back on me."

He waited for us to turn around before he continued, "Finally, one of you will be the leader for this obstacle. But remember—this is a team effort. Team members are encouraged to participate in the decision-making process. Any questions?"

Nobody moved.

"Like I said," Cadet Sabo continued, "you'll have a maximum of thirteen minutes to breach my obstacle. So far, Bravo Company's Second Squad, First Platoon, holds the record." He folded his arms across his chest. "Seven minutes and twenty-six seconds."

I heard a few of my squadmates whistle under their breath.

Cadet Sabo nodded. "That's right, people. Bravo Company kicked some serious butt. Their time will be hard to top. But you've still got H Company's squad competition. Your times for all the obstacles are going to be averaged when you complete the LRC. And the squad with the best composite score will win the company's squad competition." Cadet Sabo looked at his watch. "Incidentally, that squad from Bravo Company I told you about? They also won Bravo Company's squad competition. They smoked everyone."

"Yeah," I heard Hickman mumble behind me, "and I bet they didn't have any females in *their* squad."

I looked at him. He was staring at Cadet Sabo, the expression on his face blank, like he hadn't said anything at all. But standing beside Hickman was Bonanno. I caught his eye, and he quickly shifted focus to the ground.

He thinks it, too. Well, I just was going to have to prove them wrong.

"Okay," Cadet Sabo said. "If you've got no questions for me, stack arms over there." He pointed to the edge of the woods. "Your squad leader and I will keep an eye on them. Move out!"

We unslung our M-16s and scrambled for the trees. With the butts on the ground and barrels in the air, we balanced our M-16s, one against the other, until the clump of weapons stood on its own, looking like a miniature tepee. When we had returned to the edge of the sawdust pit, Cadet Sabo said, "After Cadet Daily picks the leader, I'll start the clock."

I kept my eyes on Cadet Daily's boots as he paced back and forth, eyeing each of us. The voice in my mind was in sync with his steps: *Don't pick me! Don't pick me! Don't pick me!*

"All right," he finally said. "Combat, show 'em how it's done."

Ping! I closed my eyes, relieved. *Thank God!*

"Yes, sir!" Ping yelled.

"Remember," Cadet Sabo said. "Thirteen minutes. Or less." He and Cadet Daily went to stand beside our weapons. "Starting . . . *now!*"

Ping started the timer on his watch and clapped his hands together. "Okay, guys. Let's do it. First thing . . . McGill, I need you to do a quick recon. Climb up the wall and tell me what you see. And don't forget the mines." He pointed at the red piping bordering the pit. About four feet of sawdust lay between the piping and the base of the obstacle.

"Not a problem," Jason said, jogging over to the aluminum partition behind us. "You're looking at an expert jumper here."

Ping laughed. "Whatever you want to believe about yourself, McGill. Okay, Cero. Grab a couple guys and drag the supplies"—he waved toward the partition—"over to the edge of the pit."

Cero nodded at Kit and Bonanno, standing near him. "Mind giving me a hand, guys?"

I watched the flurry of activity explode around me, amazed. I knew Ping would be good, but I didn't think he'd be that good. He didn't even have to stop and think. While I just stood here trying to process all the information, Ping already had a plan and was rattling off orders. And everybody followed them, just like that. No questions asked.

Jason had his back to the partition now, sizing up the obstacle. After he took a few deep breaths, he sprinted toward it. Clearing the sawdust gap with one huge leap, he planted one foot in the center of the wall, grasped the rope, and pulled himself up, hand over hand, until he reached the top.

"Okay," he called down to us over his shoulder. "Here's the deal—we've got another wall, mirroring this one. The two walls kinda form an A. But with a gap between the walls that we've gotta cross of about . . . oh . . . four and a half, maybe five feet or so."

"That's about as wide as I am tall," Gabrielle whispered to me, her eyes large.

I nodded—a little impatiently, I realized. But I couldn't reassure her right then; I didn't want to miss a single detail about the obstacle.

"Any mines up there with you?" Ping asked.

"Nope."

"Then move across the gap and tell me what you see."

Jason reached for the other wall, then disappeared from sight.

"Hey, Ping!" Cero yelled from the partition behind us. "Check this out." In his arms he held the flat crate that Cadet Sabo had called an ammo box. "This thing's heavy. Like forty pounds heavy. It's filled with rocks or something."

"So's this," Bonanno said, tipping the fuel barrel. "I'd say it weighs eighty pounds, easy."

Ping turned around, a frown of concentration on his face.

"Okay," Jason yelled from the other side, "this wall looks exactly like the one you're looking at—minefield at the bottom and all. Except there's no rope."

"Move it, Third Squad!" Cadet Daily yelled from the sidelines. "Time's a-tickin'!"

Ping wiped his forehead with the back of his hand and, nodding at Cero, said, "Look, just get that stuff moved, okay? We'll get this figured out."

Jason grunted as he pulled himself back across the gap

between the walls. "And you got to clear like three or four feet of sawdust, I mean *water*, to get all the way over to the other side. And the edge of the pit is mined." He nodded at us. "Just like on that side."

Ping let his breath out slowly.

"One more thing," Jason said, swinging his leg over the top of the wall to straddle it. "I don't know if it's important or what, but there's this board lying on the ground over on that other side."

"A board?" Ping squinted up at Jason. "How long?"

Jason shrugged. "About ten feet, maybe? It looks like a plank. You know, the kind pirates walked."

"It's twelve feet long, people," Cadet Sabo yelled from where he stood beside our weapons. "And the answer to your next question is 'yes.' If you find a useful purpose for it, go for it."

Ping nodded. "Thank you, sir." Then he looked up at Jason. "Good job, man. Just hang tight." He slowly turned back to us, removing his Kevlar to scratch the top of his head.

As I watched him think, I wondered what he'd come up with. A bunch of facts about the obstacle milled around in my mind, but that was all. I had no idea where *I'd* start.

But it didn't take Ping long. "Okay, guys," he said, "this is what's gonna happen. We're going to pass this stuff up the wall. Cero, Bogus, you're our tallest men, so you're going to be doing most of the passing. One of you, go up there with McGill," he said, replacing his helmet. "And the other, stay down here." He paused to snap his chin strap. "I know the reach will be tough, but we've got to make it happen, guys."

"What are we gonna do with the stuff?" Jason yelled from the top of the wall. "You know, once it's up here? I mean, we're talking zero storage space up here."

Hickman shrugged. "That's a no-brainer. Just toss the stuff off the top."

No-brainer, huh? And I wasn't even able to come up with that! How would I function when my turn came around to be leader?

"Can't do that, people!" Cadet Sabo yelled. "You've got very sensitive items there."

Hickman and Cero looked at each other and swore.

"No need to get *illiterate*, guys," Kit said. "We'll just put a couple of guys on the far side, too."

Ping nodded. "Then two on top, and two on this side. We've got three guys tall enough to make the reach—"

"You can count me out of that job," Gabrielle said, and laughed.

Everyone looked at her vaguely, then turned away.

Gabrielle scooted closer to me and whispered, "These guys are wired a little too tight."

I shrugged. I thought of myself. Better than not being wired *at all*.

"Then that's it," Ping said. "McGill and Bonanno, take the far side."

"I'm on my way," Jason yelled, and started climbing back across the gap.

"Me, too," Bonanno said.

"Then Cero and Hickman, you take the top. That'll leave Bogus and me to the lift the stuff from this side. We'll pass it up, then down, like an assembly line. Okay? Let's hit it!"

Gabrielle and I looked at each other. Everybody had a job but us.

"And I suppose Andi and I will just stand here," Gabrielle said, "cheering you guys on."

Kit smiled. "I'm sure you're a very good cheerleader, Gab."

Gabrielle crossed her arms and turned away from him.

"But you'll be helping Ping and me with the lifting," Kit continued. "Socrates said, 'Know thyself.' And I *know* I'll need all the help I can get."

When everyone was in position, Ping said, "We'll start with the ammo box. It'll be our test run. Kind of like a warm-up."

Kit nodded. "You're calling the shots, Boss Man. I just work here." He squinted up at Cero. "Okay, Big Guy. Let's get those biceps burning." He lifted the ammo box over his head and leaned toward the wall. "Keep an eye on my feet, guys. Don't let me get too close to the piping. I'd hate to finish the obstacle sitting on the sidelines."

Cero moved partway down the wall, rappel fashion. Then, hanging on to the rope with one hand, he stretched the other toward the box.

"Not even close," Ping said. "Come on, Bogus! You've got to angle it toward Cero more."

I couldn't just stand here, watching. "Is there something I can do?" I asked.

Ping shook his head, waving me away. "Just wait one, Andi. Okay?"

I stepped back, chagrined. I got the message—I was in the way.

Ping looked up the wall. "Hey, Cero. Face Bogus, if you can. I think it'll give you a couple more inches."

Cero nodded, and holding the hand with the rope behind his back, he twisted around to face the box.

Kit slowly tipped the box forward, his arms shaking. "Give me . . . some support . . . here? Ping? Somebody! This . . . this thing's . . . slipping!"

I stepped forward. "I'll—"

But Ping was already there. "I'm all over it, Bogus." He stooped in front of Kit and, reaching upward, partially supported the weight of the box. "Okay. Forward now . . . a little more . . . more . . ."

Gabrielle and I hovered around them, wanting to help but not knowing how. I hated feeling useless like this.

Several inches still remained between the box and Cero's flexed fingers.

"Doggone it!" Kit yelled, letting the box slide to the ground. He paced back and forth, rubbing his right shoulder with his left hand. "Sorry, guys. We don't have the reach. Guess I'm just not tall enough."

"What if I get up on your shoulders?" Ping asked. "And I hand it up to Cero?"

"I don't know . . . yeah." Kit shrugged. "That might do it."

Ping looked at Gabrielle and me. "Then you guys can lift the ammo box up to me?"

I looked at the ammo box, then at Gabrielle. "Sure. We can handle that."

"Yeah." Gabrielle tugged at a red curl that had escaped the confinement of her Kevlar. "Sure."

Ping climbed on Kit's shoulders. I dragged the heavy ammo box over to Gabrielle, and even lifting it together we struggled to boost it up to Ping. Ping and Kit grunted and gasped until finally Cero yelled, "Got it!" And with one hand, Cero passed it up to Hickman.

"Good job, guys!" Ping slid off Kit. "But I think you're going to have serious problems getting that thing down the other side."

Cero nodded. "You ain't kidding. There's no rope on the other wall to help us out."

We all watched Ping turn from the obstacle. I saw him studying the fuel barrel and rope that still needed to get over.

Maybe that *rope? Is he thinking about using that rope somehow? Like tying it to the top of the wall on the other side or something? Maybe I should say something about it!* I could feel my adrenaline pumping. I *could* be useful. I finally had something to contribute! I took a deep breath and . . .

"But we've got that board . . ." I heard Ping saying to himself. He looked back up to the top of the wall. "I've got an idea. Listen. Have McGill and Bonanno take that board they've got over there and prop it up against the wall and over the sawdust. Then you guys slide the ammo box down to them. But watch the mines."

I'd been wrong. At least I hadn't opened my mouth; that was something to be grateful for. What was my problem? Why couldn't I think?

Cero gave Ping a thumbs-up. "Sounds good to me." Then Hickman and Cero disappeared with the ammo box across the gap between the walls, out of sight.

Ping turned to us. "One down." He walked over to the barrel, then circled around it. "This is gonna be the killer." He stepped over the rope coiled on the ground beside the barrel. "I don't know—one guy lifting this thing?" He shook his head. "I can't see it happening. Not with that reach. And we're going to run into the same height problem that we had with the ammo box." He glanced at Gabrielle and me before turning back to the barrel.

I bet he's thinking about Gab and me. That we'll never be able to lift that barrel up to him. And I knew that if that was what he was thinking, he'd be absolutely right. We'd had enough trouble with the ammo box. The thought made me feel even more useless.

Ping bent over and picked one end of the rope off the ground. "Anyone remember how long they said this rope is?"

"Twenty-six feet," I answered without thinking. *Hey, that helped!* Was he thinking of using the rope now?

"Okay, then this is what we're gonna do, guys. It'll be a stretch"—he grinned—"but we're going to risk it. We're going to wrap the rope around the barrel, secure it with a sturdy knot, and then toss the free end up to Hickman and Cero. Then we'll boost, lift, swing—whatever it takes to get the barrel high enough so those guys can pull it up and over the mines with the rope." He handed me the end of the rope. "Sound like a plan, guys?"

Kit nodded. "Sounds like a plan."

Well, at least I'd been on the right track. Sort of. They were using the rope for something, even if it wasn't what I had come up with. I felt slightly encouraged. I stared at the rope in my hand, then at Ping and Kit. They were pointing at the wall and discussing the barrel, their backs facing me. I looked at Gabrielle. "So . . . I guess we should get started on this."

"Sure." Gabrielle glared at Ping and Kit. "Maybe we'll get a few cool points by taking the initiative."

I watched Gabrielle as we looped the rope around the barrel. Her mouth was tight, and her hands worked fast with stiff, jerky movements. Something was bothering her. *Does she feel as useless as I do?*

Ping came up behind us. "Slide the rope down a little, guys. Keep it center of mass. No need to have physics working against us."

"No kidding," Gabrielle muttered after he stepped away. "We're not complete idiots." She twisted the rope into a half knot. "Isn't it interesting how people change when they're handed a little power?" She scowled over her shoulder in Ping's direction. "Absolute power corrupts absolutely."

I snuck another quick look at Gabrielle, confused. She *wasn't* feeling like I was. She seemed angry at them—at Ping—not at herself. "Gab, what's up?"

She didn't answer.

"You mean . . . Ping?" I almost laughed. I'd never seen Gabrielle criticize Ping before. She practically worshiped him! "You're mad at Ping?"

"Not mad," she said, forming a second half knot. "Disgusted. Thoroughly and utterly disgusted."

"Disgusted? Why?" I couldn't believe her 180-degree turn. It was almost schizophrenic. I sighed. "Because he double-checked us? Gab, he's the leader. Isn't that what he's supposed to do? You know, make sure everything's 'just right'?"

She stopped tugging the rope and stared at me. "Doesn't it bother you, Andi," she whispered, "that we're being excluded in this whole stupid thing? And it's just because we're girls! I mean, I'd think you of all people—"

"Excluded? Gab—"

"All right!" Jason's voice rose from the other side of the obstacle. "Beautiful, guys! We got it! The ammo box is now under our control!"

I looked at the wall, then smiled at Gabrielle. "Great! They did it! I mean, *we* did it!"

"You got it right the first time," Gabrielle said.

Cero appeared over the top of "our" wall. "First mission accomplished! What's next?"

Hickman crawled beside him. "We're ready for that barrel, guys."

After Ping explained the plan to Hickman and Cero, and inspected our knot, he held the end of the rope out to me. "Andi, you're good at throwing . . ."

"Better than most of you guys," I heard Gabrielle mutter under her breath.

I stared at the rope, my chest tightening. Was he going to ask me to do something?

". . . so how about tossing the end of the rope up to Cero? Kit and I are gonna be lifting this thing." Ping nodded at the barrel. "That leaves both of us out."

"Your generosity astounds me," Gabrielle muttered again.

I looked up at the wall, wiping my hands on my pants. "Sure." This was it. My big chance. I couldn't blow this. It wasn't like running—just me against myself and the clock. The whole *squad* was depending on me. If I failed, we'd all fail.

"You've basically got one shot, Andi—you can't miss. If it falls into the sawdust or hits the mines, well, you know the deal."

Gabrielle snorted. "How quickly they forget. Only this morning, what did Andi do? Huh? Let me give you a little hint: *Who* was one of the two individuals in this squad to qualify Expert on the Hand Grenade Assault Course? Hmm?" She shook her head. "Who not only threw her grenades within the bursting radius, but got bull's-eyes on all five targets? You guys are pathetic!"

I looked at the dirt. *Thanks a lot, Gab.* Why was she trotting that out? All she was doing was building up everybody's expectations, setting me up for failure. I didn't need that kind of pressure. I created enough of my own.

"Come on, Gab," Kit said, "Take 'er easy. We're all in this together. Okay?"

"Gab," Ping said, "I don't know what your problem is, but—"

"I'm not the one with the problem!" Gabrielle pushed up her TEDs and crossed her arms. "No one was surprised when Hickman got Expert this morning. Oh, no—everyone expected *that*. He's a pitcher, after all! But when Andi gets Expert, well, it must've been luck or—"

"Look," Ping said, "Andi's performance this morning didn't go unnoticed, okay? That's why I asked her to do this!"

"Oh, really?" She was all sarcasm. "Well, you certainly didn't exude confidence in her ability—"

I clenched my teeth. Here I was again, just like at home. Somehow getting dragged into an argument I wanted no part of. Being held up as the poster child for someone else's personal agenda. I was sick of it.

Ping frowned. "What? I never doubted her ability, Gab. Just because I—"

"Just stop it!" I yelled. "I can't believe you're arguing about this now! We've got a mission to do!" I grabbed the end of the rope out of Ping's hand. "Just tell me when you want me to throw this stupid thing."

I could feel everyone, even Cero and Hickman on the top of the wall, staring at me.

I don't care. Let them stare. I was tired of always getting pushed around. I squeezed the end of the rope in my left fist. *After that huge deal Gab made, you better not screw this up.* I tossed the rope from one hand to the other, feeling its weight. *This needs to be heavier, or I'll never get it up there.* I made a quick, tight knot close to the end of the rope, watching Ping and Kit each take a side of the barrel.

"Okay, Andi." Ping grunted as he lifted the barrel with Kit. "Now!"

I made sure I had enough slack and, holding my breath, tossed the rope underhand, up to the top of the wall.

"Bull's-eye!" Cero yelled, snapping his hand around the rope.

Yes! I wanted to jump up and down, but I knew it wouldn't have been the thing to do right then. I had to act casual, like I hadn't expected anything but perfection out of myself.

"Now, Hickman," Cero was yelling, "pull!"

With violent jerks, Cero and Hickman tugged the barrel upward as if they were hauling an anchor out of the sea. The barrel crashed against the wall, just missing the minefield, and banged and bumped its way up to the top.

"Okay, Ping," Cero yelled down to us. "The barrel's secure up here, but I sure hope you've got some ideas on how we're getting the thing off of here, 'cause Hickman and I, we don't have a clue."

"No problem. Just tell McGill and Bonanno over on the other side to take that board and reach it up to you guys. Then you guys place it over the gap and roll the barrel across it. Got it?"

Cero nodded. "Then what?"

"I'm on my way up," Ping said, jogging toward the aluminum partition. "I've got it all worked out."

Cero gave Ping a thumbs-up and disappeared across the gap.

I watched Ping sprint toward the obstacle, bound up the wall, and disappear across the gap.

About a minute later Hickman returned to our side of

the obstacle. Looking at Kit, he said, "Ping wants you—" He glanced at Gabrielle and me. "I mean *all* of you to get across to the other side ASAP." He looked at Kit again. "Ping wants you over first to help with the barrel. And I'm supposed to stay here to make sure that, well . . ." He looked back at Gabrielle and me. ". . . just until everyone gets across. Safely."

"There's nothing like being lumped together with ammo boxes and fuel barrels," Gabrielle whispered to me as Kit jogged back to the aluminum partition. "I feel like just another bothersome piece of junk that has to be lugged across that obstacle."

I glared at her. I was sick of her negative comments, but that particular comment really riled me. She was blaming her own incompetence on other people. "*Lugged* across that obstacle? Who's going to be 'lugged across that obstacle'?" I felt shaky inside, because I knew I was about to say something that would probably make Gabrielle mad at me. But I *had* to say it, because she just wasn't getting it on her own. I knew that until Gabrielle started taking responsibility for herself, she'd never earn her place in the squad. And because she was my friend, I wanted to help her, stand by her, and not let her lose the respect of the squad.

What I'd somehow figured out and wanted her to understand was this: Just because we were members of the squad, we weren't automatically a part of the team. A gaping difference existed between the two positions. Like the difference between knowing that someone sat beside you in class because the teacher had assigned seats and knowing that someone chose the seat beside you because she was your friend. Or like the difference between people who can barely tolerate each other calling themselves a family and people who truly love each other *being* a family.

More than anything I wanted to be part of Third Squad from the inside; I'd spent seventeen years standing on the outside. And I wanted Gabrielle to be there with me. "Listen, Gab. If you let yourself be lugged across that obstacle, then you aren't any better than an ammo box—a wood box full of rocks. A—what did you say?—a 'bothersome piece of junk'?" I turned back to the wall, my eyes on Kit as he swung over the top. There. I'd said it.

"But Andi," Gabrielle said, "they don't want to hear our ideas. They just do their own thing without asking what we think."

Our ideas? What ideas? "No one stopped you from throwing out suggestions, Gab. You can't get mad at them for not listening to you"—I paused, softening my tone—"if you had nothing to say."

I kept staring up the wall, wondering how she'd respond, worrying that I'd come across like some know-it-all.

"Well," she finally said, "they aren't letting us do anything. Don't pretend that—"

"What do you want to do? Lift the eighty-pound barrel? Or even better, hold some guy on your shoulders while *he* lifts the eighty-pound barrel?" I shook my head. "If we have to do that kind of stuff, we're going to fail."

She stared at the ground, winding a loose strand of hair around and around her finger.

"I might not be able to lift that barrel, but I know what I can do. I can follow orders, even if that includes staying out of the way, without complaining. I can take care of myself without getting someone to pick up the slack. And," I said, pointing at the wall, "I can get across that obstacle without being lugged."

"I can't believe it," Gabrielle said. "You sound exactly like Cadet Daily."

I couldn't tell if she was annoyed or impressed. But I wasn't going to worry about it. I'd finally said what I needed to say, what I thought she needed to hear. And if she didn't like it . . . well, she'd just have to get over it.

"All right, Bryen," Hickman called down to us from his perch on the wall. "Kit's over. You're next."

"Okay," Gabrielle said, her eyes bouncing between Hickman, the slanted wall, and the minefield bordering the sawdust. "Sure. I'll just . . . just shimmy right up that thing." She glanced at me and whispered. "Without being lugged."

I smiled. She smiled back.

"That's right." Hickman pointed at the bottom of the wall. "Just get a good running start and jump high enough so your feet hit the wall above the mines. Then all you gotta do is grab that rope and hang on. If you get that far, I'll pull you up the rest of the way."

Suddenly, yelling erupted from the other side of the obstacle. Hickman looked over his shoulder, then down at us. "The barrel's over! That means as soon as we're all across, the clock stops! Let's go!"

Gabrielle took a deep breath, then charged toward the obstacle. But she slid to a halt inches from the red piping.

I closed my eyes. *Oh, Gab!*

She laughed nervously. "Just practicing, guys." She jogged back to the partition without looking at me. I noticed that she was limping a little. *Oh . . . her knee!* I had forgotten about her knee. I felt a tiny twinge of guilt, then, about going off on her. She'd complained about a lot of things today, but her knee wasn't one of them.

Gabrielle licked her lips and tried again. This time she

made it over the piping. The heel of her boot just barely cleared the wall's mined area, but there she was—hanging on to the rope, squealing, "I did it!"

I jumped up and down, clapping my hands. "Way to go, Gab! Now all the way to the top!"

Gabrielle inched her way up the rope, and Hickman pulled her over the top of the wall and steadied her. "See the board?" I heard him say. "Crawl across it, over the gap." Then he looked down at me. "Whenever you're ready, Davis, I'm ready."

You don't need to be ready for anything, Hickman. I swallowed and wiped my hands on my pants, studying the wall, then the sawdust pit, and finally the red piping. I closed my eyes and breathed slowly. *Just get a good start— and jump. Simple.* When I opened my eyes, I was speeding toward the obstacle. I saw the red piping. I saw the sawdust sailing under my feet. I saw my right foot hit the slanted wall. I saw hand over hand walking up the rope. I saw Hickman's face. He was smiling.

"Not too shabby, Davis. Need a hand?"

"No, thanks." I threw my leg over the top of the wall and pulled myself up. Straddling the top, I paused a moment to catch my breath. Ping was on the top of the wall across the gap leaning over the edge, his back toward me. Excited voices were coming from the other side of the obstacle. I crawled across the gap, over the precariously placed board, which shook as I moved. *Gab must've loved this!* I squeezed next to Ping and looked over. And there was Gabrielle, hanging halfway down, clinging to Ping's hand. Jason, Kit, Bonanno, and Cero were yelling advice to her from the ground beyond the red piping. "Okay, Gab," Ping said, dragging her back up. "We'll give you another shot in a second. You're thinking too much."

"Yeah, Gab," Kit said. "It's not much different than going down a slide. Just like doing the jungle gym when you were a kid."

"I didn't do jungle gyms, Kit," Gabrielle said, her voice shaking. She squirmed over the top of the wall, looking down at the sawdust below. "The only experimenting I ever did with gravity was jump rope!"

"Okay, Andi," Ping said. "Show Gab how it's done. All you've got to do—"

"—is slide down and push off the wall before I hit the mines." I looked at Ping. "Right? And hope I make it over the sawdust."

"Excuse me, Andi," Gabrielle said, swinging her legs over the top and elbowing me out of her way. Without another word she pushed herself over the edge, slid down the wall, and landed safely on her hands and knees in the dirt outside the red piping.

"Hu ah!" Kit and Jason yelled, slapping hands.

Gabrielle got to her feet, picked her TEDs out of the dirt, shoved them on her face, and brushed herself off. "Piece of cake. *Now* it's your turn, Andi."

I do not ask for any crown
But that which all may win;
Nor try to conquer any world
Except the one within.
Be thou my guide until I find,
Led by a tender hand,
Thy happy kingdom in myself
And dare to take command.
　　　　—LOUISA MAY ALCOTT, "MY KINGDOM"

CHAPTER 14

SATURDAY, 7 AUGUST
1520

"DAVIS, IT'S YOUR TURN." Cadet Daily stopped pacing and stood in front of me.

My eyes jerked to his face, my heart shifting into high gear. This was our fifth obstacle. Half of Third Squad had already led. The inevitable had come. "Yes, sir."

He folded his arms across his chest. "This is your chance to excel."

"Yes, sir." I thought about that word. *Excel.* Just this morning I had excelled, qualifying Expert on the Hand Grenade Assault Course by throwing bull's-eyes on all five targets despite long charges uphill, smoke burning my eyes, and simulated bombs thundering from every direction. Earlier in the week I had excelled, running through the muddy Bayonet Assault Course, stabbing straw-filled dummies, low crawling under barbed wire, and jumping over log barricades. All summer I had excelled, dogging the guys during P.T., memorizing knowledge, drilling on the Plain, rappelling and ruck marching and withstanding the hazing. *But that was different. That was you against yourself. You weren't* leading *anyone.*

I hadn't been afraid to hold a live grenade and pull the pin, then lob it over the top of a concrete bunker. And I hadn't been afraid to load forty rounds of live ammunition into my M-16, then fire them into a target downrange. But I was afraid now.

"Okay, Cadet Tooley," Cadet Daily said, stepping away from me and turning to the fidgeting upperclassman behind him. "They're all yours."

"Right-o." Cadet Tooley gave Cadet Daily a thumbs-up and marched over to us like someone had just wound him up and let him go. He quickly scanned our group, his eyes darting from one face to the next. "All right, New Cadets. As your squad leader has already informed you, my name is Cadet Tooley, and I will be the Safety for this obstacle." He snapped his head into a nod. Actually, everything about him was snappy—his movements, his quick speech, his high-pitched nasal voice, his darting eyes.

That guy must've been a squirrel in a prior life. I'll never relax with him around.

His eyes flicked around our group again. "Cadet Daily has informed me of your outstanding effort on the LRC thus far, New Cadets. According to *him* you are in the running for taking H Company's squad competition."

"HU-AH!" We all knew that was an exaggeration, but we liked hearing it, anyway.

Cadet Tooley clasped his hands behind his back and

nodded again. "That's all well and good. But if you're not safe while you're at my obstacle, you'll be sorry. 'Blood makes the grass grow' might be a catchy phrase, New Cadets. But I've never cared much for grass. Especially when it grows in my sawdust pit." He thrust an arm toward the obstacle behind him. "Take a minute to view the obstacle to my rear, your front." Then he waited, whistling tunelessly.

Okay. Concentrate. You've got to take everything in. I stared down the length of what looked like ten feet of waist-high monkey bars, painted red. Except instead of actual bars it had slack chains that were partially covered with gray padding. Where the monkey bars ended, a wooden wall towered about ten feet high.

"Time's up, New Cadets. Now listen carefully. This is the scenario. Exactly two hours ago your team received an urgent radio call from forward elements of your battalion, operating twelve kilometers from your position."

I leaned forward, my mind struggling to keep pace with his speech.

"The enemy has conducted biological warfare in this forward element's area of operations, contaminating their water supply with an extremely aggressive strain of cholera, known to kill the average human within two hours after initial symptoms are evident. For your professional development, New Cadets, these symptoms are debilitating abdominal cramps, massive diarrhea, and violent vomiting, leading to dehydration, shock, and finally death. Not a pleasant way to go."

"Nothing like leaking out of both ends," I heard Jason whisper to Kit. "That's got to suck."

"Leaking out of both ends?" Kit whispered back. "More like *blasting*. Ol' Faithful strikes again."

I rolled my eyes at them while they snorted to keep from laughing. *Guys!* They could be so immature sometimes! I had to take this seriously even if they weren't.

But unlike me, Cadet Tooley was oblivious to Kit and Jason. "Your mission, New Cadets," he continued, "is to get the newly developed—and only existing—cure for cholera to the affected personnel before they die. For the past one hour and forty-seven minutes your team has been hacking its way through dense jungle when you come upon a terrain feature not indicated on your map." He flicked his hand toward the sawdust pit. "This ravine. A very deep ravine." He executed a crisp about-face and marched away from us, into the pit. "Spanning this very deep ravine is a rather deteriorated, heavily booby-trapped suspension bridge."

You mean completely *booby-trapped.* The gray padding encasing each chain was the only exception. And even then, about six inches of red chain stuck out of the padding on either side.

"This bridge is your only way across the ravine." Cadet Tooley walked along the length of the red monkey bars, making each padded chain swing as he passed, until he reached the wall. "As you can plainly see, the suspension bridge is anchored, on this end, *nine feet* below the top of the ravine. Therefore, if you make it across the bridge, you must scale this nine-foot cliff to complete the mission." He patted the wood wall.

Okay. The wall's nine feet taller than the bridge. Remember that—nine feet.

"According to the latest intelligence reports, the cliff is not believed to be booby-trapped." He spun around and flashed us a crooked smile. "But . . ."

Great—that means it probably is booby-trapped. But the side of the wall that I could see was free of any red paint. *So maybe the top is mined?*

"Finally, the enemy has laid a narrow minefield along the edge of the ravine on your side; hence the red piping encircling the pit. And located directly to your rear are your supplies." He paused for us to look. "Two ammo crates, representing two cartons of glass vials that contain the rare cholera cure; one fuel barrel, containing an isotonic replacement solution to slow the effects of dehydration; one twenty-one-foot rope; and one six-foot-by-two-foot board."

A board? Maybe we could lay it over the chains, then crawl across it to the other side! I squinted at the obstacle, my mind working fast. *No, six feet won't be long enough . . . but we'll need something stable . . .*

"Remember, to successfully accomplish the mission, you must get all the equipment and all personnel across the bridge . . ."

Personnel across the bridge . . . I had a sudden vision of BDU-clad bodies forming a bridge over the chains, and the rest of Third Squad crawling over them. *Yes! That's it! A human bridge!*

". . . and over the cliff within thirteen minutes, no exceptions. Are there any questions?" He waited, his eyes traveling around our group. "No? Okay, then. Who's the leader? Front and center!"

I took a step forward. "Sir, Cadet Daily assigned me as the leader for this obstacle." My voice sounded distant, as if it were coming from outside myself. I hoped it didn't sound odd to everyone else.

He nodded. "Well, I hope you were listening to my

safety speech, Miss . . ." He jerked his eyes to my name tag. ". . . Miss Davis."

I swallowed. "Yes, sir. I was listening, sir." *I may not have a clue about what I'm doing, but I can listen.*

"Good. That's exactly what I want to hear." He checked his watch. "You have thirteen minutes. Starting *now!*" And Cadet Tooley marched out of the pit.

Well, here goes. I wiped my hands on my pants and turned to face my squadmates. Seven pairs of eyes stared back at me, waiting. *I don't know—what if they think my human bridge idea is completely messed up?* I took a deep breath, trying to conjure up the confident, almost indifferent, façade I wore at the starting line of every race. *Come on. You've got to at least make these guys think you've got it together.*

But Third Squad took my hesitation as uncertainty and clamored to fill the silence with advice:

"How abouts we see how heavy those supplies are?"

"No, the first thing we've gotta do is send someone up the wall to recon what's on the other side."

"Sure, *after* we stabilize the chains. We can't just let someone go across."

"What about using that board over there?"

You're supposed to be the leader, right? Come on—you're losing them.

I knew if I stood back just a little longer, someone would jump in and take over. But I couldn't let that happen. *I* had to do the leading, and that's all there was to it.

I shook my head. "No, I don't think the board's long enough. But what about this? I was thinking: We could use a couple of us to make a sort of human bridge across the chains. And then, you know, have the rest of us crawl over them?"

So much for coming across confident. I hadn't dictated a plan, I had tossed out a suggestion. Why couldn't I just tell them what to do like Ping and Kit and the rest had done when they were in charge?

I saw Jason and Kit look from me to the obstacle. Cero had his hands on his hips, kicking a stone between his feet. Hickman shrugged his shoulders and crossed his arms. Gabrielle and Bonanno hovered behind the others, watching everyone's reactions. Only Ping held my gaze, nodding slightly.

Encouraged by the lack of dissent, I turned back to the obstacle and talked faster. "Two people should be enough, don't you think? If they're tall? Like . . . maybe Cero and Kit, if they want to. Or Bonanno." I pointed at the chains. "The first guy could lie down on the chains and cover the first half of them. You following me? And then the second guy could crawl over him and cover the rest." I looked over my shoulder. "They'd have to be really careful and only lie on the gray padding part because of the mines . . ."

Kit clapped his hands. "I'm in, Andi. I'll even volunteer to be one of your bridge guys."

"Me, too." Cero jabbed himself in the chest with his thumb. "But I'm going to be the first guy on. No guts, no glory. Right?" He looked at me. "You think you can arrange that, Boss?"

I smiled. "I think I can arrange that, Cero." *This isn't so bad. Acting confident, that's the key.* I looked at the rest of Third Squad. "Then after those guys are set, someone will have to crawl over them and climb up the wall to see what's on the other side." I raised an eyebrow. "Anybody really good at climbing?"

"And what if the top of the wall's booby-trapped?" Hickman asked, squinting at me out of one eye. "That 'someone' just might get wasted."

"Well . . ." I started picking the dirt out from under my fingernails. I hadn't thought that far ahead.

But . . . how could that be? Clearing the obstacle would be impossible then, wouldn't it? But then again, hadn't Cadet Tooley hinted that the top might be mined?

I knew I had to say something; the entire squad was waiting.

I shook my head. "I don't think we really need to worry about that. I mean, we've got to get *over* the wall, right? There's no way around that. Maybe in a real-life situation it would be mined. But"—I shrugged—"unless we're supposed to lose one guy right off the bat—and who knows? That may be the case—I still think mining the top of the wall just doesn't pass the common-sense test." I quickly checked the faces in the group; I was babbling, but they were still with me.

"So I guess we'll just have to take that chance. Of losing someone, I mean." I cleared my throat. "Any volunteers?" I waited as my squadmates exchanged glances. *Why did I ask for volunteers? What will I do if nobody says anything?*

"Yeah, sure," Hickman finally mumbled, looking at the ground. "I'll do it."

Kit thumped Hickman across the back. "Like Cero was saying, 'No guts, no glory.' Ain't that right, Tommy old boy?"

When I turned back to Cero, he was already leaning over the sawdust that lay between the red piping and the booby-trapped bridge. With his toes as close as possible to the red piping, he dove for the chains. Flopping on top of the first two, he wiggled forward, his body bucking as he wormed his way over the chains. Finally, after a lot of gasping and cursing, he reached the halfway point.

"Man!" Cero said, wiping his face on his shoulder. "That was like wrestling an octopus or something." He squirmed around, repositioning himself so he had both fists securely around the third chain, his chest across the second, and his thighs weighing down the first nearest our end.

"Good job, Cero! You did great." I turned to Kit and said, "Ready?"

Kit winked. "I was born ready."

I watched until Kit had grabbed onto Cero's calves and was pulling himself over the small sawdust gap. Then I went over to where Ping and Gabrielle were checking out the equipment.

"Well," I said, "I guess Cero and Bogus have everything under control."

"Look, Bogus," I heard Cero from the sawdust pit behind me, "you're really not a bad guy. But don't be getting close and personal on me now."

"On second thought . . ." I laughed, then nodded at the supplies. "So tell me. Is that stuff as heavy as usual?"

Ping shook his head. "Well, the ammo boxes aren't filled with rocks this time, so they're considerably lighter."

"Yeah," Gabrielle said, "Even I can lift them. And that barrel—how much would you say it weighs? Not more than forty pounds?"

Ping shrugged. "Forty, fifty, something like that. But I'll bet you anything"—he patted the barrel—"this baby, going over those chains and all, will be our Achilles' heel."

"Hey, Bogus! Watch those knees! I've had those kidneys

for twenty-two years, and I sort of want to keep them!"

We turned from the supplies to watch Kit pull himself over Cero's head and reach for the last chain.

"Quit . . . your . . . sniveling, Big Guy," Kit grunted. "You're yowling like a cat in a poke."

"Listen here, *Country*," Cero said, "instead of beating me in the face with your size twelves, hook them on this chain *here*." Cero grabbed one of Kit's feet, guiding it to the chain weighed down with his own chest. "That's it. Now the other one."

I had an improvement. "Hey, Cero," I yelled. "Can you also try holding Kit's legs while grabbing the chain? You know, by linking your arms under his shins? It might be more stable that way. You think?"

"Yeah, probably," Cero said. "And that way I can be *sure* his feet stay clear of my face."

Sending Hickman over our manmade bridge produced more groans and grunts as he went from lying on top of Kit to balancing on hands and knees to squatting, and finally, to standing. Then, with a little bounce, Hickman bounded up the wall.

"I might not be the most buffed guy in the world," Kit said, "but just for the record, Hickman, I am not a springboard." Kit momentarily released the chain with his left hand to rub his right shoulder. "I tell you what: I've always admired those ol' martyrs of the faith. But I just don't feel like being drawn and quartered today. Maybe tomorrow, but not today."

"Quit your bellyachin', Bogus," Hickman said from his perch on the top of the wall. "I'm not the guy giving the orders around here. Davis said to cross the bridge and climb the wall, remember? I did what I had to do." Then he looked down at me. "And we're in luck, Davis, 'cause I'm still alive. And we've got no more mines to worry about up here or on the other side."

I felt a slight relief. "Great!" *One less thing to worry about.* I smiled to myself. *Things are really starting to come together. I can't believe it—I'm actually doing this!* I glanced at the ammo boxes and fuel barrel, rope and board. *So what's next?* I ran my jagged thumbnail across my upper lip, thinking. I had a pretty good idea of what to do, but I needed to bounce my plan off someone else, just to be sure. I turned to Ping. "So, send more people across? What do you think?"

Ping smiled. "What do *you* think, Andi?"

He was right. I was the leader. I had to be the one making the decisions. I looked back at the obstacle. "Well . . . I guess we should pass the stuff across assembly-line style, like we've done on most of the other obstacles."

Ping nodded. "Probably."

"So that means we'll need people on the obstacle— someone on the other side of the wall, someone on top of the wall, someone at the far end of the bridge, and someone here"—I stamped my foot near the red piping—"to, you know, start passing the stuff."

Ping leaned closer to me. "If it were me, Andi," he said casually, "I'd put one man in the middle of the bridge, too."

I nodded. "Oh, that's right! Because otherwise, the reach will be too long." I quickly counted the people I'd already planned on using and came up with five. "And we have a couple extra people, so that won't be a problem."

I looked at my watch. Five out of the thirteen minutes were already spent. *We've got to hustle!* A new burst of adrenaline spurred me on. "Okay, guys. This is the plan. We're going to pass the supplies across. But to do that, we'll need people at different spots on the obstacle. Bonanno, I want you to cross next. Okay? All the way to the other side of the wall."

Bonanno nodded and reached over the sawdust for Cero's calves.

"Hickman, I want you right where you are. Okay? And if Bonanno needs help, you can give him a hand."

Hickman leaned over the side of the wall and spat into the sawdust. "Whatever."

His attitude bothered me, but I wasn't about to let him intimidate me now. Ignoring him, I turned quickly to Ping. Of all the members in my squad, I felt the most awkward giving Ping orders. "And Ping, you can be the guy on the far end of the bridge, closest to the wall. You'll be passing the stuff up to Hickman. Is that okay by you?"

"It's okay by me."

That left Jason, Gabrielle, and me without jobs.

I looked over at the supplies. One of us would have to reach them over the sawdust to the obstacle. The barrel was lighter than usual, but still heavy. And remembering the other obstacles, I figured the ammo boxes would be awkward. I knew *I* wasn't strong enough for the job . . . and neither was Gabrielle.

Unbelievable—I'm the leader and look what happened—Bryen and Davis out of the action. Again.

I turned to Jason. "Well, it looks like you'll be doing most of the lifting." Then I looked at Gabrielle. "And you'll . . ."

"Don't tell me," she said. "You want me to take the middle of the bridge, right?" She glanced at the obstacle and licked her lips. "So, where do you want me? You want me to sit on Cero?"

I nodded. She was staring at the barrel and twisting her

hair, looking doubtful. I could tell she was worried about the weight.

"You can do it, Gab. You're the Push-up Queen, remember? Just go where you can reach the stuff that Jason passes to you *and* stay clear of the mines."

Less than four minutes later everyone was in position. Jason and I started passing the stuff across, starting with the ammo boxes. I decided that the six-foot board was nothing but a distractor and sent it over too, saving the barrel for last.

"We are smokin'!" Hickman yelled, slapping his hands together. "Send that puppy over!"

Jason moved to pick up the barrel. "One barrel of sugar water, coming right up."

"Hold on," I said. "What about the rope?"

Jason sighed. "What *about* the rope, Andi? One of us will just take it when we cross over."

"Yeah . . . but maybe we'll need it to, you know, pull the barrel up and over the wall. We could tie one end of the rope around the barrel. And once the barrel gets across the bridge to Ping, he can toss the other end up to Hickman."

"Whatever you want, Andi," Jason said. "You're the boss." We got right to work, looping the rope around the barrel, securing it with a tight square knot.

"That oughtta do it," Jason said, moving to pick up the barrel again.

"Uh . . . shouldn't we wrap the excess rope around the barrel first? You know, as a precaution? So we don't lose the rope to the mines?"

Jason sighed again, but he wound the excess rope around the barrel anyway. "I'll tuck the end . . . right under . . . here . . . and she's ready to travel." He picked up the barrel.

"Wait one more second, Jason," I said. "Let me think this through one last time." I looked from the barrel to Ping, then from Ping to Hickman, straddling the top of the wall. *That thing may be too heavy to just pass across. Especially since the bridge is so unstable. . . .* I looked at Gabrielle. She was staring at the barrel again, twirling that strand of hair. *What if the barrel is too heavy for her and she drops it? And her knee . . .* I chewed on my thumbnail. *Oh . . . I don't know! Would it be better to toss the end of the rope up to Hickman now instead of later? Then he could alleviate some of the weight while they're passing the barrel across. Or won't the rope be long enough for that?*

"So?" Jason said, looking at his watch. "Is there some kind of problem, Andi? Or can we get on with this? We've only got about five minutes left!"

For the first time all summer Jason actually looked annoyed with me. And it made me nervous. I tried to smile. "Uh, no. I mean, *yes*—go ahead. Forget it. It was . . . nothing."

Jason shook his head and reached the barrel over the sawdust to Gabrielle.

"Wait!" Gabrielle screamed, her hands fluttering between one end of the barrel and the rope around its middle. "Don't let go, Jason! I don't have it yet. Oh, where should I grab it?"

"How should *I* know?" Jason yelled. "Am I there with you? *Just grab it!*"

"Grab the rope around the middle, Gab," I yelled, pointing. "Then pass it to Ping—quickly!"

"Okay, okay, okay!" Gabrielle grabbed the rope with both hands. "It's . . . way . . . too heavy! I'm going to drop it! *Somebody help!*"

"Ping!" I yelled.

"I'm on my way!" Ping crawled over Kit from his post near the wall.

"Put it down on my back, Gab," Cero said. "I can take the weight for a couple of seconds. Just keep it steady so it doesn't roll off."

"Okay . . ."

"All right, Gab," Ping said, now straddling Cero's back behind Gabrielle. "Scoot over. I'll take it from here."

Gabrielle cautiously edged around the barrel. Then she crouched over Cero's calves. Ping had taken her place, the barrel between them.

Ping quickly unwrapped the excess rope from around the barrel, then looked up the wall at Hickman. "Hey! Catch!"

Hickman nodded, and Ping tossed the end of the rope up to him, underhand.

I chewed on the inside of my lip. *That's what I wanted to do! Why didn't I say something?* Jason had unnerved me. But I knew that was just an excuse.

"Now, Hickman," Ping said, "on the count of three, I'm going to push the barrel toward the wall. At the same time, you've got to pull like there's no tomorrow and get that barrel up there. We probably should've done this in the first place." I noted a tone of aggravation in his voice. It was slight, but it was there.

"Well . . ." I cocked my head and smiled, trying to make everyone like me again. "I had thought of that, guys, but—"

"*Thinking* about it," Hickman said, "doesn't count for squat." Then he nodded at Ping. "I'm ready when you are."

I blinked, like I had just been smacked across the face.

Well, what did you expect? A "That's good, Andi! It's the thought that counts"? Well, Hickman's right. You didn't trust yourself, and you blew it. I focused on the barrel, wishing I were anywhere but where I was.

Ping looked at Gabrielle over the barrel. "I could sure use some help pushing this thing from your end." Then he turned back to Hickman. "Okay, ready? One . . . two . . . three!" Ping and Gabrielle pushed the barrel, and Hickman pulled the rope. The barrel slammed against the wall, then bumped its way up, inch by inch, until it stopped, dangling at the end of the rope about three feet from the top.

"Ping," Hickman gasped, "give me . . . a hand here . . . will you?"

Ping scrambled back to his original position on Kit's shoulders. Steadying himself against the wall, he stretched upward until he was just able to tap the barrel with his fingertips.

Then it happened, quick as a camera flash. But to me the few seconds took hours to play out, stretching before me in slow motion, frame by frame.

I saw Ping's upward shove and Hickman's tug, the barrel clearing the top of the wall. I saw Hickman grab the rope around the barrel's middle and shout, "Yes! I've got it!" before he twisted around, lowering it down to Bonanno on the other side of the wall. I saw Ping throw his arms back, giving Hickman a thumbs-up, then stumble, his left foot slipping off Kit and slamming onto the padded chain held between Kit's hands. I saw the padded chain move forward, Ping lurching with it, and Kit collapse, slipping between the chains. I saw Kit's face hit the sawdust, his feet shoot upward, smashing into Cero's face, then catching on the chains. I saw Cero rear his head back and yell. Blood from his nose ran down Kit's boots and drip . . . drip . . . dripped onto the sawdust below.

And then I heard heavy footsteps charging through the sawdust, and Cadet Daily, with Cadet Tooley right on his heels, yelling, "Don't anyone move! Davis, talk to me! What happened?" But all I could do was think about Kit, moaning beneath the obstacle, and Cero, his blood darkening the sawdust.

"Sir . . . I"—I waved weakly at the obstacle—"Kit, I mean . . . *Bogus*, sir . . . and Cero—"

Kit dragged himself out from underneath the obstacle and staggered to his feet, holding his right arm tightly against his chest.

Cadets Daily and Tooley turned away from me and rushed over to Kit. "I thought I said, 'Don't move!'" Cadet Daily yelled. Then his tone softened. "What's with the arm, Bogus?"

"Sir . . . it's my . . . shoulder, sir. It hurts. Bad."

"Where?" yelled Cadet Tooley. "Which one?"

Ping sprang from the obstacle. "Let's get his shirt off, sir. I'll bet he's got a dislocated shoulder. The way that chain flew forward . . . I bet it yanked his arm right out of its socket."

I heard Jason swear under his breath.

Kit's arm . . . yanked out of its socket? I closed my eyes. *This can't be happening!*

"Dislocated shoulder?" Cadet Tooley yelled. "That's serious stuff! We need to get a medic here ASAP!" He glared at Ping. "And just what do you think *you're* doing, Bonehead? Get back on the obstacle where you belong!"

"Relax. We already have a medic here," Cadet Daily said, nodding at Ping. "New Cadet Ping. Don't tell me you didn't recognize the Combat Medical Badge on his chest. Looks like you need to review your *Bugle Notes*, Tooley."

"Wasn't exactly looking for it," Cadet Tooley muttered, shuffling over to Cero on the obstacle.

"Besides your shoulder," Ping said, helping Kit out of his shirt, "do you feel pain anywhere else? Like your head? Or dizziness? You feel dizzy at all?"

Kit shook his head. "No . . . I don't know! All I *can* say . . . is my shoulder's . . . killing me!"

Ping nodded. "Okay, Kit. Take it easy. Now, this is what I want you to do. Try to stand at attention. Okay? Just drop your arms to your sides, sl-o-o-w-ly . . ."

Kit winced. "This . . . is . . . the best . . . I can do."

"You did just fine," Ping said, staring intently at Kit's limp arm and drooping shoulder. "Well, sir, I'd say it's definitely dislocated. See how one arm looks longer than the other, and how his skin is stretched here?" He pointed to a hollow area where the curve of Kit's shoulder once was. "And the head of his humerus bone here?" He tapped the sickening bump under Kit's stretched skin.

I averted my eyes, staring instead at the back of Ping's helmet, feeling weak.

Ping shook his head. "He's going to have to be medevacked, sir."

Medevacked? What in the world does that mean? I looked down at my hands; they were shaking.

"I could try to put his shoulder back in, sir, but I'd feel more comfortable letting the emergency-room personnel handle it. Shoulders can be pretty tricky."

The emergency room? I took a step back and hit something solid with my heel. Suddenly, I realized where I was. I had been slinking away from the obstacle, step by step, the entire time. And now I could feel the ridges of the corrugated partition digging into my back. *Kit has to go to the emergency room, and it's all my fault! My brilliant idea— making a human bridge. What was I thinking?* I reached behind me and squeezed one of the aluminum ridges.

"Don't sweat it, Ping," Cadet Daily said. "I wouldn't put that kind of responsibility on you. That's what the docs at Keller Army Hospital get paid the big bucks for." Then he looked around. "Let's see . . . Bonanno. You're over the obstacle already. Go and light a bonfire under those medics' butts. Tell them we have an emergency here and need an ambulance. Move out!"

"Yes, sir!" And I watched Bonanno disappear down the dirt road, wishing I could follow him.

"Okay, Cero," Cadet Daily said, elbowing Cadet Tooley aside. "What's up with *you*? It looks like someone beat you with an Ugly Stick."

"Bloody nose," Cadet Tooley answered. "Possibly broken. We'll need a medic to check him out, too."

Broken nose? The hot afternoon air seemed to be pressing down on me.

Cero shook his head. "The bleeding's stopped, sir. I'm okay." Then he smiled, dried blood smeared from his nose to his chin. "It's not the first boot that's met my face, sir."

"I could've told you that, Zero," Cadet Daily said. "You've never been pretty to look at, that's for sure. But we'll get you some ice, anyway." Then he smacked his hands together. "Okay, Third Squad. The excitement's over. Cadet Tooley, what's the clock say?"

"I stopped the clock"—Cadet Tooley checked his watch—"at four minutes and eleven seconds."

"Four minutes and eleven seconds?" Cadet Daily grinned.

"That's enough time to get in one serious power rack session and clear the obstacle! Okay, Third Squad. Except for Bogus, who's about to take a little tour of Keller Army Hospital, I want everyone to resume their positions on the obstacle—"

Resume our positions on the obstacle? But how can we when Kit . . . I swallowed. *He's kidding. He just wants us to think we're going to* . . . I pulled at the hem on my BDU shirt, twisting it between my fingers, and looked over at the obstacle, at Third Squad. Some studied the ground, some glanced at each other, some eyed Cadet Daily uneasily. But nobody moved.

"—and drive on with the mission," Cadet Daily said, turning to leave the sawdust pit. "Cadet Tooley, start the clock!"

Drive on with the mission? He really wasn't kidding. *But what about* . . . I glanced over at Kit. He was slumped against a tree, holding his arm tightly against his body, an empty, defeated look in his eyes. *See what happens when I'm in charge?* My lips started trembling. *I can't do this leader stuff—my ideas are stupid* . . . *and I get people hurt. I don't belong here.*

Cadet Daily spun around, facing me. "Didn't I just say, 'Drive on with the mission,' Davis? You *are* the leader around here, aren't you?" He stared at me with narrowed eyes, then followed my gaze to Kit. His jaw flexed.

"Yes, sir." I swallowed, pushing myself away from the partition and into the position of attention.

He whipped back around toward the obstacle, his face turning red. "And didn't I say resume your positions on the obstacle? That wasn't a request, Third Squad! So why are you just standing there, looking like a pack of whipped dogs?" He flung his arm with disgust and growled, "Stop the clock, Tooley! I've got a little attitude adjustment to make. These lamebrains seem to have forgotten everything I've taught them this summer!"

He stirred up the sawdust as he paced back and forth. "You think that because you've got a casualty, the mission stops? Is that it? You think that because this is 'just a scenario,' because this isn't 'for real,' you can just hang it up and go home? Well, think again. Because your performance in combat one day will depend on scenarios just like this one. Lots and lots of them. And someday these *scenarios* will come back to you and give you strength!"

I took a deep breath, listening to Cadet Daily.

"I'm not as cold and heartless as you think, Third Squad. I know it's no fun to see a buddy get hurt. But guess what? You're lucky today. Because he's still alive. But what are you going to do, Third Squad, when the bullets *are* flying? When you look to your left and there on the ground are pieces of skull and a pile of mush that seconds ago was your platoon sergeant's head? Tell me! What are you going to do? Sit down on the ground and cry? No! You're going to grit your teeth and drive on, because the lives of your soldiers depend on you. Because leadership is not just about making plans and executing them. Leadership"—he stopped pacing, his eyes meeting mine—"is about *leading!*"

Then he stomped out of the sawdust pit. "Cadet Tooley, as you were. Start the clock."

Leadership is about leading! I looked at Third Squad, trying to read the expressions on the faces that looked back at me. *What are they thinking? That I'm weak? That my plan was stupid? That Kit's shoulder is all my fault? That I suck as a leader?* I bit on my lip. *How can I lead these guys if they're thinking all those things? What am I supposed to do?*

"Grit your teeth and drive on," Cadet Daily had said. But I felt exhausted. Inadequate. Weak. Not at all like the leader—the *soldier*—he demanded I be.

Let someone else take over, I wanted to say. *I just don't have what it takes.*

But then something deep inside kicked in, and scenes from the past six weeks began to replay in my mind. Scenes of when I'd felt exhausted, inadequate, or weak and had, somehow, pulled through. Standing in the gas tent, reciting the national anthem . . . leaning in a foxhole, propped up with sandbags, a loaded M-16 in my hands . . . performing the Manual of Arms on the Plain . . . making West Point's Track and Cross Country teams . . . running the P.T. test and beating the guys . . . surviving West Point—the inspections, the hazing, the memorizing, the pinging, the sleepless nights, the early mornings, the ruck marches, the minute calling, the Four Responses, the meals in the mess hall.

Then older scenes, scenes from back home, forced out the recent ones. Facing the kids at the bus stop on mornings after the cops broke up a fight at my house . . . waking up to shattered dishes and slamming doors . . . coming home from school to find my trophies and medals smashed, littering my bedroom floor . . . hearing all the promises, then watching them break . . . surviving all those years at home—the fighting, the threats, the pain, the guilt, the pretending, the crying without tears, the hope that someday things would change and fearing that they would.

"And someday," Cadet Daily had said, "these *scenarios* will come back to you, and give you strength!"

Suddenly, I knew I could be the soldier Cadet Daily wanted me to be. The soldier I *needed* to be. The soldier I'd always been.

I stepped up to the red piping. I didn't drop my eyes or chew my nails or cock my head to one side. My time for approval seeking was over. It was time to take charge. I looked at Third Squad, looking back at me, and said, "Anybody know exactly how much time we've got left?"

"THREE MINUTES AND FORTY-SIX SECONDS!" Cadet Tooley yelled.

I nodded. "Let's do it, guys! Ping, take Kit's place on the chains."

Ping nodded and moved to cover the vacant spot.

"And, Gab, once Ping's set, crawl over him and climb up the wall. Then I'll go"—I pointed at Jason—"then McGill, then Cero, and finally Ping." I looked up the wall at Hickman. "And Hickman, just be ready to give a hand to whoever needs one." I shrugged. "I know I will."

"Me, too," Gabrielle said quickly.

The next few minutes unfolded like we'd spent all summer practicing the obstacle. And only after Ping had touched down in the sawdust, with nineteen seconds to spare, did I realize that the ambulance had arrived. Two medics were helping Kit into the back of it. And a dull ache tugged at my heart.

But as I returned all the Third Squad high-fives and received the countless thumps across my back, I smiled. I couldn't help myself.

Yes! It's over! We did it!

I had made the plan. I had executed it. And I had led.

You must understand men. . . .
Study their habits, impress upon them and be
impressed by them,
Until they realize that you not only possess
More book knowledge than they,
But that you equal, if not surpass them,
In all qualities of manhood.
—GENERAL WILLIAM T. SHERMAN,
WEST POINT CLASS OF 1840

CHAPTER 15

SATURDAY, 7 AUGUST
2015

"HEY, GUYS," Jason said, pointing his boot brush at a figure moving toward us up the line of Third Platoon tents. "Kit's back."

Jason, Gabrielle, Bonanno, Cero, and I looked up from where we sat together on the grass in front of my tent, brushing Kiwi on our boots. In the fading daylight the figure looked like a silhouette against the twilight sky. No facial features, no mannerisms that I could see distinguished him as Kit. Just a body in BDUs, plodding forward. Both his M-16 and his unbuckled LCE were slung over his left shoulder, looking like they might slip to the ground at any second. But when he got closer, I knew it was Kit. I saw his face, with eyes looking large and dark behind his TEDs. And a sling—blue and white against the browns and greens of his BDUs—binding his right arm against his body.

"He looks *terrible*," I whispered.

"Hey, Kit," Gab called out. "How're you feeling?"

And then the others called out their greetings:

"You're back already? Good to go!"

"You okay, man?"

"What's with the sling? They fix you up?"

Kit vaguely glanced our way as he walked past. "What's up?" he mumbled. Then, dropping his gear in front of his tent, he crawled inside.

We looked at each other, then went back to blackening our boots, saying nothing. As the sky grew dimmer, conversations started to pick up around us. A couple of tents away four Second Squad guys were getting a game of cards going. A debate about baseball teams was heating up behind us. And somewhere somebody said the punch line to a joke, and laughter erupted.

Seconds later Ping and Hickman ran up to join us, their boots and polish in their hands and their M-16s on their shoulders. "We saw Bogus," Hickman whispered, jabbing his thumb toward Kit and Jason's tent.

Ping took a spot across from me. "So, what's the deal? What'd he say?"

"Nothing," Cero said. "Just walked on by us and crawled into his tent."

"He looked bad, guys," Gabrielle whispered. "*Really* bad." She raked her fingers through her hair, still damp from the shower we'd taken before dinner. "I just can't believe they sent him back out here. If he really had a dislocated shoulder, that's . . . *unconscionable!*"

Ping shrugged. "That's the Army for you. Can't miss any of that 'good ol' army training,' you know."

"'Good ol' army training.'" Gabrielle snorted. "Tomorrow's

our *last* day out here. We've—*he's*—already done all the hard stuff. What's to miss?" She shook her head. "It's ridiculous."

Bonanno cleared his throat. "But Cadet Daily said we're having introductory map reading all morning tomorrow. Reading a compass and all—sounds pretty important."

"And don't forget about that stud competition goin' on tomorrow afternoon," Hickman said. "Sure would be a shame if he missed out on that." He spat onto the toe of his boot and rubbed it in with his brush. "Muscle heads on parade."

Gabrielle sighed. "Oh, Hickman! Are you ragging on the Iron Man Competition again? It's so obvious that you're jealous, 'cause you know you'll never get picked to represent Hardcore." She looked up from her boots and raised an eyebrow. "An Iron Man you are not."

Everyone laughed. Everyone except Hickman.

Hickman glared at Gabrielle. "Har. Har. You are the funniest."

"Well, I don't know about you guys," Gabrielle continued, "but I'm looking forward to it because Cadet Daily said that all the nonparticipants—practically everybody— get to watch the competition from Lake Frederick's beach in our swimsuits."

"Did you say 'beach,' Bryen?" Cero laughed. "Now where I come from, there are beaches."

Gabrielle stuck her nose in the air. "Hey, I'm not picky. If it's got sand, water, and sun, Andi and I are there, working on our tans."

"The only sun Andi's gonna get, Gab," Jason said, "will be while she's out winning the Iron Man Competition. That is, if the sun can catch her."

I bent over my boots, feeling my face grow warm. "I don't think so. I mean, no one's even asked me to do it . . . and it's tomorrow, so—"

"Sure you'll do it," Hickman said, spitting onto the toe of his boot again. "They have to have a female represented on every team. Gotta have that equal representation, you know. They just haven't gotten around to asking you yet."

"Like Andi wouldn't be asked to do it, anyway," Jason said. "I know she can kick my butt. What about you, Hickman?"

"You know, Gab's right," Ping said, frowning, his mind obviously on things other than tan lines and Iron Men. "They could've cut Bogus some slack. I mean, it serves no purpose making him come back out here. Sleeping on the ground, getting no rest. He's just going to be miserable!"

"No kidding!" I shook my head, relieved the subject had changed. "Just remind me never to get injured anywhere near here, okay?"

Hickman snorted. "If you were the one that got hurt, Davis"—he narrowed his eyes—"you wouldn't be out here. Because you're a female. They would have kept you in a nice cushy hospital room instead."

Because I'm a female? I looked at him for a second, confused. What did all that have to do with Kit coming back out to the field? "I don't understand. What difference—"

"Here we go again." Gabrielle rolled her eyes at me. "Dr. Hickman's great female-conspiracy theory."

"It's no conspiracy, it's reality!" Hickman said, glaring at her.

Gabrielle rolled her eyes again. "I'm so tired of hearing about this."

"Well, Gab," Jason said, taking an unusual interest in the tongue of his boot. "I think all he's saying is . . . most of the people on profile *are* females."

Gabrielle turned to glare at him. "So?"

He was right. And once again I felt myself siding with the guys.

"So," Hickman said, "don't you think it's kinda strange that there are *three* girls to every guy on profile, but only one girl to every *ten* guys at West Point? And what do they go on profile for? Shin splints. Pulled muscles. Stupid period cramps. It's weak!"

Bonanno laughed. "Yeah, guys would never go on profile for weak stuff like that." Then his face got red. "Uh . . . I meant the, uh, shin splints and pulled muscles, not the other . . . thing."

Jason shrugged. "Guys are different. It would be like admitting they're total wimps or something. So they just suck it down and hope for the best. Most guys, at least."

"So do most of the girls," Gabrielle said, pulling one of her boots over her foot.

Hickman leaned forward. "No they don't! Most girls have no problem running to the medic about stuff that every guy puts up with. Because they know if they whine loud enough, they'll get out of the stuff they don't want to do. And it's all legit—a doc signs off on some piece of paper, they're handed a pair of crutches, and they're golden."

"Well, *I* didn't," Gabrielle said, yanking at her laces. "I didn't go to the medic when I hurt my knee the other night. And I probably should have—"

"So you're the exception to the rule, Bryen." Hickman clapped his hands in mock applause. "You're one cut above Often-slacker. Congratulations."

Gabrielle looked at Hickman, then dropped her eyes to her boots and tied her laces, saying nothing.

I couldn't believe he'd said that! *What a total jerk!* I looked at the rest of Third Squad—Jason, Cero, Bonanno, and Ping. Everyone was suddenly engrossed in his boots, except Hickman, who was messing with his watch, a smug expression on his face.

So why isn't anybody saying anything? Do they think Hickman's right? That Gab's just "one cut above Often-slacker?" I refused to believe that. At times they might have thought—as I had—that she acted too much like a "girl"— whiny, maybe even slightly on the wimpy side—but never like Often-slacker. And it made me mad that they wouldn't defend her now. That they'd just let Hickman humiliate her like that after she had tried so hard.

If I hated one thing, it was labels; I knew how easy it was to become what you were called.

I turned back to Hickman. This was one conflict I couldn't back away from. Gabrielle was my friend, and she didn't deserve this. I just couldn't let myself blend into the squad, where it was safe. I had to say something.

"That was really low, Hickman," I heard myself say. I took a deep breath to steady my voice, and then the words came, fast. "You have no idea what you're talking about. Gab's knee has been killing her all week, but she hasn't tried to get out of anything. Everything that the rest of us have done, she's done. And she hasn't complained about it one time, not even to me." I glanced at Gabrielle, who was watching me intently.

"I know how bad her knee hurts because every morning when she crawls out of her sleeping bag and into her BDUs, I see what it looks like. She won't go to the medic because she'd rather put up with the pain than be called a profile get-over like Often-slacker. But I guess she shouldn't have bothered, because the bottom line is, no matter what any of us females do around here, people like you, Hickman, are always going to think we're all just one cut above Often-slacker anyway. If we're lucky."

Everyone's eyes were off his boots now and on me.

"Whoa!" Hickman laughed, slapping his hand over his heart in mock surprise. "Davis is fired *up*!" He looked around at the rest of Third Squad. "Now, really, guys. Did *I* say that? What she said?"

They glanced uncomfortably at each other, unwilling to take sides. I knew what they were doing; it was what I'd always done until now—played it safe. I didn't blame them for not speaking up, but I was glad that I had, and I could tell Gabrielle was, too. She knew me better than anyone here. She knew how hard this had been for me.

"Just checkin'. 'Cause I didn't think I said that." Hickman turned back to me. "Why should I be impressed that Bryen didn't go running to the medic for a profile? Huh? You just said she's been doing everything with the rest of us, right? All that proves is she doesn't need a profile. If she's got a bone sticking out of her skin or a gaping chest wound or her eyes hanging out of her sockets, fine. That's a different story. She deserves a profile. And that goes for everybody—it makes no difference if they're male or female. But tell me, how many of those people who fall out to the rear of formation every day fit into that category? When I look at those people, all I see is get-over, 'cause that's what most of them are—profile get-overs with a piece of paper excusing them for being weak. They kick back in the shade while we beat ourselves up all day. They chill out in the barracks while we run P.T. They ride in a truck while we take our forty-pound rucks for twelve-mile walks. Those people didn't even have a Beast. They make me want to puke!"

"Yeah, you're right, Hickman," Ping said, "you're always going to find people who'll try to weasel out of things by going on sick call for piddly stuff. But the docs write up the profiles. *They* issue the crutches. So"—he shrugged—"who's to blame?"

"The losers who go on sick call in the first place! If they didn't have some kind of weakness to begin with—"

"Shut your stupid mouth!" Cero hissed. He jerked his head toward the next tent over, and we turned to look. There, sitting a few feet away from us, just outside the opening of his tent, was Kit, staring at a wrinkled piece of paper in his hand.

A cold prickle started between my shoulder blades and rushed up the back of my neck. *He heard!* I closed my eyes. *Kit, please don't think that* we *think that* . . .

Then Kit looked up at us slowly. "My weakness excuse," he said, looking back down at the paper. "With a doc's Johnny Hancock and all."

We all looked away, exchanging miserable glances in an awkward silence that I could almost feel.

Cero broke the silence. "Well, I don't think you're weak, Bogus."

We all jumped in then, echoing Cero. "So, are you hungry?" Gabrielle blurted out. "You look hungry. Did they feed you dinner at the hospital?"

Kit shook his head and started moving toward us, lugging his M-16 by its sling. I scooted closer to Gabrielle to make room for him, and he dropped down beside me.

"You sure missed a good one here, Bud," Jason said. "Roast turkey and gravy, mashed sweet potatoes—"

Gabrielle frowned at Jason.

Kit reached down into the cargo pocket of his pants. "I'm not real hungry." He pulled out a bottle of pills and shook it. "Anyway, I've got these."

Kit's voice was more drawn out than I had ever heard it.

"What'd they give you?" Ping asked. "Tylenol III with codeine? Or—"

"Nope." Kit rubbed his eyes under his TEDs. "Just Motrin."

"Motrin?" Ping asked. "You *did* have a dislocated shoulder, didn't you?"

Kit nodded. "Yep. Sure did."

"And they gave you Motrin." Ping shook his head in disbelief.

"Yep." Kit shoved the bottle of pills back into his pocket.

"So—" Jason said, glancing at the rest of us. "Tell us. What happened?"

"They put my shoulder back in."

"Maybe he doesn't want to talk about it," I said quickly.

Kit closed his eyes. "Nope. I got a feeling that this is a story you'll all want to hear." He let his breath out slowly. "Well, I got to the emergency room, and this orthopedic surgeon kinda looked my shoulder over for a couple seconds, and then started yelling, 'Get that stricken look off your face, New Cadet! It's just a dislocated shoulder. It's not like you've got a sucking chest wound or something.'"

I saw Hickman's gaze slowly sink down to rest on the boot brush in his hand.

Good. The irony of that statement's similarity to his own wasn't lost on him. And he seemed to actually feel bad about it. Or at least he had the decency to act like it.

"You're kidding!" Jason said. "A *doctor* said that?"

"Oh, yeah," Kit said, his eyes growing more animated at our reactions. "And then he said that I should've had the intestinal fortitude to put my shoulder back in myself."

"That man," Gabrielle said, narrowing her eyes, "should not be a doctor."

"So, what did you say?" Cero asked, leaning forward.

Kit pulled at his sling. "The ol' standby—'No excuse, sir!'" He gritted his teeth as he shifted around, trying to get comfortable.

Bonanno grinned. "Good answer, Bogus!"

Kit shook his head. "Apparently not, 'cause that's when he really went off. He said, 'No excuse is right, New Cadet! What are you gonna do when you're in combat and your shoulder goes out? You gonna wait around for some doctor to help you out? Well, there's not gonna be a doctor out there beatin' the bushes with you. You're gonna have to put it back in by yourself or get a bullet in your brain waiting.'"

I winced. *Poor Kit! If it hadn't been for me and my stupid idea* . . .

"I'm so sorry," I whispered, wishing I could reach over and pat him on the back like my sister did to me when I was hurting. But I couldn't. Not at West Point. So I just looked at him instead, hoping he'd understand.

I was surprised to find him watching me. Our eyes met briefly, and then he nodded, a slight smile on his lips, before turning back to the rest of the squad.

It only took a second, and he hadn't said a word. But

he'd let me know that he didn't blame me.

Jason snorted. "Gotta love his bedside manner."

"'What are you gonna do when you're in combat?'" Gabrielle mimicked. "Sometimes I really hate this place."

Kit sighed. "I don't know . . . maybe he had a point." He moved one leg, then the other, straight out in front of him. "He showed me how to do it, but it wouldn't work." He shrugged, then winced. "So he started pumping a bunch of drugs into me and had a whole passel of nurses hold me down. And then he shut the door. When he did that, I knew it was really going to hurt. And it did." He looked around at all of us. "And here I am. End of story."

Nobody said anything for a while. The group of card players a couple of tents away, I noticed, seemed to have gotten louder.

"Hey, Bogus," Hickman finally said, still staring at his boot brush. "I just want to say that, uh, well—" He cleared his throat. "I don't know what you heard, you know, *earlier,* but I hope that you don't think that, uh, we—" He cleared his throat again. "I mean that *I* was talkin' about you or anything. 'Cause I wasn't, okay? I was just makin' a general statement about—"

Kit waved his words away. "Don't sweat it, Tommy."

Then the conversation changed, just like that—to the Patton movie we'd be watching later that night in the field beyond Tent City to favorite pizza restaurants to the rules for playing spades. Hickman took out his cards, and he and Jason played a hand against Gabrielle and Kit. I held Kit's cards for him, and he told me what to play. And before we knew it, the sky was black, and we were walking down the line of tents to the outskirts of Tent City.

It was like being at an old drive-in movie without the cars—the screen was about that big, set up near the wood line at the edge of the field. Or like an outdoor concert without a band—people everywhere, sitting on the grass with an excitement in the air that was almost electric.

"I don't believe it," Cero said. "A movie during Beast. The upperclassmen must be getting soft."

"Soft?" Gabrielle shook her head. "Leave it to this place to provide entertainment, and what do they come up with? The Patton movie. I don't call that soft, Cero. That's hardcore indoctrination."

"Third Squad!"

The voice behind us made us jump to our feet in a conditioned response and yell, "YES, SIR!" New cadets nearby stopped talking and eyed us nervously.

Cadet Black walked around to our front, shaking his head. "Glad to see your motivation level's still high, Third Squad, but this is recreation time. Sit down, sit down." He waved toward the ground, and as we resumed our positions on the grass, he sat with us. "So tell me." He smiled. "You guys ready for a good dose of Old Blood and Guts?"

"YES, SIR!"

"Glad to hear it, Third Squad. General George S. Patton is a big hero of mine, ever since I saw the movie during *my* Beast. It's kind of a tradition around here, to get you all fired up about being American soldiers. And George C. Scott, may he rest in peace, did a pretty decent job playing him, so enjoy."

"YES, SIR!"

"Well," he said, checking his watch, "I do have one order of business to take care of before this thing kicks

★

off." He looked at me. "Davis, Cadet Daily says you're a swimmer. That right?"

"Well, sir, I . . ." I swallowed. "I'm not a swimmer, exactly. I worked as a lifeguard for a couple years, taught little kids how to swim and stuff, but I never swam competitively or anything, sir."

Cadet Black nodded. "Just wanted to make sure you're not gonna sink on me, Davis." He leaned closer. "Okay, here's the deal. I'm sure you've been hearing noises about the Iron Man Competition that's going on tomorrow afternoon."

Jason reached over Kit, sitting next to me, and jabbed my arm.

I ignored him. "Yes, sir."

"Every company needs four individuals to represent them in the competition," Cadet Black said. "And Hardcore's entire chain of command—from the squad leaders on up to the Company Commander and First Sergeant—had a little powwow this evening and came up with a list of names. And yours, Davis"—he leaned closer—"was at the top of our list."

Me? At the top of their list? I looked down at my hands, not really seeing them. *Everyone was talking about me? All the squad leaders, platoon leaders, and platoon sergeants—even First Sergeant Stockel?* I looked up at Cadet Black, and all I could do was nod.

"Understand," he went on, "this is totally voluntary." He held up his hand. "It's highly encouraged, mind you, but if you really don't want to do it, we won't hold it against you." His lips twitched. "Too much." He paused, watching me. "So what will it be, Davis—Go or No-Go?"

I didn't hesitate. "Go, sir!" *My name was at the top of their list!*

He grinned and slapped me across the back. "Didn't doubt it for a second."

I stopped myself from smiling up at him. I had to act cool. Not too excited. As if I'd expected it all along.

"Our Athletic Officer, Cadet Barrington, will be meeting with you sometime tomorrow morning to give you the details, but basically, what you'll be doing is swimming out and back to this raft that'll be in the middle of Lake Frederick. Then, as soon as you hit the beach, you've got to knock out fifty push-ups—"

Fifty push-ups? I cringed inside. *Great. I've never done fifty push-ups at one time in my life!*

"—and fifty sit-ups as fast as you can, and finish up by running a couple of miles around the lake. Piece of cake."

"Yes, sir," I said.

"I'll be counting your push-ups and sit-ups, okay? But we'll talk about all that tomorrow."

"Yes, sir."

Cadet Black stretched to his feet, and I stood with him. "We're expecting big things out of Hardcore, Davis. We've got an awesome team. We've got this guy from Fourth Platoon, Ziegler—he's a nationally ranked swimmer—and some water polo player from Second Platoon named Fritz. And then there's Valente from First Platoon. You probably know him, Davis—he's a recruited track guy."

I shook my head. "No, sir."

"Well, supposedly he can run the mile in 3:58 or something. But we"—and I thought I saw him wink at me then—"haven't been able to try him out in the Black Group because he's been on a no-running profile most of the summer." He shrugged. "Looks like he's got some recurring heel injury, and your coach doesn't want to take any chances with it. Tomorrow will be the first time he's run all summer."

I nodded. *A 3:58 miler? A nationally ranked swimmer?*
Suddenly I didn't feel so excited anymore. *How could I be
at the top of their list with those guys on it, too?*

"Oh, yeah!" He slammed his fist into the palm of his
other hand. "We are going to kick some serious butt, Davis!"
He laughed, shaking his head. "The rules say that each
company has to have at least one female on its team—"

At least one female? I felt my heart collapse in on itself
and sink into my stomach.

"—and well, in our case, Davis, that was clearly a no-
brainer. For obvious reasons." He slapped me across my
back again. "Get some decent sleep tonight, Davis. After
the movie, of course. We'll need you nice and rested up for
tomorrow."

"Yes, sir," I mumbled.

"Have a good one, Third Squad!" he said. And he was
gone.

I sank back into the grass, feeling numb. And stupid.
At the top of their list. Yeah, top of their female *list, he
meant. I should've known—Hickman was right. Why . . .
how could I have expected anything else?*

Gabrielle nudged me. "Hey, Andi, what's wrong?
Bummed you won't be lounging under the sun with me
tomorrow?"

"No, Gab." I sighed. I didn't have the heart—or energy—
to go into it now. "Just tired, I guess."

"No, that's not it," Kit said. "It's what Cadet Black said
about needing at least one female on the Iron Man team.
You think that's why you got asked to do it, don't you, Andi?"

I looked at him, not being able to read clearly what his
face said in the dark. Was I that transparent? I always

★ 255

thought I'd been so good at hiding things at home.

"No way," Gabrielle said, shaking her head. "Cadet Black said picking Andi was a no-brainer." She leaned closer and peered into my face. "That *is* what's bothering you! I don't believe it." She crossed her arms and huffed. "Andi, sometimes you are so . . . weird! So what if they needed a female on the team? What's the big deal? I mean, what are you trying to prove, anyway? That you're a guy or something? Well, guess what, Hon?" She reached behind me and snapped my bra. "You're not!"

I glared at her as I adjusted my bra, then looked down at my hands. "Look, guys. It's not that big a deal, okay? It's just that . . . well, it would've been nice to be asked just because . . . I can do it, you know? Like the three other guys were asked 'cause they can do it? Everyone's just going to think that the only reason I'm out there is because I'm a female, not because anybody seriously believes I can win the thing."

"If that's what you think, Andi, then you're just going to have to prove them wrong," Kit said, "and smoke everyone. You know, beat 'em at their own game."

Beat 'em at their own game? I hadn't thought of it like that before. But . . . maybe I could.

"You've only been doing it all summer," Gabrielle said.

Then I noticed the new cadets around me were turning their attention to the screen at the edge of the field. The image of an American flag filled the entire screen, almost glowing in the night. A buzz of conversation came over the sound system, and then a commanding voice boomed over the buzz, "ATTEN-*HUT!*" And all was quiet, over the sound system and in the field in front of the screen, except for the muffled click of footsteps, moving closer. A man in uniform rose up from the bottom of the screen as if he were climbing a flight of stairs into it. First the helmet appeared, black with four silver stars emblazoned across its front. Then the face, stern and unsmiling, looked at us out of a pair of narrowed eyes. Then the chest, covered with medals and sashes and braids, and gleaming black riding boots completed the picture. A trumpet fanfare announced his presence—a ramrod-straight, crisp, military figure superimposed over the flag.

"Be seated." The figure on the screen paused for the sound of shifting chairs to cease. "Now, I want you to remember," he continued in a gravelly voice, "that all this stuff you've heard about America not wanting to fight, wanting to stay out of the war, is a lot of *horse* dung!" The man slowly paced back and forth as he spoke, punctuating his words with a riding crop he held in his hand but never taking his eyes off us. "Americans traditionally *love* to fight. All *real* Americans *love* the sting of battle."

"HU-AH!" cried the new cadets around me. I glanced at Kit beside me. He was clutching his hurt shoulder, but he was leaning forward, his eyes locked on the screen.

He's really getting into this! For some reason Kit's intensity surprised me. I'd just been grateful to have something—anything—take my mind off the Iron Man Competition. But now I turned back to the screen, intrigued.

"When you were kids," the soldier went on, "you all admired the champion marble shooter, the fastest runner, big league ball players, the toughest boxers. Americans *love* a winner and will not *tolerate* a loser! Americans play to win *all the time*! I wouldn't give a hoot in Hell for a man who lost and laughed. That's why Americans have *never* lost and *will never* lose a war. Because the very *thought* of losing is *hateful* to Americans."

Kit leaned toward me, his eyes still on the screen. "That's why," he whispered, "you got picked for the Iron Man Competition, Andi. Not because they needed a female, and not because you were the best they could get. But because you're *that* kind of person." He nodded at the screen. "You're a winner. And everybody knows it."

"Shhh!" Gabrielle hissed at us. "Can't you see I'm trying to watch a movie here?"

SUNDAY, 8 AUGUST
1430

The sun was bright and hot overhead, causing little waves of heat to shimmer over the surface of the lake. The air was soaked with heat, but more suffocating was watching the tense faces of my competitors as they prepared themselves for the race, bouncing and stretching on the strip of silty, rocky sand that bordered the water.

I stripped off my Gym Alpha as the King of Beast had instructed over the bullhorn, then began to warm up, wearing only my swimsuit. I stretched my quads and hamstrings, and I ran in place, all the while sneaking glances at my competition, thirty-six of us in all. Most of them were guys; I had expected that. I counted only nine females, including me—one from every company, and no more. One of them I recognized—the girl with the Asics I had seen at the Field House during track tryouts earlier in the summer. We hadn't run in the same group that day, but I remembered watching her lope across the finish, easily nailing her mile time at 5:30 on the dot.

I shook out my arms and faced the water, trying to choke down my mounting nervousness. *Doesn't mean she can swim. Most runners sink like rocks when they hit water. Plus she's not a guy.* The guys were the ones I was really concerned about. Kit had clarified my mission last night. Beat 'em at their own game, he had said. And that was exactly what I'd set out to do—prove that I wasn't out here just because I was a girl. I couldn't worry about another girl beating me, too. I'd go crazy if I did.

I watched two upperclassmen swim out to the raft in the middle of the lake. The King of Beast had said they'd be there, watching us. "You may use any stroke or combination of strokes to get there," he had said during his prerace briefing, "but you must touch the raft before returning to the shore. Anybody who fails to do so will be disqualified."

Most of the guys around me looked like swimmers— stocky, big upper bodies, strong legs. It only made sense; they also had the kind of arms that could crank out pushups forever. *But it doesn't mean they can run.*

I played my strategy over in my mind. I would get a decent start during the swim, struggle through the pushups somehow, then make up time during the sit-ups and the run. Especially the run.

"All new cadets participating in the Iron Man Competition, fall in at the start line at this time!"

Cadet Black scooped up my running shoes and Gym Alpha from the sand at my feet. "I'll be looking for you when you exit the water, Davis," he said. "Go get 'em!" And he was gone before I could say, "Yes, sir."

In a few seconds it'll be all over. Once it started, I knew my nervousness would leave me. My body would take over then, and whatever would happen would happen. I moved with the others to find a spot in the front rank between the two orange cones that marked the starting line.

I stared out at the water. *I'll swim mostly crawl. It's fastest.* I chewed on the inside of my lip. *I don't know . . . the water looks pretty murky. And there's going to be lots of people, too. Lots of splashing, lots of waves.* I let my breath out slowly. *Maybe switch off between breast stroke and crawl . . . probably more breast than crawl since I'll need to see where I'm going.* Then it struck me. See where I'm going! A panicky feeling flared up in my gut. *I've got contacts in! If I lose them in the water . . .*

Without contacts I couldn't see past the tip of my nose. I'd never be able to find my way out of the water, let alone make the run. *And if I don't make the run . . .*

I frantically scanned the bystanders for Cadet Black. *Maybe he's got goggles!* But I knew the thought was idiotic. *Why in the world would he have goggles? And even if he did, who says they'd let me wear them?* Goggles weren't part of the prescribed uniform, and exceptions never happened during Beast.

Come on. Just calm down. You used to lifeguard all the time with contacts in. Just deal with this. I turned back to the water, drumming my fingers on the sides of my legs. *I'll just have to swim lifesaving strokes, with my head out of the water most of the time. It's almost as fast.* I knew the thought wasn't very convincing, but it was all I had.

The King of Beast was standing off to the side of us now. "Remember what MacArthur said, New Cadets: 'Upon the fields of friendly strife are sown the seeds that upon other fields, on other days, will bear the fruits of victory.'"

MacArthur's Opinion of Athletics. I had memorized it out of *Bugle Notes* two weeks ago.

"Only one of you can be the victor, so have fun." And the buzzer on the bullhorn went off.

Only one can be the victor. I sprinted down the sand and into the lake, already churning from the others around me. I plunged forward, attacking the water with strong thrusts of my arms, my head above the waves with eyes fixed on the raft before me. The water was warm, like sweat.

Bodies were pulling ahead of me. I knew I couldn't keep the pace I had set much longer; doing this modified crawl stroke was anaerobic—my lungs felt like they were about to explode. I changed to breast stroke until I recovered my breath, then switched back, alternating between the two. *Come on! Come on! Come on! Push it a little harder!*

After I had slapped the raft with the palm of my hand and was on my way back, I realized that swimming the modified strokes was slowing me down. More people were passing me, it seemed, than I was passing. So I squeezed my eyes shut and stuck my head under the water, counting out six strokes of crawl before coming up for air. Then I'd do three strokes of modified breast to get me heading in the right direction, and dunk my head again, counting out six more strokes. At last my fingertips touched bottom, and I was stumbling out of the water and up onto the sand, my lungs clamoring for air. Blood pounded in my ears.

"Davis! Davis!"

Cadet Black was running toward me, my shoes in one hand and the rest of my clothes in his other. "Get into the Leaning Rest, *now!* You're the third female out. Let's go!"

Third female? That's it? I collapsed into the Leaning Rest position, heaving lungs full of air at the ground. "What . . . about . . . overall? Sir?"

"I don't know . . . upper third, maybe? Come on, Davis! Knock 'em out! Every second counts!"

Upper third. I clenched my teeth and started pumping out push-ups. *I've got to do better than that!*

"One . . . two . . . three . . . four . . . five . . . six . . ." Cadet Black counted.

My arms and legs were trembling from muscle fatigue. I pushed my rear end upward, keeping my arms fully extended, and rested for a few seconds. Then I dug my hands deeper into the sand and hit it again.

"Ten . . . eleven . . . twelve . . . you've gotta break the plane, Davis . . . fourteen . . ."

I felt like I had a hundred-pound ruck on my back, pushing me into the ground. "Can I go . . . down . . . on my knees . . . for a second?" I gasped. I was at twenty-five, halfway there.

"Yeah, sure," Cadet Black said. "It's allowed." But he sounded disappointed.

I sank down on my knees and shook out my arms. My hair, matted and sandy, had fallen across my face. Sand coated my arms up to the elbows. I looked around, pushing my hair aside. Some of the guys were already on the sit-ups. I forced myself back into the Leaning Rest and squeezed out more push-ups, two and three at a time. Muscles I never knew I had burned.

"You're at forty, Davis. You're lookin' good. Don't stop. Just ten to go. One female's already on the sit-ups. You've gotta hustle now."

Come . . . on now! After . . . it's all over . . . you won't . . . even . . . remember . . . the pain!

Somehow I cranked out the rest, one by miserable one. Then I flipped over on my back for the sit-ups.

Cadet Black grabbed my feet to anchor them. "All right, Davis. Hit it!"

Soon my ears were filled with my rhythmic breathing. *Now's the time to start making your move.* I shut my eyes and concentrated on hammering them out. *Push it! Push it!*

"Good to go!" Cadet Black said. "Now you're cooking, Davis. Just like a machine. Forty-nine . . . fifty! Now, get those shoes on. Every second counts!" He thrust my socks into my hands.

I looked around me, panting, as I crammed my sand-covered feet into my socks. One by one, guys were staggering out of the sand and heading for the trail around the lake, but the Asics girl was nowhere in sight. *Thank God!* I licked my lips and crunched sand between my teeth.

Cadet Black shoved one of my shoes on my foot while I tied the other shoe's laces. My hands shook.

"One female's just started the run, Davis!" he yelled as I scrambled to my feet. "Go get her!"

And then I was gone, chasing down the bodies in front of me. *Three events down, one to go. This last one's got to count.*

The trail consisted of dirt with a few rocks and tree roots to trip over, and it was narrow, barely wide enough for two running abreast. But as my feet pounded over it, I felt good. It reminded me of the trails I had run in cross country races. I started to relax and got into a rhythm. The King of Beast had said that the trail around the lake was just under three miles, so I adjusted my pace. Even though my body was tired, I felt energized. I was running! It had been over a week since I'd run.

I easily caught the only girl ahead of me and said, "Good job! Keep it up!" as I passed her. She was short and had arms that would've been big for a guy's. *A swimmer.*

Then I got to work, picking off the guys in front of me, one by one. *Just keep it controlled. Don't rush it.*

Every so often new cadets and upperclassmen standing in twos or threes lined the trail, cheering us on.

"Way to go!"

"Keep it up!"

"You're the number one female, Miss!"

The lake was always on my left, with an occasional cluster of trees blocking my view of it. I knew I'd be able to tell that I'd hit the halfway point when I saw the beach area, rows of bodies in black swimsuits sprawled across white towels over the sun-fried grass. Even during free time new cadets congregated in uniform rows. *I guess that's what happens after six weeks of Beast.*

The sun was really beating down now, causing streaks of grimy sweat to run into my eyes and down my arms. At the same time, the sun had dried my swimsuit, which, I noticed with irritation, started to ride up on my rear. But the biggest discomfort I had to deal with was my chest. The Lycra of my swimsuit was just not matching the performance of a Jogbra.

"Go, Andi, go!"

It was Kit, standing with Cadet Daily and Ping along the trail. They had come all the way out here just for me. In all my years of running, my own dad had never managed to do that.

"You're number thirteen, Davis!" Cadet Daily yelled as I passed them.

Thirteen? I felt my stomach tighten. *That's not good enough!*

"Those guys are flaggin' up there! Take 'em!"

"Do it, Andi!" I heard Ping yell. "Do it!"

I glanced over at the water. The rows of black on white were directly across now.

Halfway. Gotta pick it up. I turned up the pace a notch. Slowly I increased my speed, like winding up a spring, until the moment I'd start my kick. Then I'd let everything go.

I focused on my breathing, keeping it steady. I fixed my eyes on the bare back of each guy ahead of me, passing one . . . two . . . three. I vaguely remember thinking, *That's interesting!* when I passed Hickman and Gabrielle, standing together, cheering me on. I passed another guy and another. The rows of new cadet sunbathers came into view. *Okay— now!* I started kicking it toward the finish, though I couldn't see it yet. The trail, now lined with shouting new cadets, widened into the stretch of sand that bordered the water.

"Finish strong, Davis!" I thought I heard Cero's voice booming above the others.

The orange cones stood about two hundred yards away, looking like tiny fluorescent triangles in the distance. One more guy was within reach. *You've got to give it everything!* I started sprinting faster, faster. The cones were getting closer. One hundred and fifty yards . . . one hundred . . .

I blew past the guy and kept cranking toward the finish. Fifty yards . . . twenty . . . ten . . .

I saw Jason in the crowd, red-faced and yelling, his fist pounding the air. "Go! Go! Go!"

And then some guy out of nowhere came from behind and lunged across the finish before me, landing facefirst in the sand.

I slowed to a trot, then doubled over, nearly collapsing on the ground myself.

"Gotta keep walking, Davis," Cadet Black said, draping one of my arms over his shoulder.

Jason ran up to us and took my other arm. "Way to go, Andi! You did great!"

"Awesome," Cadet Black agreed, nodding his head. "Awesome. You came in eighth, Davis. Almost seventh. If that guy hadn't dived across the finish right at the end . . . Anyway, you beat all the females. None of them even came close. You've done Third Platoon proud."

Eighth. My throat tightened, pressing against that growing, aching lump. I took deep breath after deep breath, trying to choke it down, but it remained. *Eighth.* I could feel tears settling in the corners of my eyes. I hadn't done what I had set out to do. I hadn't won.

"Davis! Way to kick some butt!" I looked up. Three bodies were running toward us. One of them, his arm in a sling, lagged behind the other two as they wove through the cadets clustered near the finish line. Then I heard Cero's voice behind me. "You were flying, Davis!"

And before I knew it, all of Third Squad was with me at the finish—surrounding me, congratulating me—as if I *had* won, after all. It didn't seem to matter to them that I wasn't the best. I had done *my* best. And that was enough. For them.

I pulled my arms away from the shoulders that had supported me and swiped my hand across my eyes.

"Thanks. I think I can walk on my own, now."

And then I smiled. It was enough for me, too.

Your left, your right,
Your left, your right.
You're out of sight,
You're dynamite.
And it won't be long,
Till you get back home.
—U.S. ARMY MARCHING CADENCE

CHAPTER 16

MONDAY, 9 AUGUST
0520

BESIDES THE STARS and a sliver of moon, the sky was black. This morning beams from hundreds of flashlights and the *clink-clank* of entrenching tools had beaten the sun in driving the crickets from the field. It was too early for conversation, and even if it hadn't been, I doubted anyone would have felt much like talking, anyway. In just a few hours, when we had marched back from Lake Frederick, Beast would be over.

Gabrielle and I dragged our gear out of our tent and up-rooted the tent pegs that anchored our tent in the ground. Then we stood, staring at the canvas collapsed on the grass.

"Tonight we get to sleep in a real bed," Gabrielle whispered.

"Yeah." I took a deep breath and let it out slowly. "Can't wait."

We looked at each other. The thought, we both knew,

wasn't entirely comforting. We'd be back in the barracks, which would be filled with upperclassmen we'd never met. And their mission: to make our lives miserable.

Fifteen minutes later H Company was all formed up and standing at attention, wearing Kevlars and LCEs, our rucks at our feet and M-16s on our shoulders.

First Sergeant Stockel stood before us, our guidon waving atop its staff, stuck into the ground behind him. And beyond lay Tent City, now nothing more than an empty field.

"H COMPANY, STAND AT . . . *EASE!*" First Sergeant Stockel waited as we shifted into position.

"Six long weeks ago you stumbled through West Point's gate as dirty, nasty civilians, shuffling behind your mommas and daddies. Today you're going to march through that very same gate as soldiers. You're gonna have a pack on your back and a weapon in your hands and the most miserable summer of your lives behind you. So hold your heads high, Hardcore. This is your victory march."

"HU-AH!" we yelled in response.

"That's right, Hardcore. You've earned it." He nodded his head slowly. "But remember, one decisive battle doesn't win the war." He paused. "You've come a long way, Hardcore. But you've got even longer still to go. If you think because Beast is over, the worst is over, think again. It's *never* over, Hardcore. Not today. Not after Plebe Year. Not even when—if—the day comes that you get to stand in front of a formation like I am, now. At West Point, it's . . . *never* . . . over." Then First Sergeant Stockel came to the position of attention. "Just a little something for you to ponder while you're marching back. H COMPANY—"

"PLATOON!" bellowed the four platoon sergeants.

"ATTEN-*TION!*"

And in one solid movement the one hundred and twenty members of H Company snapped to attention, head and eyes to the front with heels locked.

"The following individuals, report to the front of the formation!" First Sergeant Stockel yelled. "New Cadets Valente, Fritz, Davis—"

Me?

"—and Ziegler, *front and center!*"

I saw a new cadet from First Platoon, then one from Second Platoon, step away from their squads and hurry to the front of the formation.

Oh! They're the guys that did the Iron Man Competition with me! But why—

"Go!" Ping whispered beside me.

I scurried through the narrow space between Third and Fourth Squads, and up the aisle in the center of the formation to the front. The other three new cadets were already there, standing in a row facing First Sergeant Stockel. I slid into line at the end.

"Okay, New Cadets," First Sergeant Stockel said to all of us. "About, face!"

We spun around. The entire company stood before us—four platoons, neat and square. My eyes jerked toward Third Platoon. I spotted Cadet Black first, out in front, then Cero, way back in Third Squad, his head sticking up above all the others in the platoon.

First Sergeant Stockel stepped around in front of us, our company guidon in his hand.

"Just as the battle flags of the Civil War bore their units' scars, this guidon wears your history. I know it hasn't been shredded by bullets or sullied by blood, but the rain has stained it, the wind has worn it, and the sun has faded it. It's been with you at every formation and on every P.T. run. It's marked where we camped and flown before you when you drilled on the Plain. It's been your rallying point for six weeks, Hardcore. And today, it'll lead you home."

His words gave me goose bumps. *Home.* Yes, West Point was a great place to call home.

"Traditionally, a unit chose its guidon bearer by his character. Only the most courageous and honorable man was entrusted with protecting the guidon, because to the soldiers in combat, their guidon was more than a piece of cloth hanging off a pole. It was their standard, the heart of the unit, the rock that everyone clung to in the thick of battle. And so the guidon bearer was charged to defend it, even if it cost his life." He paused, turning to look at the four of us, standing behind him. "Our guidon needs soldiers worthy of carrying it. Your four classmates here have demonstrated that they possess the physical strength and mental toughness to carry out the job. They proved themselves during the Iron Man Competition yesterday, and they won't let us down today."

H Company roared its approval.

They're cheering for us . . . for me*!* I could feel the pride and excitement bubble up inside me, warming my heart and prickling my skin. I was experiencing something close to what I'd always imagined gold medalists must feel at the Olympics when the Star-Spangled Banner unfurls and the anthem is played. It was the most awesome feeling in the world. I peeked over at Third Platoon again, and a smile started at the corners of my lips. *Be military. Don't you dare smile!* I forced my eyes to stare past the formation, at the horizon. The sun was working its magic, slowly changing the night into day. Streaks of pink wove in and out of the thin gray clouds, causing everything hidden by the darkness to become visible.

I wondered: If my parents were here now, would they be cheering for me, too? But I let the thought go. I knew, deep down, that my parents' seeing me now wouldn't change a thing. To them I'd be the same Andi I'd always been; it was unrealistic for me to expect anything else. But *I* knew different, and that's all that counted now.

First Sergeant Stockel had disappeared behind us. "New Cadets," I heard him say, "about, face!"

We turned to face him.

He nodded. "All right. When I say, 'Post,' I want you to render a salute and move out." He took a step back and fell into the position of attention. "POST!"

I saluted with the others and hurried back to my spot in Third Squad.

I can't believe it—I'm going to carry the guidon back!

"SICK CALL, FALL OUT AND FALL IN BEHIND CADET BARRINGTON AT THE REAR OF FORMATION!" First Sergeant Stockel bellowed.

Down our squad on my right, I saw Kit reach for his ruck at his feet.

Kit's not marching back with us. The realization of that fact hit me—hard—for the first time. If I could've carried all his gear and his M-16 in addition to my own so he could make the march back with us, I would have done it. But it was impossible—West Point had its rules, and I wasn't strong enough.

Kit's face looked strained as he heaved the ruck over his one good shoulder, trying to hide his pain. Then with one unsteady step backward, he was gone.

I couldn't whisper good-bye or even nod as he passed behind me. I could only stand there, staring blankly at the stubble on the back of New Cadet Monroe's neck. Then I scooted my ruck and myself one space to the right with the rest of Third Squad, and the void that Kit had left behind was filled.

When the injured new cadets had disappeared behind the formation, First Sergeant Stockel ordered the platoon sergeants to conduct safety briefings, then turned the company over to them.

"Okay, Third Platoon," Cadet Black yelled. "You've got twelve miles to go today, so I want to see you emptying those canteens. You get three short breaks, so make the most of them. We're gonna take a slightly different route back. We've got this little detour through Camp Buckner to break up the monotony." He grinned. "That'll be a rush, Third Platoon. Those yearlings will be watching you, seeing what you're all about. Remember, they just finished spending a year in your shoes a couple of months ago, so they're gonna be hopping in their little booties to see somebody else on the bottom of the totem pole."

A *whole year of this*. I could hardly imagine life past this formation, let alone all the way to next summer.

"First Platoon!" I heard First Platoon's platoon sergeant yell. "Right . . . *face!*"

I turned my attention to First Platoon in front of us. The new cadets, hunched from the weight of their rucks, wobbled and bumped into each other as they turned ninety degrees to the right. "Guidon bearer, post! Columns from the left, forward . . . march!" And First Platoon started across the field in double file. New Cadet Valente sprinted to get himself in front of them, his ruck bouncing on his back, and the guidon, held in his hands, waving above his head.

That's going to be me soon. I couldn't wait.

Then I heard Cadet Black say my name. I snapped my eyes to his face.

"You'll get the handoff after the second break."

"Yes, sir." *The guidon.*

"Second Platoon!" shouted Second Platoon's platoon sergeant. "Columns from the left! Forward, march!"

"Get it up and get it on, Third Platoon!" Cadet Black yelled at us. "Let's go!"

Hickman asked me to hold his M-16 for him while he hoisted his ruck onto his back, then he held mine for me. And before I knew it, I was one cog in a long, camouflaged marching machine that stretched across Tent City and into the woods.

0610

The first part of the march was mostly downhill, and the canopy of branches overhead dimmed the woods, making the march seem almost effortless. My mind slipped into neutral as I watched the ground in front of me pass beneath my boots. It was almost like sleepwalking. Only my aching arms and shoulders from yesterday's competition reminded me that I was, indeed, awake.

We took our first break in a large clearing, stopping barely long enough to top off canteens and check feet, then scrambled down a rocky path to a dirt road, out of the shade and into the sun. By then the morning was stifling, and as we marched, lining either side of the road, clouds of dust kicked up under our feet, choking our lungs.

Cadet Daily stayed close to us during most of the

march, striking up short conversations to pass the time. I heard him behind me talking to Ping about how he had spent last summer, working with a bunch of drill sergeants at a place called Fort Jackson. He talked to Hickman in front of me about major-league baseball players. I even heard snatches of the discussion he had with Gabrielle about Philadelphia cheese steaks. But before he got to me, the column halted.

"Okay, Third Squad," Cadet Daily said. "Camp Buckner's just ahead."

I squinted. Up ahead new cadets were abandoning the edges of the road to make a formation in the middle.

"We're gonna march through that place like we own it. But no gazing around, you got that? You don't want those yearlings to think discipline was slack this summer. Do you?" He smirked. "I don't think so. First impressions are lasting impressions, Third Squad. It's trite, but it's oh so true. Now, move out to the road and get in platoon formation. Let's go!"

We formed up and started moving down the dirt road, Cadet Black marching to our left, calling cadence. *"YOUR LEFT, YOUR RIGHT. NOW KEEP IT IN STEP. YOUR LEFT, YOUR RIGHT, YOUR LE-E-EFT!"*

My heart started pounding in my chest just from the thought of seeing the yearlings looking at us. We marched up a hill, across a hardtop road, and through an opened gate. A weathered metal sign with a West Point crest stood off to one side: Camp Buckner.

Cadet Black looked at us as he marched. "Now, I want three things outa you. I want you standing tall. I want you looking good. And I want you sounding off. You got that, sports fans?"

"YES, SIR!"

We marched past a steep hill that rose up sharply on our left with long tin trailers stuck into its side, like stair steps, to its rounded top. Bodies in BDUs streamed out of them.

The yearlings!

The road curved to our left. I could hear the boom of voices from the other companies ahead of us, growing louder. As the road straightened out, we were suddenly flanked on both sides with yearlings in BDUs. Waving, cheering, some grinning, others scowling, but all looking at us, a river of camouflage flowing forward, for as far as I could see.

"ALL RIGHT, THIRD PLATOON!" Cadet Black shouted over the roar. "SEEING US ISN'T GOOD ENOUGH. I WANT THEM TO HEAR US!"

I could hear the excitement in his voice, and it was contagious.

"I'M A STEAMROLLER, BABY!" Cadet Black sang. The veins of his neck bulged and his arms flexed at his sides, reflecting his effort.

"AND I'M ROLLIN' DOWN THE LINE!"

I could feel Third Platoon's tension mounting all around me. I peeked at the throng of upperclassmen watching from the sidelines. *They don't look any older than we do!* When I looked at the Beast cadre—First Sergeant Stockel, Cadet Black, Cadet Daily, the King of Beast—in my mind I knew they were only three or four years older than I. But they seemed ancient, like they'd been around forever, had seen the world, and had come back again to disclose its secrets to us.

"SO YOU BETTER GET OUTA MY WAY, NOW—"

No gazing around, remember? I stared dead ahead, with

the most serious, military, "Don't mess with me!" look on my face that I could muster, belting the phrases back.

"'FORE I ROLL ALL OVER YOU!"

"Way to go, Third Platoon!" Cadet Black said after we had gone through Camp Buckner and pulled off into the woods for our second break. "You looked great out there. Now, fall out and take a load off."

I changed my socks and leaned back against my ruck, the sling of my M-16 wrapped around my leg. "Wake me up when it's time to go," I mumbled to Gabrielle and closed my eyes.

"Davis!"

My eyes flew open. Cadet Black was standing over me, the guidon in his hands.

"You've got a job to do, Iron Woman." He raised the guidon above his head and drove it into the ground between his feet. "Get on your ruck and report to First Sergeant Stockel."

I pushed myself to my feet and grabbed my gear. "Yes, sir."

Cadet Black hovered around me as I pulled on my ruck. "Don't forget to sling arms, Davis, since you'll need your hands free to carry the guidon. Carry your weapon across your back with the barrel pointing down. It'll bother you less that way. All right?"

"Yes, sir," I said, swinging my M-16 across my back the way he said.

"Your canteens filled?"

"Yes, sir. Both of them, sir." I was amused that he was fussing over me like some kind of mother hen. I slapped my Kevlar onto my head and snapped the chin strap.

He smacked me on the shoulder, almost making me

topple over. "You'll be setting the pace for the company, Davis." He grinned. "Don't dog us out too bad. And whatever you do, don't let that guidon touch the ground. Do us proud. Now, get on outa here!"

"Yes, sir!" I yanked the guidon out of the dirt and ran as fast as my load would allow over to First Sergeant Stockel. I raised my right hand in a salute and gasped with the little breath I had left, "Sir! New Cadet Davis reports to First Sergeant Stockel as ordered!" *Whew!*

First Sergeant Stockel stared at me in his intimidating way, then looked at his watch, making me hold my salute. "You're late, Davis. I was starting to think I was gonna have to find a replacement for you. Thought maybe you fell out back there or something."

"No, sir!" I gritted my teeth. *I've never fallen out on* anything, *sir.*

He smirked, as if he had read my mind. "Leading the company won't be like going on a little run, Davis. Or like marching back in formation. There's no accordion effect up there to give you that little breather, now and then, you know. It's just plain hammering." He narrowed his eyes. "Sure you can handle it?"

"Yes, sir!" I shouted, louder.

"Okay, then." First Sergeant Stockel returned my salute. "We shall see."

He spun away from me and bellowed, "H COMPANY, FALL IN!" New cadets scrambled for their gear, their squad leaders herding them into two columns. When all the platoons were ready, First Sergeant Stockel marched me to the front of the company.

"H COMPANY!" First Sergeant Stockel shouted over his shoulder. "FOR-*WARD*, MARCH!" And we stepped off, side by side, onto a narrow trail in the woods, the equipment of one hundred and twenty new cadets in two columns thumping behind us.

First Sergeant Stockel was right about one thing: Leading the company was no stroll in the park. He started out at a furious pace, more like speed walking than marching, and when I jogged to keep up with him, he snarled, "Save your running for the track, Davis!"

He wasn't much of a companion. He said very little, but when he did speak, he grunted in one-sentence statements: "Over that rise the trail will open up," or "You're crowding me, Davis," or "Let's pick it up a little." I felt no comfort from his presence like I had from my squadmates, plodding out the miles with me.

Finally we came out of the woods and into a huge grassy area packed with new cadets resting—boots off, rucks opened. Guidons stood, marking off each company's turf.

"West Point's golf course." First Sergeant Stockel said to me over his shoulder. He led us to an empty spot and halted the company.

"Good job, Davis," he said. "Now, plant that standard"—he waved at the guidon—"here and ground your gear. I'll release you to your platoon when your replacement comes. Be sure to drink plenty of water. You look like some wet rat I just dragged outa the Hudson." And he was gone before I could respond.

"Good job, Davis." I smiled. The only positive thing First Sergeant Stockel had said to me all summer. I raised my weary arms above my head like Cadet Black had done, and drove the guidon into the grass between my feet. It was as good a feeling as ripping through the tape at the finish line.

I shrugged off my ruck and yanked off my Kevlar. I rubbed my arms and stretched my back, looking at the new cadets around me. *First Platoon*. Nobody I knew well enough to recount my experience of marching beside First Sergeant Stockel. *Where's Gab when I need her?*

I took out my canteen and poured some water over my head, feeling the relative coolness sink into my skin. Then I emptied the rest of it down my throat.

"Heat stroke?" I heard First Sergeant Stockel's voice from somewhere behind me.

"Yeah. It's rough," another upperclassman said. "The guy wins the Iron Man yesterday and can't make the march today." They were getting closer. "Had to be picked up by the truck. It's really rough."

Ziegler? New Cadet Ziegler from Fourth Platoon had won yesterday, killing everyone. Ziegler *fell out of the march? No way!* I'd be sure to mention this to Hickman later on.

"Yeah," First Sergeant Stockel said. "Yesterday probably wiped him out."

They were only a few feet behind me now. I just stood there, my back toward them, watching the breeze toss the guidon back and forth, back and forth.

"Well . . ." I heard First Sergeant Stockel sigh. "You got a replacement for him? I mean, at this point I'd take just about anyone. *Somebody's* got to carry it in—"

Before the thought was fully formed in my mind, I turned around and said it. "I'll do it, sir!"

First Sergeant Stockel and the other cadet, whom I recognized as Fourth Platoon's platoon sergeant, just stood there, staring back at me.

I swallowed and tried again. "I'll carry the guidon, sir!"

I held my breath, my eyes locked on First Sergeant Stockel's face. *You said you'd take* anyone.

But he shook his head. "You already carried the guidon, Davis."

"Aw"—the upperclassman waved his hand—"let her do it, Stockel. It saves me the headache. Plus"—he smiled at me—"I don't think anyone's gonna object to Davis carrying it in the rest of the way."

First Sergeant Stockel took off his glasses and rubbed his eyes. "All right!" he snapped, squinting at me. "But just make sure you blacken your boots and dust yourself off, Davis. I don't want the whole world thinking I let a grub ball carry in my guidon!"

"Yes, sir!" I yelled. "Thank you, sir!" And I ripped into my ruck, a huge grin spreading across my face. I couldn't help myself.

And, shock of all shocks, First Sergeant Stockel grinned back.

1055

The entire regiment of new cadets assembled on the golf course parking lot, platoon behind platoon and company behind company—A Company through I.

"ALL RIGHT, HARDCORE!" First Sergeant Stockel yelled, his eyes bright behind his wire-framed glasses. "THIS IS IT—THE FINAL STRETCH. THE *HOME* STRETCH. ARE YOU MOTIVATED?"

"MOTIVATED! MOTIVATED! MOTIVATED, SIR!" we screamed in response.

"I CAN SEE THAT!" First Sergeant Stockel yelled back. "BUT . . . ARE YOU ALL FIRED UP?"

I could feel the power building behind me. *"FIRED UP! FIRED UP! FIRED UP, SIR!"*

"THEN LET'S GO DOWN THERE"—he threw his arm behind him in the direction of West Point—"AND SHOW 'EM WE'RE THE MOST MOTIVATED, DEDICATED, HIGH-SPEED, LOW-DRAG COMPANY OUT HERE!"

"HU-AH!"

"DO IT, HARDCORE! COMPANY, ATTEN-*TION!*"

I heard the sharp clap of equipment behind me like the snap of a whip.

Cadet Haywood, our company commander, strode to the front of the formation and exchanged salutes with First Sergeant Stockel. He must've seen my face when he took First Sergeant Stockel's place, because he smiled at me and said, "There's nothing like leading the company in. We COs get all the glory." Then he shrugged. "Hey, what can I say? I didn't make the rules."

I was supercharged by the time we finally stepped off, Cadet Haywood and I perfectly centered on H Company behind us. We entered Washington Gate and continued down a long hill. The companies stretched before us, their guidons like golden beacons urging them forward. The sun was directly overhead, pouring down on us out of a bright sky—the hottest time of the day. But I hardly noticed the heat. I was bearing the guidon—straight out in front and angled at forty-five degrees—like a warrior of old, a sort of Joan of Arc, gallantly leading my legions home.

"Keep your eye on G Company," Cadet Haywood said to me over his shoulder, "and stay in step with them if you can't make out the cadences. They're kind of hard to hear, marching up here."

The road curved to the right at the bottom of the hill, then flattened out. *Washington Road!* I had traveled it many times before, double-timing in formation at six in the morning, admiring the brick houses with enclosed porches that bordered the road. It had been quiet then, except for the cadences. But today the street was alive. People wearing sundresses and shorts, baseball caps and sunglasses, Army uniforms and jeans covered the sidewalks, waving banners that said, "Welcome Back!" and "Congrats!" and cheering wildly as we passed.

A chill tingled over my body. I stood a little taller. I raised the guidon higher. I concentrated on staring straight ahead. *"LET 'EM BLOW, LET 'EM BLOW! LET THE FOUR WINDS BLOW! FROM THE EAST TO THE WEST, HARDCORE IS THE BEST!"* I heard H Company thunder behind me.

Cadet Black said the march through Camp Buckner would be a rush, but that has nothing *on this!*

As we drew closer to the Plain and the granite buildings, the crowd grew thicker, and suddenly its tone changed. The reds, blues, and yellows blanched to white, gray, and black. The beaming smiles became screaming mouths. The waves turned to fists, and the cheers to threats. Red, screwed-up faces pushed closer, filling my vision, and I felt my body involuntarily flinch like I'd faced a wall of fire.

"I'm gonna be your worst nightmare, Bonehead!"

"You won't last one hour in my company, Smack!"

"You want some TLC? I'll give you TLC—Terror, Long and Continuous! Lots and lots of it!"

Don't look at them! As I forced my eyes back on G Company, the mob blurred around me. I gripped the guidon harder, holding it even higher than before. I knew this demonstration was designed to frighten us, to intimidate. Well, their effort was wasted on me. This was just another battle, and I was going to win.

And then I saw it. The Plain, that huge expanse of perfect green, extended to our left. And the barracks, six stories of immovable granite with the medieval mess hall in the middle, towered before us, overlooking the Plain. And beyond, the Gothic chapel atop a wooded ridge, standing watch like a quiet sentinel. A sight more inspiring than a "Welcome Back" banner. It was home.

We passed the two mansions on our right, their quaint charm marred by the crowd screaming in front of them. We veered left, filing past the statue of General MacArthur, and marched over the cement walkway that separated the barracks from the Plain. Upperclassmen leaned out of the barracks' windows, their insults raining down on us and reverberating across the Plain.

One by one the companies ahead of us turned to face the Plain, and pulling into their slots in front of the barracks, they stopped.

Then it was H Company's turn. Cadet Haywood yelled over his shoulder, "H COMPANY! LEFT TURN, MARCH!"

And H Company occupied its place facing the Plain, the place where we had stood every day for countless formations in all kinds of weather during the past six weeks.

"MARK TIME, MARCH! RE-DEE, HALT!"

The march back from Lake Frederick was over.

First Sergeant Stockel took over the company from Cadet Haywood, then called the upperclassman who normally carried the guidon to the front of the formation.

"Hand off the guidon now, Davis," First Sergeant

Stockel said, his voice just above a whisper, "and return to your squad."

"Yes, sir." I thrust the guidon into the upperclassman's hands, saluted First Sergeant Stockel, and bolted for Third Platoon.

As I fell in on the end of Third Squad beside Gabrielle, she turned slightly toward me and smiled. Sort of. It was a shaky smile.

I know, Gab. I know. Today's going to be tough. I wished I could grab her hand and squeeze it. But you just didn't do that at West Point. We'd handle today like we'd handled all the other days.

"All right, H Company!" First Sergeant Stockel said from the front of the formation. "I'm not real big on good-byes, so I'll keep it short."

This is it. Any second now we'd be released to the barracks, and Beast would be over.

"You did it, Hardcore. You conquered Beast. We were with you every step of the way, but the time has come to let you go."

Let you go. It was almost a sad expression. So final. But I was ready. I wouldn't have believed it a week ago, but I *knew* it now. My beast was gone; I'd conquered it.

"The year you have ahead of you is gonna wear you down," First Sergeant Stockel was saying. "Each of you has a weak spot, and West Point's gonna find it. But you have the ability to succeed, Hardcore, because we've trained you to succeed. You have all the tools." He paused. "But the only thing that'll *keep* you here . . . is yourself."

First Sergeant Stockel raised his arm in a salute and yelled, "DRIVE ON, HARDCORE!"

"DRIVE ON, HARDCORE! DRIVE ON, SIR!"

"PLATOON SERGEANTS, TAKE CHARGE OF YOUR PLATOONS AND RELEASE THEM TO THE BARRACKS!"

My eyes snapped to Cadet Black at the front of our platoon. *This is it. It's really over now.*

Cadet Black returned First Sergeant Stockel's salute, then turned to face us. "You know what you've gotta do, Third Platoon. 'Nuff said. Squad leaders, take charge of your squads!"

New cadets from the other platoons and companies were already scattering, headed for the roaring barracks.

I squeezed my eyes shut, waiting for Cadet Daily's voice above the storm. *Okay, here goes—*

"Third Squad—"

I held my breath.

"Fall out!"

I hesitated a second, but there was really only one thing to do.

I whipped around and charged toward the barracks with the others.

As I reached the dim sally port, I heard Cadet Daily yelling after us. "NEVER SURRENDER, THIRD SQUAD!"

That's right, Cadet Daily. Never *surrender.*

Several books on West Point publish a whole glossary of
West Pointisms.
It will be well for the new cadet if he has seen these words
And perhaps memorized some of them.
But here is a word of caution.
He should never use such terms until he has heard them
authoritatively employed,
For he may well . . . reveal him[self] to all
As a student of a glossary.
—E.D.J. WAUGH, AUTHOR OF *WEST POINT, 1944*

GLOSSARY OF CADET SLANG AND MILITARY TERMS

AO: Area of Operation. Also slang for "the immediate area."
ASAP (pronounced as a word, *ay-sap*): "As Soon As Possible."
At West Point this means "immediately."
as you were: the command to disregard the previous statement of the speaker. Literal meaning: "as you were before
the last statement or command was issued."
balloon goes up: a saying that refers to the moment a war or
battle begins. Possibly originated from the barrage balloons used
in World Wars I and II to protect cities from air raids. When the
balloons went up, it meant a bombing raid was about to begin.
Battle Dress Uniform (BDU): the Army's woodland-
patterned camouflage fatigue uniform.
beanhead: slang for NEW CADET. Possibly originated from a
new cadet's head that, when shaved, resembles a bean.
Beast: slang for Cadet Basic Training.

big bites: slang for putting a normal-sized portion of food on the fork when eating.

Black Group: the fastest ability group of the three running groups during Cadet Basic Training.

brass: the insignia that UPPERCLASSMEN wear to designate their year at the Academy. FIRST CLASSMEN wear black, SECOND CLASSMEN wear gray, THIRD CLASSMEN wear gold, and FOURTH CLASSMEN wear none.

***Bugle Notes*:** also called the "PLEBE Bible," a pocket-sized handbook containing West Point trivia, quotations, and general information about the Army and West Point for recitation. See also KNOWLEDGE.

butt: 1. the remains of anything, the remaining portion of any whole (e.g., the butt of a minute). 2. the base or bottom (e.g., the butt of a rifle).

C-130: a military aircraft used to transport equipment or troops.

Cadet in Charge of Quarters (CCQ or CQ): an upperclass cadet whose duty for the day is to sit at a desk outside the orderly room and answer the telephone, relay messages, and guard the barracks.

Cadet in the Red Sash: the first upperclass cadet to whom NEW CADETS must report. Characterized by a scarlet sash worn around the waist.

Camp Buckner: the eight-week military training camp for THIRD CLASSMEN, located on the USMA Military Reservation and named after General Simon Bolivar Buckner, West Point Class of 1908.

CO: short for Commanding Officer, usually used to refer to the Company Commander.

Combat Medical Badge: a decoration awarded to Army medical personnel who were attached or assigned to infantry units as medics during combat.

company: a unit of approximately 120 to 140 soldiers or cadets, consisting of four PLATOONS.

cover down: the command for soldiers within a formation to align themselves from front to rear.

dammits: clasps on the back of name tags, BRASS, or service ribbons which are pinned to the uniform.

deuce-and-a-half: a two-and-a-half ton truck used to transport military supplies or troops. Also referred to as a "LMTV" (Light Medium Tactical Vehicle).

dick: to look out for oneself at the expense of others; to take advantage of.

dress right: the command for all soldiers within a formation to align themselves with the soldier on their right.

dress right, dress: perfectly ordered; correct. Comes from the command for soldiers to DRESS RIGHT.

drop: command to get into the Leaning Rest, the push-up position.

entrenching tool (e-tool): a lightweight fold-up military shovel that soldiers carry to dig foxholes.

fall out: 1. the command for dismissing soldiers from a formation. 2. command to relax or disperse. 3. to fall or lag behind, as in a run or ruck march.

fall-out: a person who consistently lags behind; straggler.

first classman: also "firstie"; a senior at West Point.

First Sergeant: the Company Commander's chief assistant, responsible for unit accountability and administration; the highest-ranking sergeant in a COMPANY.

fourth classman: also PLEBE; a freshman at West Point.

get-over: a person who consistently doesn't pull his or her own weight or tries to get by with a minimum amount of effort.

hu-ah: 1. a guttural grunt used by people in the military to show motivation or excitement. Slang for anything except "no." Also, the primary method for soldiers to emphatically affirm or agree with a speaker (i.e., Amen! Yes! Great!). 2. motivated, tough, hard-charging.

Jody: slang for the boy back home who is dating a soldier's girlfriend.

knowledge: the information that each NEW CADET or PLEBE is required to memorize and recite on order, especially from BUGLE NOTES.

M-14: primary rifle used by the Army between World War II and Vietnam. Currently used at West Point for drill and ceremony.

M-16: a semi-automatic, magazine-fed combat rifle weighing approximately nine pounds. Primary weapon currently used in the Army.

medevac (*medical evac*uation): to remove wounded soldiers from an area by helicopter, military aircraft, or ambulance.

military time: the designation of time of day using a twenty-four-hour clock. The day begins at one minute after midnight (12:01 A.M.), which is written as 0001.

new cadet: status of a FOURTH CLASSMAN during Beast.

phonetic alphabet: a standardized system of words spoken in place of each letter of the alphabet. Used during oral communication to clearly distinguish and minimize confusion among letters of the alphabet.

A —Alpha	J —Juliet	S —Sierra
B —Bravo	K —Kilo	T —Tango
C —Charlie	L —Lima	U —Uniform
D —Delta	M—Mike	V —Victor
E —Echo	N —November	W—Whiskey
F —Foxtrot	O —Oscar	X —X-ray
G —Golf	P —Papa	Y —Yankee
H —Hotel	Q —Quebec	Z —Zulu
I —India	R —Romeo	

ping: to walk quicky (i.e., 120 steps per minute) in an erect posture with head and eyes to the front and hands cupped.

platoon: a unit of approximately thirty to forty cadets or soldiers, consisting of four SQUADS.

plebe: a FOURTH CLASSMAN; freshman at West Point.

police: 1. to clean or straighten up; to groom. 2. to collect, gather.

Prep School: short for the United States Military Academy Preparatory School.

rack: 1. to sleep. 2. cadet bed or cot.

R-Day: Reception Day. The day in which the NEW CADET reports to West Point for the beginning of Cadet Basic Training; the first day of BEAST.

regiment: a unit of approximately twelve hundred cadets or soldiers, consisting of three battalions.

second classman: also cow, a junior at West Point.

smack: Soldier Minus Ability, Coordination, and Knowledge. Slang for a FOURTH CLASSMAN or NEW CADET. Originating from a time when FOURTH CLASSMEN were required to smack against the wall in the position of attention when encountering an UPPERCLASSMAN in a hallway or stairwell.

squad: a unit of approximately ten soldiers; the Army's smallest tactical unit.

third classman: also YEARLING, a sophomore at West Point.

upperclassman: a cadet in his second, third, or fourth year at West Point.

USMA (often pronounced as a word, *yoos*-may): United States Military Academy.

Woo Poo U: slang for West Point.

yearling: a THIRD CLASSMAN; a sophomore at West Point.

zoomie: slang for a person who attends the United States Air Force Academy.